SURVIVAL

THE EMERGENTS TRILOGY, BOOK ONE

K. A. RILEY

A NOTE FROM THE AUTHOR

Dearest Fellow Conspirator,

Survival is the first book of the *Emergents Trilogy*, which picks up where the *Resistance Trilogy* leaves off.

What you have in your hands is one-ninth of what's called an *ennealogy*, a rare and hard-to-pronounce word meaning "a nine-part series." It's basically three sequential, interlocking trilogies. (Think *Star Wars* or *Planet of the Apes*)

Here is the Reading Order for the *Conspiracy Ennealogy*...

#1: **Resistance Trilogy**
Recruitment
Render
Rebellion

#2: **Emergents Trilogy**
Survival

Sacrifice (Coming in November 2019)
Synthesis (Coming in early 2020)

#3: **Transcendent Trilogy**
Travelers
Transfigured
Terminus

SUMMARY

In the year 2043, with the nation destroyed by war, seventeen-year-old Kress—accompanied by her Conspiracy of friends and by Render, her companion raven—embarks on a perilous cross-country mission through a violent, dystopian land to locate and recruit Emergents, the scattered group of fellow teenagers who have begun to exhibit strange evolutionary abilities.

Not all Emergents are ready to accept who and what they are, however. Some have even started using their abilities for personal gain or to commit acts of terror. Now Kress has to figure out who is friend and who is foe as she risks everything to expose the government's lies and take down the tyrannical President Krug once and for all.

Blending the best elements of sci-fi and fantasy and picking up where the *Resistance Trilogy* leaves off, the *Emergents Trilogy* follows Kress and her friends on a daring and dangerous quest to recruit allies, save sufferers, restore truth and freedom to their corrupted country, and, if at all possible…to survive.

To the Survivors. Vengeance will be yours.

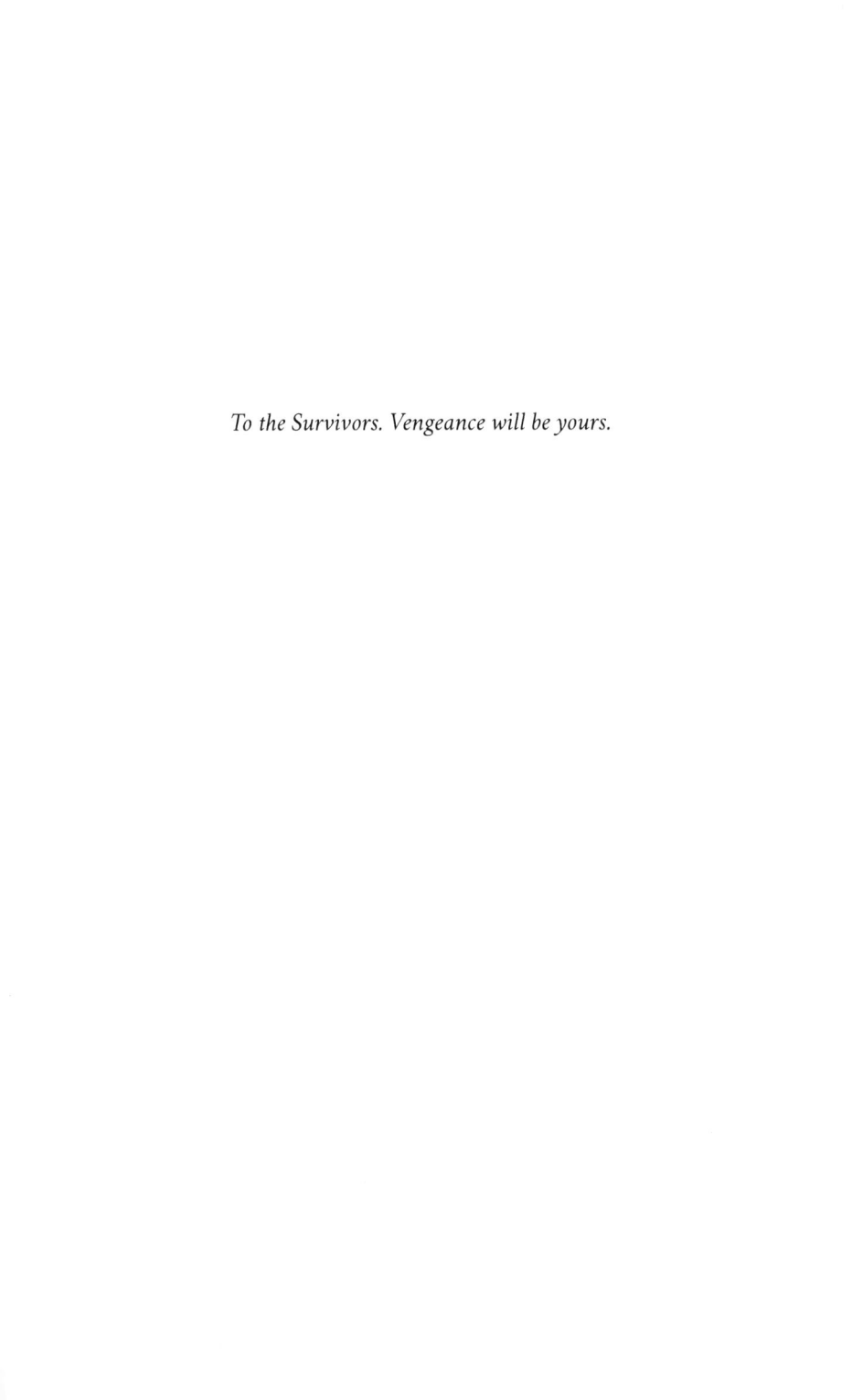

"Extinction is the rule. Survival is the exception."

— Carl Sagan

PROLOGUE

NEARLY A YEAR AGO, on the day I turned seventeen, the Recruiters came to my tiny, bombed-out and war-torn mountain town and took me and the other seven members of the Cohort of 2042 to a secret location where we were trained to be soldiers in the ongoing war against the invading Eastern Order.

We were nervous about going, of course. It's not every day that a platoon of huge men with canon-sized guns rumbles up in a fleet of military trucks to take you away from your home and out into the middle of a war.

But it was our duty. We owed it to our country and to all the people who died. And we thought we owed it to President Krug, who appeared daily on the viz-screen broadcasts to remind us about our duty, to warn us about the threat we faced as a nation, and to panic us into compliance.

Which is to say that I grew up afraid. We all did.

That fear followed us onto the transport trucks as the Recruiters took us on a two-day drive to a training facility in the middle of nowhere.

Confined to the Processor—a campus of eight cube-shaped buildings surrounding a giant field with an enormous floating lab called the Halo rotating above it all—we spent months immersed for twenty hours a day in puzzles, mind-games, escape rooms, relentless martial arts instruction, and a wide variety of weapons and combat training. We were tested to our physical, emotional, and psychological limits. It was all carefully designed to prepare us for the ruthless enemy we'd seen terrorizing their way through our country for as long as any of us could remember.

But then, our clear path and straightforward direction took a sharp left turn.

Toward the end of our training, we got suspicious and uncovered a reality too mind-blowing to believe but too insanely credible to ignore:

The Eastern Order—the so-called ruthless enemy—was a hoax.

The Order was an invented enemy created by President Krug as a way to keep everyone afraid and the country in a perpetual state of war.

Realizing we were nothing but subjects in a shadowy government experiment, the eight of us escaped from the Processor and went on the run. But not before two of our friends—Karmine and Terk—were brutally killed.

Later on, our friend, Kella, distraught over all that had happened to us, fell into a deep pit of despair, and we had to leave her behind with another group of teenage runaways we found hiding out in the mountains of Colorado.

Over time and through many encounters and adventures in the apocalyptic wasteland our country had become, my remaining four friends and I began to exhibit certain enhanced abilities.

Brohn, the unapproachable Mr. Perfect and, eventually, my boyfriend—although I'm still trying to get my head around that last fact—developed impenetrable skin and augmented strength. Cardyn, my best friend and confidante since I was six, had a way of hypnotizing people through a type of psychic persuasion into doing his bidding. Rain, five feet tall but with a giant brain and the fighting skills to match, had an unusually advanced gift for logistics and strategy. Our shy and enigmatic friend Amaranthine —we call her Manthy—evolved something called "cyberpathy" that enabled her to "talk" to certain kinds of digital technologies.

Me? I had Render, the oddly intelligent black raven my father entrusted to me when I was six years old. Over time, we began communicating through what Cardyn dubbed our "telempathic bond." Render and I began to immerse ourselves into each other's consciousness, until many of his abilities—telescopic vision, acute hearing, predatory instincts, superior agility, and even a kind of prescience—started to become my own.

Oh, and I can kind of fly sometimes.

But this isn't a story about superheroes.

There's nothing super or heroic about watching helplessly as your friends and family are slaughtered, about your tiny town getting burned to the ground, about living under the crushing weight of a colossal lie, or about being scared all the time, wondering if each day will be your last.

Together, burdened with the new weight of truth—about who we were and about the deadly world we had so far survived—the five of us made our way west to San Francisco and fought alongside Brohn's younger sister Wisp and her rebel Insubordinates in a battle against the Patriot Army, a branch of our own government, and, as it turns out, the real enemy. It was there that we ran into General Ekker, who captured me and Brohn and revealed some more of the truth about who and what we were.

He called us "Emergents."

According to Ekker, through a fluke of nature combined with a compromised climate and a culminating event in binary technologies, we were identified as some kind of next rung on the ladder of human evolution.

I would have thought we'd be something to celebrate. Instead, the Emergents became sought after as human guinea pigs by an underground division of government-funded geneticists called the "Deenays," pursued back and forth across the country, rounded up, tested, tortured, and, ultimately, killed if we didn't cooperate.

Now, the five of us are heading back east in a decked-out and fully-loaded government truck the size of a small house with our new cyborg friend Olivia, a Modified who is literally plugged into the remnants of a dying global digital network.

Together, we've been tasked with helping to assemble an army that can liberate the country in the same way we liberated San Francisco. To do this, we're first going to track down other Emergents and spread the truth about all the lies we've lived with for so long.

Our victory in San Francisco ended with hints about who we are. We found out that our town and others like it—all at or near the 39th parallel—had been targeted deliberately. Anyone over seventeen had been killed to leave the rest of us to fend for ourselves in isolation and under a state of constant confusion and fear. We also discovered that our abilities are enhanced by our proximity: The closer we are to each other, the stronger we become.

While we were being weeded out over the past eleven years, powerful men were plunging our nation ever deeper into chaos, violence, and injustice.

Now, for the first time after a lifetime of helplessness, we have the ability to do something about it.

We're together, the five of us, and we're determined to stay that way.

Our personal survival—and the survival of our nation and everything it was supposed to stand for—depends on it.

1

When I was six years old, my father brought me into his lab on the fourth floor of Shoshone High School in the Valta, our small village of just a few hundred people tucked away in the mountains of Colorado. We called my father's room a lab but really it was just an old classroom with chunks missing out of the exterior wall from one of the first drone strikes we were told had been orchestrated by the Eastern Order.

The Eastern Order was the enemy back then, an invading army of merciless marauders, who thumbed their noses at God and shot on sight. They blew up buildings and schools. They attacked our infrastructure, bombed our food and water supplies, rounded up and imprisoned anyone they considered a threat, and they sadistically killed countless children and innocent civilians with the same casual callousness of someone stepping on an ant. They held nothing sacred, they hated our country, they were savages, and they lived only to destroy.

Or so we were told.

Long before my friends and I discovered the Eastern Order was a fabrication, my father already knew two things to be true:

that President Krug had invented the Eastern Order and that one day, Krug would be coming after me.

That's why my father sat me down at his glossy white and glass lab table and had me roll up my sleeves. It's why he told me to relax as he lowered one of the diagnostic magno-hydraulic articulating limbs he'd rigged to a power conduit running through the ceiling. And it's why he spent an entire afternoon, bent over tiny showers of orange sparks, implanting a maze of circuitry and data filaments into my forearms.

I watched as the inky dots, looping spirals, and arcs emerged until my forearms were decorated with a motherboard pattern of elegant rings and circles, curved lines, and swooping strokes of obsidian black.

The procedure took a long time, and it hurt. A lot. But I trusted my father, and I loved him, so I sat still while he tinkered and fidgeted, his head tilted down as he peered into the holo-magnifier projected from the ocular emitter clipped onto his safety glasses. When he was done, he pushed his glasses up onto this head and gave me a big hug and told me how proud he was of me.

"These are part of you now. Together, you are a bridge."

That confused me. I knew what a bridge was, and I knew I wasn't one. But my father went on to explain how I was a "bridge across the Digital Divide."

When I looked confused, he laughed and told me not to worry about it.

"The technology you see here," he said, gesturing with a sweep of his hand at the assortment of holo-displays, viz-screens, and racks of delicate silver tools around the room, "it's not all that different from what we have up here."

He tapped his temple and then mine. Then, he walked me over to his other long table on the opposite side of the lab.

Under a purple thermal lamp, a single egg sat in a makeshift nest.

My father said, "It's time," and on cue, the egg moved.

I marveled at his magic trick. "How—?" I started to say, but he put a finger to his lips.

"You are going to have many important moments in your life," he said, "moments whose meaning might not seem like much at the time, but that you'll discover later on mean everything in the world. This is one of those moments. Your first of many. Enjoy it for what it is. Cherish it while it lasts."

I was quiet after that, and my father and I sat on the lab chairs with the wobbly wheels and watched the egg hatch. Although I wanted to believe him, it was hard to imagine any scenario where the tennis-ball sized bundle of ugly gray fuzz that emerged from the speckled greenish-brown egg could ever qualify as important. My father assured me he was telling the truth.

Then he said the craziest thing: "You and this raven have the potential to save the world."

He scooped up the quivering ball of fuzz and placed it into my cupped hands.

"Kress. Meet Render."

It's been over eleven years since that day in my father's lab. Now, I'm on a road trip with five of my friends—we call ourselves the Conspiracy—to Emiquon National Wildlife Refuge in the northwest corner of Illinois. According to Wisp, who's still running the show back in San Francisco, it's where we'll find the Processor we called both home and prison after our Recruitment.

Brohn is taking the first shift at the helm of the enormous, rumbling truck. Most wheeled vehicles couldn't handle this neglected highway with all its pits and dunes and with the waves of fused black asphalt roiling its surface. But this truck is top-of-the-line government grade and was specially commandeered for us back in San Francisco, a gift for our help in defeating the Patriot Army there.

Actually, it used to be President Krug's. He rode into town in this thing. But, thanks to us, he left town without it, his tail between his legs.

Brohn and I sit up front in the truck's cab and laugh at the irony of using President Krug's own sacred vehicle to find and gather the very people we hope will help us take him down.

As much as we would have loved to stay in the amazing city of San Francisco with its colorful buildings, relatively clean air, and its steeply slanted streets, our continued presence there would have set the whole cause back. Along with taking down the garrisoned Patriot Army, we captured General Ekker, and we sent a message to the world, announcing we were on our way to stop Krug and his made-up war.

But sending a message across the remnants of the old info-net is one thing. This particular project, this "meeting" with Krug where we make him pay for what he's done, we need to do that in person.

So, we're off to gather recruits for the cause before heading to Washington D.C. to get our country back. An ambitious task, to be sure. But like my best friend Cardyn says, "What's life without a little impossibility to overcome?"

2

"Where to, Olivia?" Brohn asks into the intracomm holo-display projecting out into the air from the cab's front instrument console.

Olivia's voice, in all of its oddly mechanical cheerfulness, hums into the cab.

"We'll continue heading back the way you came. East on Interstate-80, past Reno and Salt Lake City."

I haven't gotten used to hearing her voice come at us like this. It's like the truck has an A.I., only it's not artificial. Well, not totally. As a Modified, Olivia has a lot of synthetic and manufactured parts. But she's still, at her core, an organic human being like the rest of us. She's stationed in the Pod, the small security apartment in the back of the truck. She's not artificial. But she's very intelligent.

With Brohn at the wheel and with Olivia serving as remote navigator from her Pod, we're soon out of the city, beyond the Oakland slums, and back on the ravaged highway heading east.

The rest of us, along with Render, who has claimed a perch on a small shelf above the kitchenette, settle into the main cabin and marvel at our good fortune.

Render watches us, his heavily-feathered head swinging side to side, probably wondering why our usually glum and beleaguered gang suddenly seems so celebratory and carefree.

Calling this "a luxury apartment on wheels," Cardyn has spent the last half hour twirling around on one of the loungers, which operate on a grav-pad system and are nearly friction free for a smooth ride. Revolving pointlessly in place, his coppery-red hair splayed out as he spins, he goes on and on about our victory from last night and about the thrill of combat.

"Isn't it marvie?" he squeals, his arms and legs making a big "X" as he continues his annoying rotations. "We got a victory, we saved a city that didn't even really know how much danger it was about to be in, and to top it all off, we get this!"

I tell him I don't share his enthusiasm and would be perfectly happy not rehashing recent events.

Finally, Rain scolds him and tells him to stop goofing around, but, secretly, I'm happy to see him having a good time, even if it is ridiculous, and even though it's making me dizzy just watching him.

It took only an hour, but Rain has already mastered the controls for all the gadgets and gizmos in the truck. She's taken a full stock of our supplies, inventoried the weapons, and even figured out the trick for releasing the latches holding the fold-out cots in place within the cabin's interior walls. Even though we were given the truck's specs before we climbed aboard, I'm still surprised at its spaciousness. It's got a roomy cab up front with enough space for all of us to keep the driver company and an even bigger cabin with eight fold-down beds, six mag-chairs, loungers, viz-screens, a game console, a kitchenette, two bathrooms, and a shower.

Who would've thought we could be so comfortable or have this much fun on our way to lead a coup d'état?

Manthy spends most of the drive talking to Olivia up in the Pod. Makes sense, I guess. Manthy has always been a loner. She's also gifted with the ability to talk to tech. And, since Olivia is mostly tech herself, the two of them together make for a nice kind of symmetry.

Brohn's been at the wheel, guiding us through what's basically Hell. The huge fields on either side of the road are one giant rug-burn. The road is littered with the blackened shells of cars and trucks, many of them with skeletal remains of people inside. Brohn weaves us expertly through the wreckage, taking great care not to drive over the bodies we find strewn along the highway from time to time.

"Out of respect," he tells me as he slows the truck to a crawl whenever we approach more human remains.

I reach over and put my hand on his forearm, and he leans over to kiss me before sitting back up to continue steering us down this sad, unending highway.

Cardyn's voice comes rolling to us from over in the cabin.

"I saw that," he shouts.

"Stop being such a snooper!" I shout back.

Cardyn laughs, points at me, and goes back to spinning in his mag-chair while Rain rolls her eyes and returns to scrolling through the holo-manual she's been reading as she continues to explore the ins and outs of the truck.

As for me, I've been passing back and forth between the cab and the cabin, chatting with Cardyn and Rain, keeping Brohn company up front, and generally gazing out the narrow windows, mesmerized by the wrecked and wretched state of the outside world.

Because of the heat and the potential for high levels of radiation on parts of our trip, Olivia advises through the truck's commcaster—its internal communications channel—that we keep the windows closed and the blast screens down. Fortunately, the truck is outfitted with external cameras that project outside images onto black glass displays on the inside of the windows.

Although the tech is impressive and provides excellent resolution, the sadness of everything it shows is overwhelming. All the things we used to hear people sing about our country—the spacious skies, the amber waves of grain, the purple mountain majesties—it's all in ruins. And forget about "good" and "brotherhood." We've got terror and alienation from sea to poisoned sea.

If God had grace to shed, he shed it somewhere other than here.

I can't imagine a time when the world will look healthy again, and it's even harder to imagine anything my friends and I do during this next part of our journey will really make any difference. Then again, we did liberate San Francisco. We took down Ekker and the Patriot Army, the local contingent, anyway. And we did all that in a week.

So who knows? Imagine what we can do in a month.

For the next leg of the ride, we all sit together in the cab with Brohn. There are two cushioned, high-back swivel seats next to the driver's seat and four equally-comfortable seats behind those, which gives us a chance to hang out together. Brohn insists he's fine driving up front by himself, but Rain and I insist just as assertively on keeping him company. For the moment, Manthy wants to be near me, and Cardyn wants to be near Manthy. That leaves Render on my lap with his head tucked under his wing and Olivia back in the Pod where she promises she's beyond happy.

"There's not much of a national grid left," she tells us through the commcaster. "But it's nice to be patched into the little bits I can find."

"She likes being plugged in," Manthy explains quietly after Olivia has signed off.

I ask Manthy if she thinks Olivia relies on her digital connections the way we rely on air to breathe, but Manthy, odd and aloof as always, either doesn't hear me, or else she just doesn't feel like answering.

I don't take her silence for rudeness. I've known Manthy long enough to know she doesn't have a rude bone in her body. She has plenty of mysterious bones in her body and several crazy ones, but not rude ones.

Meanwhile, Render has been squirming since we left San Francisco. He's still not totally recovered from his original injuries incurred at the hands of Ekker's men, the surgery that saved his life, or the effort he put into helping us to victory after Olivia and Manthy teamed up get him back on his feet. Or rather, back on his wings. Although he managed to assemble his own raven army, lead them into battle, and pretty much help save the day, the exertion has taken its toll, and whatever second wind he managed to amass along the way has mostly evaporated. He pushed himself too hard and too fast, and the worst part is that he did it for me. So, I'm thankful but also plagued with guilt.

The small golden plates and the thin filaments lining much of his coal-black body now are a reminder of what he went through for us and what Olivia and Manthy had to do to keep him alive.

Through my telempathic connection, I'm able to tell he's not totally used to his new appearance.

"You look amazing," I assure him. "And powerful. Like a sleek black knight in gilded armor."

Really? I don't want to look like a squatter.

"Squatter" is Render's derogatory word for people. I guess because we don't move around as much as he does. As for his looks, for a bird, he's remarkably vain.

Fortunately, he's in good hands. Cardyn and Manthy have been fussing over him even more than I have and have been passing him back and forth, arguing over who gets to hold him the longest.

The squabbling aside, it's actually kind of nice to have them looking after Render since it gives me a chance to shut my brain down for a few minutes at a time, close my eyes, and pretend the world we're driving through isn't in smoldering ruins. We saw all of this on our way to San Francisco, of course, but a very small, very naïve part of me was hoping maybe it was all a dream, that our nation hadn't turned on itself, that the pitted highway wasn't lined with crumbling, deserted towns and littered with the blackened bones of human beings too contaminated by radiation to even be dragged away by whatever scavengers were left alive in this devastated wasteland.

Twenty years.

From what we understand, that's all it took to take our country from the top of the world to the bottom of the barrel.

Rapid climate change, corporate greed, institutional discrimination, entrenched social hierarchies, sanctioned inequality, fear of variation and variety…all packaged and primed and ready for a tyrant like President Krug to swoop in and turn it all to his own selfish advantage.

President Krug didn't build the bomb. He didn't even really light the fuse. That was done a long time ago. He just blew on it to accelerate it into exploding.

For all we risked, for all we lost, and for everything we laid on the line, our victory in San Francisco was really nothing more than a single mending stitch on a ravaged and unraveling piece of our national fabric.

We haven't said it out loud, but I know we're hoping that one day, preferably in our lifetime, this barren and scarred tableau will once again teem with healthy, colorful cities filled with happy people free from the constant fear of eternal war hanging over their heads.

It's terrifying to think that such a future might rely on five Emergents, a Modified, and an armored raven.

That's why we're here, though. And that's why we need to survive long enough to assemble an army.

3

Over the next few hours, with me and Brohn taking turns driving, we stop the truck from time to time so we can stretch our legs and so Render can stretch his wings.

Waiting until the scorching heat of the red desert has abated, we let Render out in the early evening. He takes little fluttery mini-flights at first, and I'm filled with memories of him being a fist-sized, gruesome-looking nestling with patches of soft gray feathers I used to stroke while my father tinkered away at his lab table.

With Render becoming more accustomed to his golden armor and now finished with his short practice flights, we pile back into the truck. On Olivia's advice, we bypass Reno and Salt Lake City.

"There are reports of a Patriot Army presence. Better not to risk being discovered," her disembodied voice tells us from the front console.

We agree, but Brohn and Rain both think we should at least stop in Salt Lake to see if we can track down Vail and Roland, the nice couple who provided the original truck that got us to San Francisco. But Olivia convinces them that the risks would almost certainly outweigh the rewards.

"There are too many checkpoints close to the New Towns," she warns. "We don't want to draw attention to you. After San Francisco, people know who you are, and they know you're real."

"Too bad," Cardyn sighs, his chin heavy in his hand. "I'm going to miss being a myth."

After some discussion, we agree it won't do us any good to go back to what's left of the Valta, but we do decide to take a detour into the Rio Grande National Forest and up the foothills of Monument Mountain to see if we can track down Adric and Celia and their gang of castaways, who were taking care of Kella when we saw them last.

We're giddy with excitement about the prospect of a reunion with the two teenage leaders we came to know as friends, but we're disappointed after a full day's uphill hike to find the camp long abandoned with no clue about what happened to everyone or where they might have gone.

"At least there's no sign of an attack," Rain points out.

I tell the others some more about how I picked up a bunch of images from Kella when we freed her from her brainwashed confinement in Ekker's entourage.

"Nothing crystal clear," I remind them. "But I think Adric and Celia and their crew got away. She doesn't seem to remember much about it herself, but I'm pretty sure it was Kella who saved them from Ekker."

"Why didn't they all come back to their camp?" Cardyn asks.

Rain kneels down, inspecting the area for more clues. "Too dangerous," she says. "They were right to keep moving."

"They mentioned going east," Brohn recalls. "They had family there. Maybe they'll get there safely."

"Maybe they're there already," I suggest, and everyone nods their hopeful, enthusiastic agreement at this possibility.

Happy at least that Kella is safe with Wisp and Granden in San Francisco, and hopeful that Adric and Celia and their crew might still be alive somewhere in the world, we hike back down the mountain and reboard the truck.

A few hours later, with what I suppose is a justifiably pessimistic gloom filling the vehicle like a tangible fog, Rain comes into the cab where we're all sitting to announce that she has some good news.

"I was up in the Pod with Olivia. She's been in communication with Wisp and Granden. They think they've been able to narrow down the locations of at least twenty actual Emergents."

"The ones in the Processors?" Brohn asks.

Rain hangs her head, but not before I see her eyes go misty with tears.

"Granden thinks there are only one or two Processors left. All the others have been…cleared out," she says after a hard swallow and a cough to clear her throat.

A lump forms in my own throat. We don't ask for any more details. We all know what she means by "cleared out." We've suffered the losses. We've seen the bodies.

"Then where?" Brohn asks, his hands on the steering wheel, his eyes scanning the vacant, neglected road in what has turned into a constant effort to avoid the impact craters, the collapsed overpasses, and the many burned-out and long-abandoned vehicles we've had to weave our way around since leaving San Francisco.

Undoing her jet-black ponytail and letting her hair fall in sleek waves down her shoulders, Rain slides into one of the second-row passenger seats and folds her legs under her.

"Krug escaped from us with his life. But also with knowledge he didn't have before." She pinches her thumb and finger together, so they nearly touch. "He came this close to acquiring the five of us, his very own complete set of Emergents. Now that he knows just how much we're capable of and how dangerous we all can be to him, he's going to redouble his efforts to acquire more of us."

"What are we?" I snap. "Trading cards?"

Shaking her head, Rain pivots in her seat to face me. "Krug isn't looking to trade, Kress. You've seen him and his troops in action now, up close and very personal. If you thought he was crazy when he was coming after us, imagine what he'll do if he gets his hands on the other Emergents out there. Wisp is sure he already has dozens of us in Chicago alone. We're all just the tip of a very powerful, very coveted iceberg."

Rain swings around to face the rest of the group.

"Fortunately, thanks to Wisp and Granden, we know approximately where at least some of the Emergents are out there in the world. Other than the ones he already has imprisoned in his Chicago and D.C. labs, Krug doesn't know. At least not yet. Olivia was able to conceal their locations by wiping out or re-routing some of the tracking systems used by Krug's Patriots and by the Deenays. It won't be long before they figure out what's happened. And when they do, they're going to try to get to the free Emergents around the world before we do."

"So where to then?" Manthy asks. She's got her arms folded, and she's slouching low in her seat like she's annoyed at having to ask the question Brohn already asked.

"Better for me to show you than tell you," Rain says, withdrawing a small black disk from her pocket and placing it in the open palm of her hand. Flicking her glossy black hair behind her shoulders again, she taps her comm-link, which patches her in to Olivia back in the Pod at the rear of the truck. "Olivia, can you please call up the Global Emergent Nexus Wisp and Granden came up with?"

Through the speaker in the truck's front console, we hear Olivia's voice say, "Initiated," and a blue and green holo-display of a slowly-spinning image of the earth, about the size of a perfectly round watermelon and complete with shifting cloud cover, appears above the holo-pad in Rain's hand. Several spots around the rotating globe, mostly lined up along the same latitude, are lit up bright red.

"Is this real-time?" Brohn asks, clearly impressed.

Rain gives him a wink. We're too young to remember things like the Internet, social media, and the Global Grid, but our parents used to tell us stories that made the whole world sound like a magical intersection of commerce, communication, learning, and love.

"Olivia is slowly rewriting the network as we speak," Rain explains. "With satellite patches and access to the fragments of wireless carrier signals still out there, she's been able to gather more information in the last few hours than we had access to for our entire lives."

Rain calls out the names of the highlighted cities on the hologlobe, pointing to each of them as she goes.

"Wisp and Granden have identified Emergents in five cities in the U.S.: Kansas City. Chicago. Cincinnati. Philadelphia, and Washington, D.C. Only the Processors in Chicago and D.C. are left. Overseas, though, we've identified and located Emergents along the 39th parallel in Valencia, Spain. Cagliari, Sardinia. Ankara, Turkey. Beijing, China. There may be some underground groups in the south of France and scattered throughout some of the Greek islands. Some of these Wisp and Granden knew about. Some they had a good hunch about. Others are brand new to them, but Granden swears the intel is one-hundred-percent reliable. It won't be long before Krug tracks them down as well. And if that happens…"

"We won't let it," Brohn says, his jaw set, his hands tight on the steering wheel.

"Did they ever figure out why?" I ask Rain.

"Why on that exact latitude, you mean?"

"Yes."

Rain shakes her head.

"Olivia's working on that, too. She promised to let us know as soon as she finds anything."

Rain returns her attention to the globe. As she talks, she flicks her fingers apart to enlarge each of the cities in turn. One at a time, as she skims through the floating display, we see landmarks, which Rain explains to us.

"Krug Tower in Chicago. That's where we're headed. And here's Carew Tower in Cincinnati. The Liberty Bell in Philadelphia. The City of Arts and Sciences complex in Valencia, Spain. The Shrine of our Lady of Fair Winds in Cagliari, Sardinia. The Kocatep Mosque in Ankara, Turkey. The Forbidden City in Beijing, China. And, finally, the Krug White House in Washington, D.C."

Rain glances up at all of us to make sure we're paying attention before going on.

"So, even though we're still not sure why this particular latitude seems to be the favorite location for the Emergents to, well, emerge, we still have a duty to find the rest of them, save them, and see if we can convince them to join us in taking down Krug and his Patriots."

"Wait," Cardyn says. "Wisp is planning on having us go to all of those places?"

"Well, as many as we can get to," Rain says. "It's hard to fight a war without an army. And these Emergents, if we can find them, can give us an advantage beyond anything Krug's Patriots have ever seen." Pointing one at a time to two patches of green she says are in Illinois, Rain says, "According to Wisp, we'll start here and here. We think these are two of the Processors. The first one might be the one we were taken to for Recruitment. We'll check that one out now. After that, we go to Chicago. Then we go after Krug in D.C. At some point, though, we're going to have to track down the other Emergents around the world."

Cardyn looks puzzled and points at a big blue patch on the

projected and rotating image. "I don't imagine you're thinking of having us drive across the ocean?"

"Don't get me wrong," Brohn calls back over his shoulder while drumming his fingers on the truck's massive steering wheel. "It's a great rig, this truck, but it'd make one lousy boat."

"Some of those cities," I say, "the ones overseas…they're so far away. Brohn's right. This truck is fine for getting us to the places Wisp wants us to go in the U.S. How do you plan on getting us to the ones all the way on the other side of the Atlantic Ocean?"

"Well," Rain says, tapping her finger on her chin. "That kind of travel and all the potential danger involved does require some sacrifice. Any objections? Anyone want to quit?"

We all shake our heads and offer up a resounding, "No!"

"Well then," Rain laughs, it's on to Emiquon National Wildlife Refuge. "Let's see if the Processor is how we left it."

She heads back into the cabin of the truck, leaving the rest of us to sit in the cab in silence at the thought of returning to the place where, for a few months anyway, we suffered through the most traumatic time of our lives.

4

AFTER A FEW MORE HOURS OF bouncing and jostling in the truck's cabin, I start to get a headache accompanied by an urge to stretch my legs. Plus, Cardyn keeps spinning around in his seat while telling really bad jokes, and my stomach hurts from groaning.

"What has two legs and red fur?"

When no one answers, Cardyn says, "Half a cat."

Manthy scowls at him. "Gross."

"Okay, how about this one. Why did the dyslexic man walk into a bra?"

Again, he's greeted by silence.

"Because his wife left her laundry hanging on the clothes line, and he didn't notice when he walked under it. The man's dyslexia doesn't have anything to do with it, and I'm not sure why I brought it up in the first place."

"I have dyslexia, you chaffer!" Brohn hollers out from the cab.

Cardyn blushes and says not to worry. "I have a bunch more."

"I'm going up to visit Olivia," I grunt as I push myself out of my seat and head through the cabin to the back of the truck. In a burst and flurry of feathers, Render flutters from his perch and onto my shoulder, and together, we climb the retractable metal-runged ladder leading up into Olivia's Pod.

A sight to behold as always, Olivia is fully integrated into all of the truck's internal systems and is literally plugged into the array of consoles surrounding her.

When I tell her how impressed I am with how quickly she's turned the Pod into a sophisticated hub of technology, she swings around on her mag-chair and grins with her twisted smile of flesh and synth-steel.

"These are more than just information patchwork drives," she tells me, gesturing with her multi-colored tendrils at the three floating spheres above her head. "They also monitor my organic and digital systems and basically keep me alive."

"I didn't know that," I confess as I sit down across from her in one of the small but surprisingly comfortable mag-chairs.

The Pod is really just a small, low-ceilinged apartment, tucked away in a hidden chamber embedded in the roof above the rear-end of the truck. It's got four mag-chairs and four fold-up cots, one on each side of the room. The base of each wall is lined with long, horizontal storage lockers, which contain reserve food rations, clear tubes of water, and a back-up cache of weapons and ammo. In her investigations of the ins and outs of the rig, Rain discovered that the Pod is basically a concealable, blast-proof vault designed to protect Krug or any other government dignitary in the event the truck is attacked or taken over. So there are no windows or anything. But Olivia's consoles and the slew of Surface Mounted Devices emit pulses of bright, multi-colored lights, which give the small space a kind of carnival fun-house effect.

Annoyed by the blinking diodes and the scrolling code above the phosphor-coated instrument panels, Render pecks at my ear, and I tell him to quit it, brushing his powerful beak away from my face with the back of my hand.

"I like your relationship," Olivia says. "Yours and Render's."

"Me, too. He's not a pet or a friend, exactly. Kind of a sibling. I guess there's no real name for it."

"That's what I like about it. There are prisons and chains in the world, but there's not much out there more confining than a label."

"I know what you mean. Human. Post-human. Emergent. Modified. I get a headache just thinking about where I fit in."

"Just remember, there's an ancient, universal sameness under all that surface difference. You and I have the same kind of circulatory, skeletal, muscular, and neurological systems," Olivia emits a tinny giggle. "Mine just has a lot more ones and zeros in it."

I have to admit, I'm still slightly afraid of her. I know that's a result of my own problems and prejudices, but there's something so unusual about her and about the life she's forced to lead. She defies my expectations for what it means to be human, and it takes me out of my comfort zone. The strands of colorful fibers where her hands would normally be are snaking around and undulating in hypnotic waves. The collage of data-managing chipsets, circuit boards, and scales of rough skin making up her face contort into what I now recognize as a smile. Although she's closer to Manthy, I get the sense Olivia enjoys my company almost as much.

"Funny you should put it like that," I say. "The ones and zeros, I mean. I used to think human and digital technologies were opposites. Now I'm not so sure."

Olivia's checkerboard eyes go glassy for a second, which I know means she's processing information, probably unrelated to our conversation.

"We spend half our lives disconnected from everything, including from ourselves, and we spend the other half trying to get connected again. Modifieds like me may be tragic, but we're a reminder that people and things are really all made up of the same stuff."

"My dad once told me something similar."

"About the tech implanted in your arms?"

"Yes. And about all the ways it connects me with Render. He said one day, we could save the world."

"Well, somebody's got to do it."

"You know what I'd really like to do? When all this is over, I mean."

"What's that."

"Be a teenager."

"It has been hard on you, hasn't it?"

"I don't mind excitement and adventure. I just wish I'd had a say in it."

"That's your job now, isn't it? Helping others like you to have a say in how their lives are lived."

"I guess so."

Olivia tilts her head toward the access ladder leading back down to the cabin.

"Don't underestimate what you and your Conspiracy are doing or how important you are. And be careful not to scapegoat President Krug. He's a narcissist, a war-monger, and a dangerous fool. But he's *a* problem, not *the* problem."

"You're not defending him, I hope."

"Not at all. He's an evil man."

"Then if he's not the problem, what is?"

"There is war, famine, pestilence, and death in the world. The plagues of humankind. What you did in San Francisco—"

"What *we* did. We couldn't have done any of it without you."

"I appreciate that. But what you're preparing to do now…try not to think of it as ridding the world of the four horsemen of the apocalypse. That's the wrong goal and an impossible task. The horsemen are just the consequences of the real diseases infecting our DNA."

"Which are?"

"Ignorance and Fear. Those are the real plagues. You are the antidote. You produce the antibodies of enlightenment and courage."

"I never asked to be a hero."

"Real heroes never do."

"I don't think you're tragic."

"No?"

"I think you're inspirational."

"That might be too much pressure for me to handle," she says, her laugh ringing through the Pod in a chirpy metallic echo.

Hopping from my shoulder over to one of Olivia's consoles, Render struts through the various holo-displays and lines of green code scrolling ghostly through the air. The glowing images glint and glisten off his oil-black feathers and the strips of gold armor and gossamer threads of circuitry lining much of his body. He *kraas, kreeks,* and offers up a raspy grumble of contentment, and Olivia and I share another laugh.

It occurs to me then: Perhaps at least part of my discomfort around the Modifieds stems from being in such close proximity to someone like Olivia who represents what people have been talking about as the post-human. She's been both born and constructed, taught and programmed. All the technology humans have been amassing over however many thousands of years is sitting here in front of me, smiling, chatting, and coalesced into a network of blood vessels, neuro pathways, and fiber optic microfilaments.

It's what Render is now and what I thought I was before. Now, I'm not so sure about any of it, and I think maybe it's the uncertainty about who and what I'm becoming that's causing all my discomfort. I also think it's secretly why Olivia likes having me around. In a strange way, my discomfort and naïveté about life seem to amuse her, but they also seem to give her some sense of hope about the future of humanity. Or, at least how flexible we wind up being about defining what it means to be human.

"Can I ask you something?"

Olivia, who has turned on a slight angle as she investigates readings from a monitor off to her left, swivels back to face me. "You can ask me anything you want, Kress."

I swallow hard and ask, "What does it feel like?"

"You mean these?" she asks, her tendrils dancing in the air.

I nod.

"They feel tingly, to tell the truth."

I grin at this, happy she's not offended by my curiosity.

"But 'it'—the *fact* of me and what I've become—feels terrible."

"I'm sorry…I didn't—"

"It's okay. You're wise to ask. I have certain abilities now because I'm a Modified, and I have a lot of pain because I wasn't happy with who I was. That's my fault. Taking advantage of me at my lowest, at my emotional weakest…that's Krug's fault. Did I ever tell you how I came to be who I am?"

I shake my head and squirm in my seat, regretting I ever opened up this particularly uncomfortable can of worms.

"I was exactly your age. Seventeen. I loved digital technology and all the new possibilities for the kind of lives and world it might help us to develop. I read every scientific and engineering journal I could get my hands on. Like your father, I built things. Miniature wave turbine machines. Electromagnetic weather predictors. Interfaced hydraulic load-lifters. Nano-botic diagnostic micro-drones. You name it. The only thing I couldn't figure out was people. It was like I was speaking one language and they were speaking another. I spent a lot of time living inside my own head, mostly happy but always alone, often wondering when I'd get out and why no one was coming in to get me. When a team of genetic techno-engineers recruited me out of high school for a study, I went along with it. I was taken to a lab and put through a battery of tests over a period of months. Then years. My parents came to visit for the first few weeks. After that, they came less and less. It wasn't long before they stopped coming at all."

"Did they forget about you?"

"No. They were told I'd died."

"That's terrible."

"But not entirely inaccurate. The me I'd been *did* die in a way. The old En-Gene-eers—we know them today as the Deenays—planned to use me as a weapon, part of a team of people who could think and obey like machines and who had the mental processing speed of a computer. The idea was that we would control the global digital network, and they would control us. But some of us rejected that plan. That's when they did this."

Olivia waggles her tendrils and gestures at the consoles around her and at her legless body interwoven into her silver mag-chair.

"They tipped the techno-human balance too far in favor of the techno part at the expense of the human side of the equation."

"But you're still human."

When Olivia doesn't respond, I wonder if she's heard me, but after a second, she lifts her head.

"I'm trying to decide if that's a statement of fact, a compliment, or an insult."

I freeze, unsure if I've crossed some line of etiquette, but Olivia breaks into a grinding laugh, and I realize she's teasing me.

"I was a test subject. Then a rejected weapon. Then a discarded piece of worthless junk. And I still couldn't communicate with people. Do you know who saved me?"

I shake my head, enthralled by Olivia's remarkable story and by her even more amazing spirit.

"It was Granden."

"Granden?" I ask, incredulous. "Our Granden? As in President Krug's son?"

"He saved a lot of us back then. Just like he saved you."

"You said you spent *years* in the lab?"

"In Washington, D.C. In a bunker right under the White House, actually. Well, a few hundred feet under the White House."

"It sounds like our Processor."

"It was. It was a prototype for what became *the* Processors. Nothing as extensive as you described. It was more of a lab back then. It wasn't until Krug invented the Eastern Order and shifted his sights from the Modifieds to the Emergents that the Processors became more like the military installations they are today."

"We need to shut them down," I say, biting my lip. I'm on the verge of crying or growling in anger, I can't tell which. Instead, I'm overcome by a sudden urge to be with Brohn, to have his arms around me, my head against his shoulder, the rich waves of his voice in my ear.

The truck jolts, and I gasp and grip the arms of my holo-chair.

"Must've hit another rough patch in the road," I say, blushing at my needless panic.

"Nothing to worry about, I'm sure. Brohn's a good driver."

"That's true," I agree. "He's gotten us farther in this thing than I would have."

"He's turning into quite the hero, isn't he?"

"Brohn? He's always been a natural leader. The one we always relied on in the Valta."

"And now?"

"And now what?"

"Leader. Hero. Friend. Perhaps one day lovers? Sounds like your relationship is evolving."

I blush again, but this time out of the embarrassment of being so transparent.

"Let's just say there's no label for what we are."

Olivia laughs, her tendrils flicking in the air in time with her raspy chortle.

Giggling along with Olivia, I'm just about to excuse myself

and climb back down the access ladder into the body of the truck when Rain pokes her head up into the Pod.

"We're here, and we need you and Render to do your scouting thing," she says before disappearing back down into the truck.

Rain is trying to sound casual, but I can sense the flux of fear behind the steadiness of her voice.

5

"Well," I sigh to Olivia, "looks like my talents are needed elsewhere."

Olivia emits another of her pinging chuckles.

"No matter who you are: Emergent, Modified, or plain old blood and bone human, it's always nice to feel helpful."

"Maybe that's what it means to be human," I suggest. "Having the irresistible desire to help others."

"If that's the case," Olivia hums, "then what do we call people like Krug, who are dedicated to nothing other than helping themselves?"

"I don't know. Is there an opposite of human?"

"If there is, Krug's it, along with the ones who buy into his fear-mongering stupidity."

"I'll come visit again soon," I promise.

Olivia nods, her tendrils splayed out now like a gently-swaying sea anemone, and swivels back toward her consoles as Render and I descend the ladder and join up with the others.

Down in the belly of the truck, Rain distributes the comm-links, which we each place behind our ears. "This will let us stay connected," she says.

"How is she?" Brohn asks, tilting his head back toward Olivia's Pod.

"She's a bit of a miracle. All the things she's been through…"

Brohn reaches out and helps me tighten the straps on my tactical vest. "You ready for this?"

"No."

Cardyn sidles up behind me and rests his chin on my shoulder.

"I don't think it's possible for anybody to be ready to do something no one's ever done before."

It's true. From what we know, we're one of a kind: Emergents who escaped from a modern Processor. Maybe that makes us special. Or pioneers. Maybe it doesn't mean anything at all. Either way, stepping out of this truck right now is going to be one of the more challenging things we've all faced in our lives, and I have to admit, I'm feeling kind of foolish about the whole thing. What slave willingly returns to her master? What prisoner volunteers to go back to jail? What Holocaust survivor—or anyone with a heart and a shred of empathy for that matter—wouldn't be overwhelmed by the crush of emotion upon walking into a Concentration Camp?

"We're not just doing this for the cause," Brohn reminds me as the others head toward the door, while I hesitate.

"We've become Recruiters," I say.

"True. But we're recruiting people to join in a cause, not to perpetuate a lie."

"If it helps," Rain calls back from where she's gripping the hand-rail by the inside of the truck's synth-steel sliding side door, "we're trying to save people who are otherwise going to end up like us. Only a lot more dead."

A concerned frown on his face, Brohn puts both hands on my shoulders and leans forward to look me square in the eyes.

"It's okay," I say, shaking off the last remnants of uncertainty. "I'm ready."

He throws a quick glance at the others to make sure no one's looking before saying, "For luck" and plants a sweet kiss on my lips.

I blush as a shiver runs down my neck and a set of tingles dances straight to my heart.

Although I wish I could stop to savor the moment, we have a mission to complete.

One at a time, we hop down from the monstrous rig, our boots thumping up grim clouds of red dust as we hit the ground. The badly-cratered road leads to a rough path winding downhill through a forest of decimated trees. We march along in silence, but we don't need to talk. Every one of us knows what the other is thinking, feeling, and remembering.

It was here, less than a year ago, that we were escorted to the place that for many months would be our home, our training facility, and our jail. Although I feel better than I did in the truck and more invested, walking back to the Processor still strikes me as colossally stupid, but I also know Brohn and Rain were right and that we'll all regret it if we don't at least investigate.

Besides, our mission is to gather up Emergents, and that means going to where they are or to where they might be. And that means walking willingly into places where large men with guns will happily shoot us dead on sight.

Leaping airborne from his perch on my shoulder, Render climbs into the dry red sky and scouts ahead. He sends me back images, but I'm having trouble making them out. I scan one of the access codes into my forearm "tattoos," but that causes some kind of weird overload, and I'm forced to disconnect.

It's not unusual for our telempathic connection to go glitchy like this from time to time. Although we've technically been linked together since my father first installed the implants in my forearms and introduced me to Render all those years ago, it's only been the last few weeks that I've even come close to getting a handle on how our connection has evolved and with what effects and consequences. Even now, while I'm still partially entered into Render's consciousness through a type of internal echo leftover from before the disconnect, I can only kind of see what's right in front of me here on the ground, and I have to rely on taking Brohn's arm to keep myself from walking blindly off the thin and winding strip of dirt passing for a path.

"Can we stop for a second?" I ask.

I unhook my arm from Brohn's and take a few wobbly steps on my own with the others huddling in a protective circle around me.

"It's back," I say. "I'm with Render."

In my mind's eye, I see the Processor, its eight imposing black buildings surrounding the huge green Agora with the silver Halo rotating overhead. On my mental tableau, everything is just how I remember it. The watchtowers. The gated and guarded entrance to each building. The soldiers on patrol. The lush grass of the Agora. The Halo. Everything.

But then the images go murky again, and it's like there's a short circuit in Render's brain. Or maybe it's in mine. I'm having more and more trouble sorting out that kind of thing these days.

"It's frustrating," I confess. "I can't lock him in."

Rain tells me not to worry about it.

"Best not to push it too hard," she advises.

I agree, but before I know it, a wave of dizziness rolls over me, and I feel myself slumping in slow-motion down to the ground, but I can't seem to do anything about it. When I blink myself awake, I'm in Brohn's arms with Cardyn crouched down across from us in a small clearing, his hand on my knee, asking me if I'm okay.

I try to blink Cardyn's fuzzy form into focus. "What happened?"

"We were hoping you could tell us."

I groan and allow Brohn to help me to my feet. "I'm not sure. It was a pretty simple connection. Render sent me back what he was seeing. Then, it was like the world turned to mud and started sliding downhill."

"And now?" Brohn asks.

I brush red dirt from my black cargo pants and continue to head toward the Processor.

"I'm fine. But something's not right."

"Are we in danger?"

"Yes," I say at last. "It's pretty much the only thing I'm sure of right now."

6

With my head clearing up, we resume our hike to the Processor.

Manthy is straggling along behind with Cardyn keeping her company. Despite her obvious annoyance at his recent run of goofy humor, she still seems to be okay with him being close to her.

Brohn leads the way down to where the path ends at a wall of thorny vegetation. He rips and weaves his way through with the rest of us following close behind. The barbed brambles with spikes as long as knitting needles tear at my exposed arms, and I'm happy for my heavy-duty tactical cargo pants and the combat vest with the Kevlar inserts. Without those, the rest of me would be slashed to shreds by now as well.

"How many do you figure there are?" I ask Brohn. "Guards, I mean."

"Not sure. I counted maybe twenty or so when we were here before."

Rain says, "That sounds about right. Plus, the scientists Heller had working for her up in the Halo."

Annoyed at the density of this barbed and bristly knot of vegetation around us, I smack at one of the thick red vines and am rewarded for my frustration with a deep cut to my hand.

"I'd know for sure how many guards there are if I wasn't having so much trouble syncing up with Render," I say, pressing my palm to my thigh to stop the bleeding. "I'm not sure which one of us is having the trouble."

"He did go through a traumatic experience back in San Francisco," Rain reminds me.

"So did I."

Cardyn catches me wincing and asks if I'm okay.

"Just a little cut to the hand," I tell him. "No big deal."

"We should've worn gloves," Cardyn sighs. "Or maybe…you know…not come here at all."

He's right about the gloves, but there's nothing we can do about it now. As for being here, trudging our way to a place we risked our lives to escape from only a few months ago…it's an unfortunate step, but it's one we have to take if we want to get to all the next steps in our mission.

Brohn swings his head left to right and scans the dark treetops above us.

"We haven't seen any Patriots yet. With their tech, they would've known we're here by now."

"Or it could be a trap," Cardyn suggests from a few paces behind us. "You know, a couple hundred men with guns just around the next bend."

Rain turns back and gives Cardyn a sarcastic, "Thanks for the optimism."

But we all know he's right. We're here to find and save Emergents. The Patriot Army isn't going to just step aside while we liberate their captives and then go on our merry way.

"Do you think maybe we should have, you know, a plan of attack or something?"

Cardyn is trying to sound casual, but his voice can't conceal the undercurrent of fear.

"This is just reconnaissance," I remind him. "We scope out the area first. See what we're up against. If it looks like it's too much to handle, we'll regroup and figure out an optimal strategy."

"Strategy is Rain's thing," Cardyn mumbles, mostly to himself. "I have an allergy to bullets, especially ones shot at my head."

"No one is shooting at us," Manthy points out from behind him.

"Maybe Cardyn's right," I concede. "We're used to Render providing intel in advance. Without our connection, a bit of caution might be called for."

Nodding, Brohn takes out his nine-millimeter Sig Sauer 2040, and we all follow suit except for Manthy who prefers the two lightweight combat tomahawk axes she found in the truck's arsenal. She says she's averse to the deadly heft of the pistols and Magpuls the rest of us carry.

Hunched down, we split up and walk along the edges of the overgrown footpath, staying concealed but still able to make eye contact at intervals along the way.

Render circles overhead but then disappears from view.

"Damn. I wish he'd stick close."

"We'll be okay," Brohn assures me, his hand on my arm.

We've defeated the Patriot Army before, but we know better than to get complacent and let our guard down. Even though they're advertised publicly as being there for our own good and to protect us from the Eastern Order, the truth is, as we've experienced far too many times to count, they are actually exactly what they claim the Eastern Order to be: ruthless, vindictive, violent, and completely contemptuous of any lives other than their own. They follow Krug's commands without question or hesitation.

An admirable trait…for a slave.

When it comes to the mass relocation, deportation, torture,

and genocidal murder of civilians, I definitely prefer a soldier who's willing to question orders.

Render continues to fly sporadically overhead, appearing and then disappearing above the scorched treetops. I still can't completely connect with him, and it's making me nervous and edgy. Normally, I think of myself as having the usual five senses. With Render, it's like those five are enhanced, plus I've got a couple of extra senses beyond what's normal for a human being. When our connection fades or goes glitchy like this, I feel like I'm down to just two or three senses, and the world has gone out of focus.

Breaking into the main clearing at last, we find ourselves face to face with the Processor, looming before us like it did all those months ago. Only today, it isn't the pristine and imposing set of buildings where we were introduced to Hiller and her team of soldiers, experimenters, and torturers.

The Processor—the entire facility, the Halo, all of its buildings —has been destroyed.

The vehicle lanes and dirt foot paths are overgrown with more clusters of spikey red vines. The back of the Alpha Cube is seared with blast burns, and a giant chunk has been blown out of the top floor of the Beta Cube where some of the building's framework, bleached white as a beached whale's ribcage, now lies twisted and exposed.

Up above the rooftops of the black buildings, the slanted top of the Halo juts high into the air, skewed on a horrific angle above the tree line with parts of its surface splintered off like bone fragments in a compound fracture. The sunlight glints a fiery red off the top curve of the giant disk Hiller and her team used as a research, observation, and assessment facility, and I have to shield my eyes with my hand as I look up at it.

"What happened?" Cardyn asks no one in particular.

"Looks like it's been attacked," I suggest.

Rain agrees but only partly. "Look at the debris. The scorch marks. The angle of the I-beams. The collapsed foundations. This place *was* attacked. But not from here. Whatever happened, it started inside."

"Then that's where we need to go," Brohn says, striding right up to the laneway between two of the razed buildings with far more confidence than I think is warranted given the circumstances.

If it was up to me, I'd follow Cardyn's advice and take things tortoise slow. Maybe even call it off and get back to the truck. But we're on a mission, and Brohn has never favored a meandering approach when a direct one is available.

Slipping through the open gateway and between two of the Cubes, we follow him now into the Processor and explore the ruins of the giant campus.

Even in its best condition, the place would have brought back the worst memories. Now, devastated and quiet as a corpse, it's like walking into a nightmare. Rain was right. It looks like a bomb was detonated. A lot of bombs, actually. And not your basic run-of-the-mill bombs either. It looks like something new and unique went off in here.

"This isn't what I saw," I tell the others. "It all looked normal in my mind. Like it was when we were here. I think Render was sending me memories."

"Or maybe you were misinterpreting his signals," Rain suggests.

"What do you mean?"

Rain kneels down and starts scanning the boot prints in the weed-filled and long-neglected grass. "We all filter what we see and experience through the prism of our expectations. Render could have been sending you what he remembers plus all of this. The overlap might have been too much for your brain to handle."

"I'll try not to take that personally."

"Good," Rain smiles, standing and walking toward the middle of the Agora. "It's not meant as an insult. But let's face it. You and

Render are two different minds sharing a consciousness. We haven't even started to figure out what that means, how it works, or what the consequences might be for either one of you."

Standing in the middle of so much destruction, all I can do is nod my reluctant agreement.

7

Holstering our weapons for now, the five of us walk along, still on alert for any leftover guards or Recruiters who might be lurking around.

We're just as cautious about what's underfoot. Huge craters have been blasted into the surface of the Agora revealing the complex jumble of cogs, shafts, and gears that at one time worked to transform the field into a variety of training grounds.

Easing our way along, our heads on a swivel, we make our way across the remnants of the field where the once-lush grass is now a charred mess of deep pits and fused carbon. Long and splayed-out patches of hardened black ash dot parts of the battered site.

"Artillery flash burns?" I ask.

Rain shakes her head and toes one of the piles of fused carbon. "People."

"What?"

"I think people died here. Maybe all of them."

"Emergents?"

"Maybe. Possibly Recruiters. Either way, whatever happened looks unexpected and full-blown catastrophic."

"This could have been us," Cardyn mutters. "Last year, I mean."

"Well it's not," Rain snaps. "Let's stay focused."

Moving more gingerly now, we arrive at the center of the field where we gather around and peer down into the deep shaft leading to the Silo, the underground barracks where we slept every night after long days of training. The Capsules, the clear pods that carried us up and down, are a barely-recognizable twisted mass of composite aero-plastigel and strips of half-dissolved synth-steel support struts.

"Must be at least thirty, maybe forty feet down," Cardyn says, pointing into the abyss and shaking his head. "I can't believe we lived down there."

"We slept down there," Brohn reminds him. "I'd hardly refer to anything related to our experience here as 'living.'"

"Anyone feel like going down to investigate?" Rain asks.

"Too far to jump down," Brohn says, leaning over the deep chasm. He kneels and runs a hand along the inside rim and reaches as far down into the pit as he can. "Too smooth to climb down," he adds, standing up and brushing his hands on his pants.

There's a moment of silence and then I look up to find everyone looking at me.

"What?"

Rain points to the twisted and vine-covered synth-steel capsule leaning half out of its shaft. "There's no way down with the Capsules and mag-lift wrecked like that."

"Exactly. So why are you all looking at me?"

"Well," Rain says, glancing around at the rest of our Conspiracy before finally turning back to me. "I guess we were all kind of thinking that maybe you could…you know…fly down there?"

"You're joking."

Rain shrugs.

"I can't fly."

"Well..."

"You did kind of make an impossible leap from Krug's helibarge to the top of the Armory," Brohn says.

"And from the Halo to the Theta Cube," Manthy mutters.

I shoot her a dirty look, and she drops her head, suddenly enthralled apparently by the laces and buckles of her boots.

The truth is, I can't fly. I can barely navigate a flight of stairs without tripping and hurting myself. But I know the instances Brohn and Manthy are referring to and, although technically I didn't fly on those occasions, I know why they think I might have. I haven't talked with them about it much because, frankly, saying it out loud seems creepy and a little braggy. But what I did those times was more like gliding. Like the air wrapped itself around me and offered me a hand. All I did was accept the offer.

Preferring not to add any more fuel to their fire, I don't mention the time in the mountains when Render and I slipped away to play a game in the woods. That time, I took an impossible thirty-foot leap from a rocky overhang into a ravine and didn't get hurt.

"Okay," I sigh. "I'll try."

The others step back like they think I'm going to go exploding down into the shaft like an air-to-surface missile.

"It doesn't work like that," I tell them, and they break into embarrassed but understanding smiles.

Render is circling overhead. After two failed attempts, I connect with him successfully, and I feel my body get instantly lighter, as if my bones have gone hollow. I give a little hop over to the rough edge of the open shaft and glide down, landing safely at the bottom, pleasantly surprised and a little impressed that I don't even have to bend my knees very much.

"How's it look?" Brohn calls down.

I wander around for a minute before I yell back up. "Not how we left it. I think they had other Seventeens down here after us."

Cardyn cups his hands around his mouth and leans down over the opening above me.

"I'm sure they did," he says. "You didn't really think they were going to stop with little ol' us, did you?"

I run my finger along one of the walls in the sleeping quarters and inspect the black debris that comes off at my touch. There's light coming down the shaft, so the middle of the Dormitory is bright, but the rest—the perimeter, the Shower Room, and the Mess Hall where we had our meals—sits in eerie darkness.

I blink a few times, and I'm able to access Render's predatory night-vision.

Coils of exposed wiring hang down from the ceiling in frayed bundles along with dented ventilation ducts and the shattered remnants of polyvinyl tubes from a sprinkler system. Water plinks down onto my shoulder as I wind my way around and over a maze of twisted copper pipes and ruptured conduits protruding up through missing chunks of the floor.

"It looks like maybe there was a fire down here. And there's blood. Whatever happened, whoever was down here…I don't get the sense it ended well."

"What about the tech?" Rain calls down. "The viz-screens? The meal allotment systems?"

I shake my head before remembering they can't see me from up there. I tilt my head up toward the opening.

"Nothing. All fried."

Above me, Brohn kneels down. "Um…Are you able to get back up?"

"That's a little harder," I shout, looking up at the dark faces of my four friends forming a ring around the shaft's opening with the blaze of red sunlight in the sky behind them. "I haven't actually practiced it much. Maybe I should have considered that before I let you all talk me into coming down here."

"Too late for that now," Cardyn says unhelpfully.

"Here goes."

With Render still in my head, I bend my knees and jump out of the deep pit. I don't make it quite to the top, but I'm saved by Brohn who latches onto my forearm and hauls me the rest of the way up.

"Yeah. I've really got to work on 'up,'" I pant into Brohn's chest.

"Still," he says, his arm around me in support, "that's a pretty impressive trick."

"Thanks," I pant, holding up a "give-me-a-minute" finger.

What Brohn calls a "trick" is actually an enjoyable experience for the body, but, right now anyway, it's pretty tough on the mind.

"What now?" Cardyn asks.

Rain starts tromping back toward the base of the crash-landed Halo. "Let's see if anyone else is still around."

"I sure hope not," Cardyn mutters as he walks past me. "This place gave me the creeps *before* it was a nuclear wasteland."

We cut back across the scorched Agora to the base of the grounded Halo. With one boot up on the edge of a partially-crushed doorway, Rain peers into a black slit in the chrome-colored surface.

Cardyn asks if we're really planning on climbing into the Halo. "This thing looks like it might come crashing down at any second."

As a joke, Brohn steps over to the huge structure and pushes on its scarred and tarnished silver surface with both hands. Of course, it doesn't budge. Its bottom curve is embedded twenty feet into the earth with the rest of the disk rising up hundreds of feet into the air like a crash-landed UFO. It's leaning on the Beta and Delta Cubes, whose rooftops and upper floors have been crushed nearly down to the ground by its weight.

Even though it floated above the Agora on grav-suspenders, the Halo was a fully-stocked military laboratory and must weigh tens of thousands of tons.

"So," as Brohn informs Cardyn, "it's not going anywhere."

"But we are," Rains says, stepping into the opening in the side of the Halo and climbing her way inside.

One at a time, we follow Rain into the seam. She activates the small shoulder-scope flashlight on her vest, and we're immersed in a jungle of streaky shadows.

The corridors are steep, slippery in places and treacherous in others, but we clamber on. We hang onto door frames, handrails, recesses in the walls, access panels—anything we can get a grip on as we ascend into the gloom.

"Wait," I call up to Rain. "This is the control room."

She slides back down to the rest of us, and everyone follows me through the half-open door. As we enter, a bank of automated emergency lights flickers awake and bathes the large room in a hazy white glow.

It was in this room where we confronted Hiller and where she ultimately killed herself. Now, we gaze around at all the computers, viz-screens, consoles, and mounds of monitoring and testing equipment burned to a crisp. Anything loose in the room —chairs, tables, and a bunch of crumpled storage lockers—has slid down in a heap against the far wall.

Careful to keep my balance in the slanted room, I edge my way over to the central console which is dark except for one flickering red light at the bottom of one of the input panels.

"I know. I know," Manthy grumbles. "Talk to the tech."

Manthy slides her hands along one of the long consoles. Her eyes go gray as she shakes her head, mumbling about weak signals.

"Wait," she says. "Got it."

Now, her eyes go baby-doll black.

"The external network is fused. There's a security protocol I can tap into. The Cubes are all dark. No. Wait. There's power in…the Zeta Cube."

"Did we ever go in there?" Cardyn asks, leaning over Manthy's shoulder.

"No," Brohn says, running his hand along his jaw in thought. "The challenges and escape rooms were all in Alpha through Epsilon. Eta was a medical building. Theta gave us access to the Halo."

"Then why is the Zeta Cube the only one with power?" Cardyn asks.

"Good question. Let's go find out."

Cardyn hangs back. "Hold on a second. Are we sure we want to go poking around in this place? There's obviously no one here. Or worse, what if there *is* someone here, and this is all a trap?"

Brohn and Rain dismiss Cardyn's concerns, but Manthy tells them to wait.

"Cardyn's not being paranoid," she says.

Cardyn beams as she comes to his defense.

With her head down, Manthy reminds us about the real dangers we encountered during our time here.

"They tricked us from the very beginning. They killed Terk and Karmine, and they would have killed us if we hadn't figured things out and gotten away when we did."

"Well," Brohn says. "It looks like it's two to two. Kress, that makes you the tie-breaker. What do you say? Do we investigate Zeta Cube, or do we head back to Olivia and the truck?"

"I'm not sure I like the idea of this being on me," I say, my hands up.

"Then I say we get out of here," Cardyn insists. "I say we drive far away, and never, ever come back here."

"I don't disagree," I tell him. "And Manthy has a good point. On the other hand, if we go back to the truck, we're going to wonder what we might have discovered. We're out here for answers, after all. If we try the Zeta Cube, we'll either find nothing or else we'll find an answer. I'm tired of wondering. I'm sick of not knowing."

"And if it's not the answer you're hoping for—?" Manthy mutters, staring at her feet.

"At least I'll know more than I know now."

"And that's worth dying for?" Cardyn asks.

"I don't know about that. But finding out who you are may be one of the only things worth *living* for."

Manthy still has her head down, like she wants no further part in any of this. But Cardyn gives me a sad look and nods.

"I guess we've come this far. Besides," he concedes, "If there are Emergents here, it's our job to find them and rescue them, right?"

We all look over at Manthy, who doesn't answer one way or another.

So, with three of us agreed, the five of us clamber back down the steep corridor and out of the Halo before making our way over to Zeta Cube.

Single-file, we enter and walk along the first floor of the silent building, terrified about what might jump out at us from every room and from around every corner. At this point, I'm almost hoping for something like that. The dead quiet of this place is almost as scary as any surprise attack.

With nothing but blasted down doors and empty rooms on the first floor, we head upstairs. Still nothing.

On the top floor of the Zeta Cube, though, we discover a locked door. Manthy tries to open it, but the tech is too far gone, and she can't connect. Brohn tries to muscle it open with no success. I tap my comm-link and connect with Olivia back in the Pod.

"Manthy's tried, but we think the signals are too decayed. Any chance you could help us out?"

Olivia's slightly metallic voice chimes around in my head. "I'm patching into the Processor's security grid now." There's a slight pause before Olivia's voice returns. "Manthy's right. The system protocols are in a degeneration sequence."

"Can you bypass it and get us into the main room on the top floor of the Zeta Cube?"

"Think you may have found some more humans to help?" Olivia teases.

I whisper "Just a second" to Cardyn when he asks me what's so funny. "Not sure yet," I report to Olivia. "Courage and enlightenment, right?"

"You got it. Give me a second. I'll need to reroute the existing code."

I'm just about to say, "Copy" when Olivia's voice returns.

"There it is. Initiated."

On the wall next to the door, the input panel leaps to life, projecting a cluster of flickering multi-colored lights and a running line of green code into the air in front of it.

Manthy skims her fingers along the holographic icons floating above the scrolling code.

The door wheezes partway open, sliding into the wall but jamming without enough room for us to squeeze through.

Brohn puts one hand on the door frame and the other on the open edge of the door and pushes out with a determined grunt. Mechanisms inside the door-pocket pop and snap until the space widens enough for us to enter.

Illuminated by the dim light from the corridor and by a weak Environmental Conditions Indicator on the far wall, the cavernous room is a mess of overturned tables, smashed ceiling tiles, shattered glass cabinets, and countless distorted shadows. The walls appear to have the same dark plasma burns as we've seen in other parts of the facility. Off to one side is a bank of barred detention units with their doors ripped halfway off their hinges.

Altogether, it's a demonic-looking half-lab, half-prison. Something a love-child of Dr. Frankenstein and Nikola Tesla might have nightmares about.

As we walk around and get accustomed to the gloom, we find

long, high-ceilinged anteroom where we discover a row of eight spherical cells like the giant fish-bowl prison cells Brohn and I were held in by Ekker in San Francisco.

One of the spheres is empty. Inside each of the other seven, slumped down on the bottom, is a dead body.

8

"THEY'RE KIDS," Cardyn exclaims.

Sure enough, the collapsed heaps on the bottoms of the prison orbs look to be about our age. There are seven of them, one in each sphere with the last one empty. Even through the dark gloom of the room and the hazy glass, we can see most of them are in various states of horrific physical trauma.

The dead always seem smaller, almost as if the departed spirit once had mass.

We walk past each orb, taking in the horror of the moment as we go. Leaning against the wall at the end of the line, Manthy covers her mouth with her hand.

As for me, shocked and shaking, I'm just moving over to the circle of half-melted reclining lab chairs on the other side of the room when Cardyn shrieks.

"That one just moved!" he says with a jump.

We rush over to where he's standing in front of the third in line of the cracked and fog-filled orbs. He takes a step back, pointing at the shadowy figure on the bottom of the curved glass.

"Are you sure?" I ask. The near-skeletal remains of the boy are barely identifiable under his dirt-encrusted surgical gown.

"Look."

Sure enough, the boy's fingers unclench, and his left leg twitches and extends like he's trying to get up.

We all jump again before turning around to look for something we can use to break the glass. Although there's plenty of debris in the room, none of it looks big enough or solid enough to do the job. And I know from experience how strong these cells are.

So that leaves Brohn.

Inside of the prison-globe, the boy's eyelids flutter and then close as he slumps back down in a motionless heap. His cheek is pressed up against the glass, but the few weak breaths he's been trying to take have stopped, and the fog they were making on the glass surface has faded completely away.

"Get him out of there," I cry out to Brohn. "Hurry!"

Nodding, Brohn steps forward and takes a deep breath.

He has demonstrated some amazing feats of strength over the past couple of weeks, but, like the rest of us, he's not totally sure what he's capable of or what his limits are. Although he hasn't talked about it much, I get the sense he's as amazed and as terrified about his emerging abilities as Manthy and I are about ours.

Rain and Cardyn don't mention their abilities as Emergents much. Rain because she's always reluctant to conclude anything without a battery of scientific tests under strict laboratory conditions. I think Cardyn just doesn't want to jinx it.

Brohn is the one of us most ready to embrace who he's becoming. And it's times like this when I couldn't be happier about that.

Standing with his back to the sphere, he yells out for us to give him space. Cardyn, Rain, Manthy, and I comply as Brohn raises his clenched fist high above his head.

Like a pendulum, his fist swings down and smashes hard against the thick glass, which sends a thunderous clang ringing around the cluttered room. A spider-web crack grows and spreads with an agonizing creak like a pair of rusty shears chomping through sheet-metal.

He strikes the orb again. The boy inside shudders along with the vibrating glass.

Breathing hard from exertion and probably from the stress of the situation, Brohn pants, "One more" and gives the glass a third booming strike with the side of his fist.

A section of the glass breaks apart into a dozen plate-sized shards, which collapse, some inside, some outside of the cell, leaving an irregular shaped hole just big enough for Brohn to lean into.

"Careful!" Rain warns, pointing at the razor-sharp, angular edges of the opening.

I almost remind Rain about Brohn's bullet-proof skin, but I decide against it. No sense quibbling about trivial things like that right now.

With his torso and one leg inside the sphere, Brohn scoops the boy up in his arms and shields him with his body as he eases his way back out.

An edge of the glass catches Brohn's pant-leg as he emerges, but he wrenches himself free.

"Over here," Cardyn says, dragging an inoperative mag-chair from over by the wall.

The withered boy lurches to life as Brohn eases him into the chair.

"Who…are you?" he stammers, his unfocused eyes darting from one of us to the other. His pupils are dilated, and he's emaciated with purplish veins pulsing in his arms.

Brohn puts a firm but gentle hand on the boy's bony shoulder and points one at a time to the rest of us. "I'm Brohn. This is Kress. Cardyn. Rain. And Amaranthine. We call her Manthy for short."

We each nod to the boy and offer our greetings.

Still looking up at us like we're alien pod-people who just

beamed him up to our mother-ship, the wide-eyed boy pushes away from us, the jagged edges of the broken mag-chair screeching on the cracked and pitted floor.

"It's okay," Cardyn says. "We're not going to hurt you. We used to…live here."

"You were here?" the boy says, his rheumy, red-rimmed eyes opening to a whole new level of wide.

"We were," Cardyn assures him.

"Were you…?"

"Recruits? Yes. Prisoners? Also, yes."

"Then why…"

The boy's voice trails off, and he looks like he might lose consciousness, but we tell him it's okay and to hang in there.

The boy blinks himself awake and seems mesmerized by Rain. "Why did you come back?"

"We thought there might be someone to save," she says.

"And apparently we were right," I chime in.

The boy finally takes his eyes off of us long enough to have a quick look over at the eight orbs lining the far side of the room. "The others…are they…?"

Rain shakes her head. "I'm sorry. We can check their vitals once we get them out of there. But I don't think anyone else made it."

Through a sudden waterfall of tears and with his hands clapped over his face, the boy tells us, his voice quivering, that his name is Amani.

"They were my friends," he says. "We grew up together. We came here to help in the war."

"Us, too," Cardyn says.

Amani squirms in his seat and rubs his thin wrists like he's trying to restore circulation. His gray-brown skin is ashy and spotted with round patches where he must have had adhesive sensors attached. He's reed-thin with a creased forehead and sunken cheeks.

Still, somehow there's a striking handsomeness to his features. His hair is a mane of gold and amber ringlets. His eyes, still glossy and flushed with tears, flicker between bronze and olive-green. He's not very tall, but his wide shoulders, narrow waist, and symmetrical features hint at someone attractive and, at one time anyway, athletic.

Politely accepting my offer of a protein cube, Amani tells us about experiences similar to ours.

"They came for us every year. June first."

Brohn nods. "Ours was November."

Amani looks up at him even though he barely seems to be registering our presence.

"They took the Seventeens every year. 'For the war,' they said. We were happy to go. What did we know? All we had was the viz-screens showing us the enemy getting closer and closer all the time. The adults were all gone. Killed. Or just disappeared. We kids were all that was left. There were eight of us this year. They took us in trucks. We were trained…"

Amani's voice trails off like he's lost his memory or the ability to speak or perhaps both.

"It's okay," Cardyn assures him, a consoling hand on the boy's forearm.

"We were trained," Amani continues, his face wet with tears he doesn't even seem to notice. "Trained and tortured. After a while, I didn't know which was which."

Brohn gazes around at the horrifying room with its sinister-looking lab equipment strewn haphazardly among hunks of the walls and ceiling littering the ground.

"Stick with him a second, will you, Card?" Brohn asks, rubbing the side of his fist where he smashed the glass orb. "I want to check those instrument panels. Take a look around. Make sure we didn't miss anything. Or *anybody*."

Cardyn nods his understanding.

Manthy stands behind Cardyn, who is kneeling in front of

Amani as he continues to ply the boy, as gently as possible, with questions about his past.

Still rubbing his fist, Brohn summons me and Rain to come with him over by the door.

"It hurts?" I ask.

"Not a mark on my skin. But it's tough on the bones and stuff underneath." Flicking his head toward our new friend, he surveys the scene and whispers, "Do you think we can trust him?"

"He's probably wondering the same about us."

Brohn squints and runs his hand along his stubbled jaw line. "It's just that we've come so far and been through too much. I don't want to get him back to the truck and wake up to find him killing us in our sleep. You know what they did to Terk, how they took him away and then turned him against us."

"Rain?"

Rain looks at me and then back over to where Cardyn and Manthy seem to be a calming presence for Amani. Rain is better at sorting through variables and figuring out the best thing to do in cases like this.

"If we don't take him," she says under her breath, "he'll die all alone out here."

"We don't want to be killed," I counter with a look at Brohn who nods his agreement.

Rain turns to head over to the others. "We don't want to be *killers*, either."

Brohn and I both hesitate, mulling the possibilities, but Rain is firm.

"We take him with us," she calls back over her shoulder.

Rain is small, but when she puts her foot down, she might as well be a giant.

9

"Can he walk?" Brohn calls over to Cardyn and Manthy.

Amani looks down at his legs and shakes his head.

"I don't know how long I was in there."

A deep scowl on his face, Brohn marches back over with me jogging along to keep up with him and his long, determined strides.

"It's the thing they take," he says to Amani. "It's not just your freedom or your will. It's really about taking away time."

Rain agrees. "My grandfather was a journalist. He was in the first batch of journalists Krug locked up for treason. He spent four years in prison before he packed up the family and moved everyone to the Valta. He said in prison, if you asked a guy what he was doing, he'd always answer, 'time.'"

"And it's the one thing you can't get back," I add.

The trench between Brohn's eyes deepens, and his jaw goes rigid.

"That's why we need to use the time we have wisely, to strike while we still can."

Amani seems to appreciate this and tries to stand, but flops back down in the chair, his legs a wobbly mess.

"I'll take you," Brohn says and starts to lean over to pick Amani up in his arms.

"Wait. What about the others?" I ask.

Brohn leaves Amani in the seat and follows my gaze over to the eight spheres, two of them empty, one with a big hole in it, the other six holding the unmoving and distorted bodies of Amani's friends.

"Manthy?"

Manthy shakes her head. "The status indicator doesn't show any vitals."

"Can you get the orbs open?"

"I don't know."

"Will you try?"

Manthy pauses for a second, flicking her gaze from me to the orbs and back to me.

"Okay."

She presses the palm of her hand to the input panel on the wall and winces.

"There's not much current. And the code has been corrupted. But maybe I can…"

"What's she doing?" Amani asks, his voice barely above a scratchy whisper.

"She's getting your friends out," I say.

Manthy squints, one hand to her temples. Her lip quivers, and she tries to say something, but no words come out.

Instead, a yellowish-white seam, running vertically, appears on each of the intact orbs. They slide open, and Cardyn and Rain rush over to check on Amani's remaining six friends while I go over to support Manthy who has collapsed against the wall.

"Headaches again?"

Manthy doesn't answer or look at me, so I know the answer is "Yes."

I put my arm around her and ease her close to me. She doesn't resist, which means she's in more pain than she's letting on.

Over by the line of orbs, it doesn't take long for Cardyn and Rain to pass along their findings.

One at a time, they reach into the now-open spheres and check each occupant for a pulse. For a breath. For movement. For any sign of life. One at a time, Cardyn and Rain stand back up, shake their heads, and move to the next person, each time with the same heartbreaking results to report.

Leaning against the wall with Manthy at my side, I can feel myself starting to cry as I point at the gruesome sight of the six unmoving bodies in the cloudy spherical prison cells.

"We can't just leave them in there."

"It's as good a grave as any," Brohn grumbles.

He scoops up Amani in his powerful arms. Amani closes his eyes and presses his head against Brohn's chest as Brohn, his jaw still set tight, strides toward the door.

"Let's get the hell out of here."

Together, we leave the way we came. We climb down the debris-filled concrete stairway, exit the Zeta Cube, shoulder our way back through the walls of thorny brambles, and march up the long footpath until we arrive at the clearing at the side of the road.

Render is perched on top of the truck, waiting for us.

To our surprise, he's not alone.

Sitting on the ground with her back up against one of the vehicle's imposingly thick and heavily-studded front wheels is a young girl, her thin wisps of red hair hanging in loopy straggles around her pale freckled face.

Squirming out of Brohn's arms, Amani pushes away and tries to run toward the girl, but his muscles fail him, and he stumbles face-first to the ground in an awkward heap.

Rain slides down to the ground to tend to him while the rest of us spring into action.

Following our training given this unexpected turn of events, Cardyn and Manthy slip over to either side of the road to take up defensive recon positions. In the same instant, Brohn and I, ducking down in case of an ambush or sniper fire, dash over to the girl, and I'm startled by Render who spreads his wings wide and leans over the edge of the truck, croaking and *kraa*-ing down at the gaunt and motionless stranger.

"Quiet," I hiss up at him. "She needs our help."

The girl can't be more than ten or eleven years old and might as well be an understuffed ragdoll for all she seems to weigh. Her elbow and knee bones jut out from her thin limbs like knots on the crooked branches of a sapling. The same as Amani, her skin is rice-paper thin with the veins in her arms pulsing quietly violet.

"Who is she?" I ask.

Brohn shakes his head and puts his fingers on the girl's neck below her jawline to feel for a pulse. "She's alive."

"Sheridyn," Amani moans from over on the ground next to Rain. "She's with us. She's one of the Seventeens."

"She doesn't look seventeen," I say to Brohn.

"Either way, she's going to die if we don't help her."

"Wait," I say, swiping the implants in my forearm and pressing a finger to my temple. "Let me have a quick look around."

Brohn puts a hand up to Rain, telling her to stay with Amani. Rain nods her understanding and puts her arm around Amani's waist. Brohn and I are next to the truck with the girl. Cardyn and Manthy are off to the side. But Rain and Amani are still out in the open, and I relay the need for urgency to Render.

Signaling his understanding, he lifts silently into the air from his perch on the truck and cuts above the surrounding remnants of woods in a broad circle. It takes only a few seconds, but it feels like a lot longer before Render informs me that we are, thankfully, alone out here.

My pulse finally slowing, I put my first two fingers in my mouth and give an all-clear whistle, and Cardyn and Manthy reappear from their positions off to either side of the road.

Cardyn strides over, holstering his sidearm and gesturing back to the woods.

"Nothing?"

"No. Render says we're okay."

"So, who's our guest?"

"He knows her," Brohn says, glancing over at Amani who is being helped to his feet by Rain. "She's one of his Cohort of Seventeens."

"The empty orb," I say to Cardyn with a sudden burst of realization. "She must've escaped."

"Sounds like a good idea to me. Can we maybe get out of here with our two new friends before any new *enemies* start showing up?"

"Relax," Brohn says. "You saw the Processor. No one's alive back there."

Cardyn flicks his thumb between Amani and Sheridyn. "I think these two would beg to differ."

Brohn pauses before saying, "I see your point."

Rain and Amani join us, and both readily agree that getting moving—no matter how safe Render seems to think this place is—is by far our best and only course of action.

Besides, we came here to find and rescue fellow Emergents. We saved two out of eight. Although I'm glad we got here in time to help Amani and Sheridyn, I know the thought of how things might have played out if we'd gotten here a day earlier or a day later will haunt me for the rest of my life.

10

Piling into the truck, Rain leaps into the cab and scans the ignition on. She slots the big rig into gear and drives while the rest of us do our best to take care of Amani and Sheridyn in the truck's cabin.

"She doesn't look good," Brohn whispers as I return from the supply station with a first-aid kit.

Stretched out now on one of the fold-down cots, Sheridyn doesn't move, open her eyes, or respond as Brohn hands me an IV needle, which I uncap and plunge into the cephalic vein running along the radial border of her forearm.

"Glad I paid attention in the Life-saving and Caregiver course back home," I say.

"I should've taken that course, too."

"You couldn't. It ran the same time as the archery class you were teaching."

"Oh, right." Brohn scratches his head. "Pretty soon, you're going to remember more about us than we remember about ourselves."

"Well, look at it this way. If you all die and I survive, at least I'll have all your stories to tell."

"A grim and slightly offensive proposition," Brohn says with a light laugh and a playful push to my shoulder.

While Brohn and I do our best to care for Sheridyn, Cardyn and Manthy continue to see to Amani, who is sitting up now on the cot next to Sheridyn's, his hands gripping the bed's metal edges as he fights off waves of dizziness. Together, our two patients look like they've been all the way through Hell and barely made it back.

After we get Sheridyn hydrated and her pulse and breathing stabilized, Brohn slides over to check on Amani, who Cardyn informs us has slipped out of consciousness.

Leaving our new charges for the moment, the four of us join Rain up in the cab and update her on how Amani and Sheridyn are doing.

"Think they'll make it?" Rain asks, her eyes riveted to the pitted and pock-marked road.

"I think so," I say, plopping down in one of the passenger seats.

"Do you think they're like us?" Cardyn asks, also sitting down and heaving an only partly exaggerated sigh. "Do you think they're really Emergents?"

Brohn asks Rain if she wants him to drive, but she says she's fine. His head brushing the ceiling of the cab, he stands behind my chair, his hands on my shoulders and looks over at Card.

"Who can say? Everyone has abilities and deficits of one kind or another. My skin might be durable, but I'm dyslexic. Kress can communicate with a bird, but she stinks at singing."

"Thanks," I sneer up at him.

Cardyn crosses his hands behind his head and stretches his legs out in front of him. "I'm sorry, but he's right."

"I'm not that bad."

Cardyn calls over to Rain to back him up, but Rain shakes her head.

"I'm not getting involved."

I offer her a grateful, "Thank you."

"But it does kind of sound like someone picking up a cat... with pliers."

"Hey!"

"The point," Brohn says, cutting off our playful squabbling, "is that the only difference between us and everyone else is that Krug thinks he can use us to...I don't know. Build a super army? Prolong his reign? Prolong his life?"

"All of the above," I say, my hands on Brohn's wrists as he gently rubs the trapezius muscles in my neck, which have seized up into a constricted knot.

We talk for a while longer about Amani and Sheridyn and about our chances of getting all of us safely to Chicago and then to D.C., but it's hard for me to focus. Like Manthy, the use of my abilities can result in anything from an empowering sense of euphoria to excruciating headaches, and right now, I've got a whopper. The desolation of the road, the haze of red-hued sunlight, and the combination of fury and heartbreak over what the world has become aren't helping.

After what feels like an eternity of driving, a ping from the tele-com display module followed by Olivia's voice summons us up to her Pod.

With enough distance between us and the Processor, Rain pulls the truck off to the side of the road.

"I'm not sure if Nowhere has a middle," Cardyn says, peering out at the lifeless terrain through the slit of a window on the passenger side door, "but this has got to be pretty close."

"Will they be okay in the cabin on their own for a minute?" I ask, pointing to Amani and Sheridyn.

Brohn and Cardyn exchange a look before Cardyn assures me everything will be fine.

"They're barely hanging on. They've been through a lot. Having some time to sleep is exactly what they need."

From his perch, Render preens himself and ruffles his hackles.

As the others head through the cabin to the Pod's access ladder, I throw open the truck's side door so Render can fly out and stretch his wings some more, but he turns his head away from me.

His voice—although it's more of a sensation and a patchwork of feelings than actual words—enters my mind:

Will fly later. Must stay here to protect.

I send him a mental "Thanks" for looking out for our guests and head over to join the others up in the Pod.

Brohn, his head ducked down and his shoulders hunched over in the low-ceilinged space, greets me at the top of the entryway.

"What was that all about down there?"

"With Render? Oh, nothing. I offered him a chance to get out of here and go for a soar, but he insisted on staying in the cabin to look after Amani and Sheridyn."

"That was nice of him."

"What can I tell you? He's a really nice bird."

In the air in front of Olivia, the image of Wisp appears, and we all scramble over to talk to her.

She asks us about the Processor in Emiquon National Wildlife Refuge, and we give her the whole report from the details about the destruction of the facility to the infuriating injustice of what Krug's people did to Amani and Sheridyn and their friends.

"Information is still hard to come by," Wisp tells us. "As much as we miss having her here, it actually helps to have Olivia out there with you."

"I'm patching deteriorated networks and communication protocols on the old grid," Olivia explains.

"Which means we know more now than we did before."

Brohn crosses his arms. "For example?"

"We didn't just defeat Krug in San Francisco. We did something worse. We embarrassed him."

"Good."

"We also opened his eyes to just how powerful Emergents can

be. Until us, Emergents were still kind of a hypothetical for him. Something he'd been told could be a pathway to immortality, incredible power, total control...you know, the typical god-complex desires of your average narcissist."

"Let me guess," Brohn says. "Now he's greedy, embarrassed, and *desperate*."

"To say the least. From what we've been able to determine, Krug has ramped up the Emergents program. He's shifted a lot of resources to Chicago where we think he's got an urban Processor on the go."

"So that will be our next stop?" I ask.

"Yes. And about the ones you found..."

"Amani and Sheridyn."

"Just be careful."

"We will. If anyone knows what they've been through, it's us."

"That's not exactly what I meant—"

"How's Kella?" Cardyn interrupts, leaning in over my shoulder hard enough for me to go stumbling forward as the holo-image of a startled Wisp goes wide-eyed and laughs.

"Ask her yourself."

Wisp moves off to the side, and Kella's 3-D image comes into view on the hovering display. Her face is still pale, her blue eyes have gone gun-metal gray. But there's a flicker of life in them now. Her hair is pulled back in a neat ponytail, which curls past her neck in a sleek blond swoop over her left shoulder. She's looking more like the girl I grew up with and the talented, confident sharpshooter she became later on.

We all crowd in, hands on each other's shoulders, and chatter over each other like hyperactive kindergarteners. Even Manthy, standoffish and reserved, calls out how happy she is to see Kella "up and about and alive and well" before retreating back behind the rest of us like she's embarrassed to have spoken at all.

"I'm alive," Kella agrees, a half-smile forcing its way up one side of her mouth. "But I think I'm still a few days away from 'well.'"

"Just glad to see you moving in the right direction," I say. "After the hell that evil scrag Ekker put you through."

Nodding, Kella goes on to offer details about her experiences with Ekker.

"I don't remember everything. Bits and pieces, really. And I'm not sure what was real and what I only dreamed. Did you ever hear about something called hypnagogia?"

We look back and forth at each other, but no one's heard of the term.

"It's the state between being asleep and being awake," Kella explains. "Ekker said it's where our abilities as Emergents come from."

Rain says she finds that intriguing and asks what Ekker meant by that.

"Honestly, I don't know. It has something to do with why we dream." Kella stops, and I think for a second that our connection has gone dead. But she clears her throat and continues. "What he did to me…"

"It's okay," Brohn reassures her, reaching out in a futile but sweet gesture toward the holo-display. "He's gone, and we're still here. You're safe."

Kella covers her face with her hands and cries, her shoulders shaking as Wisp appears next to her and puts a comforting arm around her waist.

"He changed things," Kella sobs into her hands, her voice barely audible through the tele-projection. "Memories. Desires. Dreams. He erased parts of who I am. Shuffled the rest."

Wisp squeezes Kella closer and they both go quiet, as we take turns telling them about Amani and Sheridyn and how maybe a similar thing happened to them and to their six Cohorts back in the Processor.

"Be careful," Kella warns, wiping tears from her face with the cuff of her jacket. "There's something about us. Being an Emergent isn't what you think."

"What is it? What are we?"

Kella looks up at us, her eyes glossy with tears, and shakes her head. Wisp's arm is still around her waist, their heads tilted toward each other, touching lightly in solidarity.

"I don't...I knew...I knew once...But I don't remember now. Ekker took away all the answers. He took away so much."

The image of Granden appears behind Kella and Wisp. He nods to one of the Insubordinates—a tall boy I don't recognize— who guides Kella, followed by Wisp, gently out of view.

"Listen," Granden says, his voice low like he doesn't want to be overheard by whoever else might be in the room with him. "Kella's right. I've seen first-hand what Krug's people do, his soldiers *and* his scientists. We told you there was a lot at stake when we took on the Patriots here in San Francisco. It'll be twice that in Chicago and, if you can get that far, a hundred times worse in D.C."

"'*If*'?" Brohn sneers.

"I'm sorry, Brohn. I know the five of you continue to defy the odds and exceed all expectations. But you're not on the run or in the relative safety of San Francisco anymore. This time, you're going exactly where Krug hopes you'll go, and you don't have your army behind you. At least not yet. You've seen what it's like in some of the New Towns. That's just the beginning. *When* you get to Chicago, you'll need to lie low. As we hoped, word has gotten out about you. That's the good news."

"And the bad news?"

Granden clears his throat. "Word has gotten out about you. Listen, Wisp is right. Krug will stop at nothing to either capture you or else replicate you. And it gets worse."

"How can it get worse than that?" I ask.

"He isn't the only one after you anymore."

"Who else?" I ask. "Who else is after us?"

The image of Granden doesn't move, so I ask again.

Still nothing. We're staring at his face, frozen in mid-expression.

"I've lost the connection," Olivia says. "Either that or else…"

"Or else what?"

"Or else it's been severed."

On that ominous note, we ask Olivia to shut down the feed, which she does. Manthy stays up in the Pod with her while the rest of us go back down into the cabin to check on Amani and Sheridyn.

"Still asleep," Cardyn announces.

Brohn says it's probably for the best and heads into the cab to get us back on the road.

Cardyn and Rain take seats next to our sleeping patients, while I join Brohn in the cab for some rare and much-needed one-on-one time.

Brohn scans the ignition on and hits the mag-starter to fire up the truck's powerful overdrive engines, and we're back on the long and ravaged road, this time heading for Chicago and to whatever answers and dangers await.

11

AFTER A FEW HOURS, we stop at a small town. Or, more precisely, what *used* to be a small town.

Instead of the people and vehicles that might have greeted us before the so-called war, we're met with a horizon speckled with rubble, dunes of rust-colored dirt, and the remnants of a couple dozen structures rising up like tombstones in a long-neglected graveyard.

From up in her Pod, Olivia tries to tap into the remnants of an old Global Positioning Network, but, as she reports back down to us—her voice clicking and tinkling like ball-bearings from out of the truck's interior communications system—the grid is too old and has too many leftover security protocols to access, so we're not sure about the name of the town or where we are exactly.

"Somewhere between Springfield and Chicago" is all Olivia can tell us.

"Well," Cardyn shrugs. "It's a start. At least she didn't say we're between two of the nine circles of hell."

"Way to look on the bright side, Card," I exclaim, clapping him on the shoulder.

Rain suggests we get out and explore, but I'm hesitant. I understand that Rain wants to get her blood pumping. She's a thinker and a strategist, but she's also a fighter and, although she'd deny it, a bit of an adrenalin junkie.

Being cooped up in the truck for this long has taken a toll on all of us. Despite its many games, activities, and amenities, most of which only Cardyn has tried out, it's still a big box on wheels, and, with nowhere else to go, it's also kind of a prison.

After getting out of the confines of the Valta last year, we've been in mostly constant motion, and, I can't speak for my friends and fellow travelling companions, but something in the pit of my stomach warns me about the dangers inherent in sitting still. I'm just not as eager as Rain is to go tromping off into the unknown.

Parked now at the edge of the town, we debate for a few minutes, but, in the end, we decide to go exploring. Like Rain, Brohn is eager to "get out and see the world," as he puts it.

"It's not vacation," I remind him.

Spinning in his hovering mag-chair in the cabin of the truck, Cardyn scowls and tells me to quit being so pessimistic.

I look over to Manthy who doesn't seem to care one way or the other what we do.

"Fine," I sigh. "Render needs to get out for a fly-around anyway."

It's true. Render likes being cooped up even less than I do, and I can feel how desperate he is to spread his wings. He's still not one-hundred-percent recovered from his injuries, but he's never been one to sit when he can walk, or walk when he can fly.

Amani and Sheridyn, have started stirring, and Amani especially seems to be getting pretty alert. Sheridyn is glassy-eyed and keeps moving her mouth open and closed but with no sound coming out. We tell her who and where we are, but I don't think she's really processing anything right now.

Considering what they've been through, we decide they'll need to stay in the rig.

"You'll be safe there," Rain tells them. "Both of you."

His head down, his face dry and creased as a saddle-bag, Amani asks again to accompany us, but even he must know he's still too weak for such a bold foray into the unknown. His voice is barely audible, and even though he tries to hide it, the tremors in his hands and his eye-twitch speak volumes about how feeble he still is. It's not only physical weakness, either. The trauma of being recruited, imprisoned, lied to, and experimented on affects far more than just the body. It plays tricks with the mind, and it derails the soul.

I should know.

Unlike Amani, Sheridyn seems all too happy to sit this one out. I don't blame her. Her recovery has barely begun, and, at this point, a mild breeze could probably knock her for a loop. She blinks herself alert and sits up with help from Rain.

"Amani and I will be okay," she assures us, her voice barely audible. She examines the IV in her arm as she brushes loops of red hair away from her face.

"Okay," Rain says in her take-charge tone, "but don't stay in here. We'll hide you up in the Pod with Olivia."

We help Amani and Sheridyn to their feet, and Brohn guides them through the cabin and back to the Pod.

With the two of them and Olivia safely stowed and hidden away and with the access ladder retracted and the portal sealed shut and invisible, the rest of us gear up, strap on our black tactical vests, slap magazines into our nine-millimeters, and head out.

As we hop down from the truck, Render whips past us, streaking up into the crimson sky, his black wings and golden armor glinting in the hot, unfiltered sunlight. He banks hard, falters in the air for a second, and then evens himself out, gliding smoothly in sweeping circles on a rolling wave of thermals.

"This way," Brohn says, leading us along the remains of a

dust-covered road running from the highway downhill into the unbeating heart of the small town.

It feels like it must be at least a hundred-and-thirty degrees out, and I'm already having trouble breathing. I'm not sure if it's the heat, the possibility of toxins in the air, or the uncertain anticipation of what's to come, but my lungs feel like the husks of a dried-up piece of old fruit. Every breath comes with a cough. Only Manthy seems relatively unaffected as we march on.

"The air's so much worse here than it was back in San Francisco," Cardyn stammers. "Why is that?"

"Probably pollution," Rain says through a bout of phlegmy hacking. She scans the small town in front of us. "Or climate change. Or radiation from the bombings."

"Or a cocktail of all three," Brohn mutters, kicking at the remnants of some old, charred auto parts strewn along the ground.

To our surprise, the hunks of metal collapse into dust.

Brohn shakes his head and walks on.

Up ahead, an old gas station has been blasted black and flat along with six or seven other small structures—probably houses or businesses of some kind. A small neighborhood beyond the gas station has been leveled. The remains are covered with the telltale burn marks and molten ridges of plasma bombs, one of the fictitious Eastern Order's weapons of choice. The yellow brick foundation of what might have been a library or a school juts up like jagged alligator teeth embedded in a shattered jawbone. Although only about five feet or so high, the wrecked brick wall is still the tallest structure left in the town.

Brohn leads us toward the gas station. Nearby, a large tree, burned crisply black, is lying on its side, its root system rising up into the hot desert air in a thorny, dry tangle. The skeletal remains of what Rain guesses were once dogs have been shoveled up against the dead tree in a kind of above-ground mass grave of shattered and carbonized bones.

Rain scoops up a fistful of red sand and lets it sift through her fingers. "It's like no one's been here in years."

"We should get back to the truck," I advise.

It's not that I'm scared. More like cautious. I'm not afraid of a fight. Not anymore. But I'm still not interested in going out of my way to look for one.

Brohn is investigating what appears to be a steel trap door by one of the old gas station pumps when Render's frantic croaking from somewhere overhead signals danger, and we leap into defensive postures, our weapons drawn.

When nothing happens, we form a circle, guns held loosely but primed for combat. Manthy gives her two axes a few spins for good measure.

Then, there's a rustle off to the side, and a man, haggard, bearded, and brandishing a four-foot length of bent and rusted rebar, lurches out at us from behind the overturned tree. His pants are caked with dirt and what looks like dried blood. He's got one blue eye. The other eye is a milky, unseeing white. He's quicker than he looks and apparently fearless as he charges forward.

Before Rain has a chance to do her situational analysis and before Cardyn has a chance to do the trick where he's able to talk people like this down, Brohn deflects the overhead strike and delivers a blurringly fast fist to the man's floating ribs just above the pelvic bone. Dropping his weapon, the man doubles over and collapses to the ground, every molecule of oxygen bursting out of his lungs as the concussive force of Brohn's punch blasts through him.

Pressing ahead, Brohn holsters his gun and is leaning forward to grab our would-be assailant when the man rises feebly to one knee. He holds up a hand and mouths the word "Please" even though no sound comes out.

As Brohn seizes the man by the collar of the ratty tatters of fabric apparently passing for a shirt, we're swarmed by a second man, two women, and about a dozen children.

Only they're not coming for us. Instead, they pile onto the kneeling man, throwing their arms protectively around him and facing us with terrified eyes, as if we were the bad guys.

As it turns out, this time, I guess we kind of are.

"I wasn't planning to hurt you," the gaunt man pleads from his knees as he glances from us to the kids now draped over him. "We just can't risk…you know…because of the children."

"We weren't planning to hurt you either," Brohn says.

"Or anyone else for that matter," I add.

"You're armed," one of the women points out. "Your truck up the road…that's military."

"You're here for us," the other woman says through a barely audible rasp. "We won't go." Tears run down her mud-caked face in dirty rivulets.

Brohn gives an "all-clear" wave of his hand, and the rest of us holster our weapons. "We're not military," he assures the huddled group in front of us.

The first woman pushes aside a clump of matted hair that's fallen in front of her eyes. "You're not the Eastern Order," she says. It's half-question, half-observation.

Brohn shakes his head and gives the depleted-looking bunch a calming smile. "No. We're the opposite of the Eastern Order."

"The Patriot Army?" one of the little boys asks, his head wrapped in a blood-stained bandage.

"No," Brohn says, a light laugh in his voice. "We're the opposite of them, too."

"Then what are you?" the second man asks. He has his arms draped protectively around a waif-like boy on one side and a black-haired girl with emerald-green eyes on the other.

"We're friends," Cardyn says, glancing at our original attacker and at the rebar sitting in the dust beside him. "As long as we're not planning on bludgeoning each other to death."

The woman with the matted hair nods and stands up, gesturing for the rest of her group to do the same. "We can live with that."

Taking a few hesitant steps toward us, she extends her hand to Brohn.

"Naomi," she says. She gestures one at a time to the other people in her motley group. "This is Ven. This is my sister, Allie. And these are most of the kids left in Odell. The rest are down there." She points with a gnarled, yellow-nailed finger to the trap door by the gas pumps where Brohn had been standing just a moment before. "Oh, and you've already met Meynar."

Brohn steps forward, the collection of kids parting way for him like they're the Red Sea and he's Moses. He reaches down and shakes Meynar's hand, hauling him to his feet in the process. "I'm sorry about the—"

"Don't give it a second thought," the scruffy man says through a patchwork of brown and yellow teeth. "Truth is, if I was in your place, I'da done the same." Meynar feels the spot on his ribs where Brohn punched him and grimaces in a sideways lean. He wipes his dirty hands pointlessly on his equally dirty pants and tells the kids everything is under control, and how we're all friends now.

"It's safe," he assures them with a soothing smile.

For the kids, I think those must be the two most welcome words in the world right now because they drop their shoulders and let go of the collective breaths they've been holding.

Shielding her eyes with her hand, Naomi looks up into the scorching red sky and at the figure of Render gliding way out over the desert. "Where are you from?" she asks at last.

"The Valta," Brohn says.

"San Francisco," I add, knowing that the name of our tiny mountain town won't mean anything to these people.

Brohn nods. "Where is everyone?"

"It's just us," Naomi says. "They took the rest away to the New

Towns. Everyone they could find anyway. The ones who refused got killed." She glances over to a long mound of red dirt out beyond the derelict gas station. "They're in there. Buried. We're all that's left."

"Why didn't you just go to the New Towns with the others?" I ask.

Meynar spits on ground. "Because fuck them, that's why."

"We've been down that road before," Ven adds, his hand on Meynar's arm. "It's how every act of slavery begins. With the brutality of force and the cruelty of insecurity on one side and an act of compliance on the other."

He sounds angry and more educated than I would've guessed given the circumstances. But I see his point. Kind of.

"Still," I offer, "compliance is better than death. Isn't it?"

Ven shoots me a condescending scowl. "Live a little longer, kid, live under a small-minded tyrant, and ask me again someday."

"Come with us," Rain insists, pointing with a flick of her thumb back toward the highway. "We have a truck. You've seen it. It's big. We have supplies."

"We're on our way to Chicago," I add. "One of the New Towns. You can start over there."

Naomi shakes her head. "There's no 'there' to get to. You'll see. The country's huge. But the Wealthies have seen to it there's only enough room for survivors and for the dead. And they get to decide who's who."

"Then be a survivor," I practically shout.

"We already are," Naomi says with a determined calm. Her composure counteracts my anger, and we're left in a stalemate.

"At least let us leave you with some supplies," Brohn offers.

"We don't have a lot," I add. "But we can spare some weapons. Some food."

Naomi shakes her head, but the kids behind her look pleadingly at us, their eyes wide, their mouths open and eager.

"We've had problems…" she says, her voice trailing off. She shakes her head as if to clear it of whatever thought had occupied it. "We haven't had a lot of luck with strangers bearing gifts."

"We're not all that strange," Cardyn says, a good-natured smile playing at the corners of his mouth. "And it won't be gifts. It'll be the few supplies we can spare. Same as you'd do for us, I'm sure, if our positions were reversed."

"It'll keep you all going a little longer, anyway," Rain says.

"Not sure how much longer we want to live like this," Naomi says quietly. "Or how long we *can* live like this."

12

BEHIND NAOMI, Ven puts his head down but not before I see him tearing up.

Before anyone else can argue or object, I say I'll be right back, and I sprint, legs burning, up the dirt access road to the truck. My lungs ache the entire way, and my skin is soaked with sweat and tacky with red-tinted dust, but I don't care anymore. Leaping into the truck, I grab a canvas rucksack from one of the storage lockers and load it up with cartons of protein cubes and four of the loaded 2040s, one for each of the adults in Naomi's group. I tap the intra-comm panel and tell Olivia up in the Pod not to worry. "Just grabbing some supplies. Back in a minute."

"Anything I can do to help?" Olivia's disembodied voice asks.

"Just look after Amani and Sheridyn," I say. "Otherwise, I don't think there's anything anyone can do to help this time."

Without waiting for a response, I leap back out of the truck and run down the dusty road to where Brohn and the others are still talking with Naomi and her group of survivors.

One of the little girls is just saying to Rain how pretty she looks when I come sliding up.

"Here," I pant, handing the bulging sack over to Naomi. "It's not much, but it's better than nothing."

Naomi thanks us, although I get the sense she's sad. I worry all we may have done is prolong a lot of pain. But I don't know what else to do.

"They were just telling us about the Patriot Army taking everyone away," Cardyn informs me.

"For our own good," Naomi says with an eye-roll. "First the Order blows half the town to Hell and then our own government won't let us stay and rebuild."

"They say there's strength in sticking together. Say we have to go to Chicago," Ven adds. "Or any of the other New Towns."

Meynar kicks at the crusty ground like it's angered him. "Keeping everyone together is the easiest way for them to keep everyone under their thumb."

"How'd you kids get past the Eastern Order, anyway?" Allie asks. "Are they still out there?"

It's an impossible question to answer, and we all stop for a second, looking from one to the other. Do we tell them the truth? That all this was our government's own doing? Or do we let them keep thinking the government's on their side and doing its best to protect them from a hostile invasion? One answer is the truth. The other, a lie. One answer lets them live in honesty. The other lets them live in peace.

Neither lets them live for long.

Rain clears her throat and says, "We've been lucky. The roads are bad and hard to navigate, but at least we haven't run into any enemy armies or anything."

We all nod and hum our agreement. It's true, after all.

Now, a knot ties itself tight in my stomach. One of our missions, our first mission to be precise, has been to educate people. To fill them in on what's really going on. To tell them the truth about the Eastern Order and about the government's tricks. We're supposed to be building an army here. But not an ignorant one. I thought it would be easier to just run headfirst into the world and scream the truth at the top of our lungs. But here we are, standing in front of a community of moral, beaten down, and kind-hearted fellow citizens, and we can't even summon the courage to tell them the truth.

Maybe sensing my distress, Render swoops down from behind me and alights on my shoulder.

The kids gasp and jump back in unison, but I tell them it's okay. "This is Render. He's my friend."

A little girl steps forward. She's got a mane of tangled hair, pink sandals, and wide-set eyes as sparkling blue as two tiny sapphires. I expect her to ask to pet Render, but instead, she looks up at me, her eyes wide. "Are you Kress?"

At first, I think I must have misheard her, and I look over to Brohn for confirmation. But he just gives me a blank look and a feeble shrug as I turn back to the girl.

"I am. Did Brohn here tell you that while I was up at the truck?"

"Actually," Allie says, "we hadn't quite gotten around to your side of the introductions yet."

"Then how did you—?"

"You're *Kakari Isutse*," Naomi says. "The girl who dreams in raven. We've heard of you."

Cardyn shoulders past me. "How is that possible?"

Naomi shrugs. "Ven is a bit of a tech wiz. Tapped into a broadcast—"

"Apparently from San Francisco," Ven interjects, sweeping his hand in a wide arc at the decimated town. "There's a rumor about the five of you and about a girl named Kress and a raven named Render who are going to save us from all this. Get things back to good."

"I don't know about all that," I say, still shocked from this unexpected and improbable turn of events. "But all the more reason you should come with us."

"All the more reason we can't," Naomi says.

Before I can ask her why not, she holds up a hand and gives a flick of her head toward the gang of children still clinging to the three adults behind her. "Where you're going...what you're about to do...It's dangerous. And important. And it's no place for kids. If you really want to save us, save the world first."

Her voice quivers and then goes firm, emboldened by a mother's protective instinct. I understand her decision, but then a shock of sorrow shoots through me as I remember, despite all we've been through, we're really still just kids, too.

"I *am* Kress," I say, looking down at the little girl who is still looking up wide-eyed at me. "This is Brohn, Rain, Cardyn, and Manthy."

The little girl's voice squeaks out a giggle. "Is Brohn your boyfriend?"

I'm afraid the heat blasting through my face might melt her on the spot, and Cardyn and Manthy chuckle to each other behind me.

Naomi tugs the girl away and tells her to stop embarrassing me.

Thankfully, no one else presses us for the truth on that one, and I say how it's probably time for us to get going.

"We have provisions," Allie says. "Not much. We have a greenhouse down there. Kale'll grow. Desert chia. There's cholla up here. Some pygmy saguaro. Protein's mostly from whiptails and collared lizards."

"We cook them over a kerosene burner," Ven adds, his hands up like he's expecting us to object. "No sense in getting trichinosis or sparganosis or any of the other 'osises' that can get you sick as a blue-tongued dog."

"It's not much," Naomi says. "And we don't have the most comfortable digs. But we'd love to have you stay for a bit, maybe send you on your way with some rations?"

My Conspiracy and I exchange a look. The rules of hospitality say we should stay. The rules of survival say we shouldn't. These people don't have much in the way of provisions, supplies, or time. And I, for one, am reluctant to take away any of it, no matter how much kindness and sincerity is behind the offer.

The others must agree with me, because they start backpedalling toward the truck.

"We'd love to take you up on that," Rain says. "But we have two more to take care of back in the truck. They're not doing so well, and we're going to see if we can give them some medical attention on the way to Chicago."

Allie, Ven, and Meynar look at us, the kids look at them, and Naomi looks at the ground.

"You're really going then?" she asks. "To Chicago, I mean."

"We have to," I say. "There are people there who might need us."

Even as I say it, I realize the ironic tragedy of those words. There are people right here in front of us who need us, too.

"We'll be back," Brohn promises. "When we've done what we need to do in Chicago, we'll be back. With help, supplies, reinforcements…everything you'll need to get started again."

Naomi gives him a weak smile as I tug at his arm and say it's time to get going.

We say our goodbyes and wish Naomi and her crew well, all of us knowing they've already made all the wishes a person could wish for with nothing to show for it but poverty, anger, and a lifetime of being locked into a no-win situation.

13

On the way back to the truck, I tell Brohn maybe he shouldn't have promised that.

"Why not?"

I just shrug. He knowns why not. We can barely keep ourselves alive. We're on our way to break into a major government-run tower and try to free a bunch of kids, who may or may not be Emergents and whom we've never met and who may not even be there for all we know. We hardly have the standing or status to promise salvation to a bunch of stragglers, weighed down by hunger and pride and struggling to hang on to any wisps of hope left in their hearts.

I hear an erratic series of breaths and sniffles from behind me. It's Manthy. She's crying.

"What is it now?" Brohn asks, sounding tired and exasperated and not at all in the mood to have to deal with an emotional crisis.

Shaking his head, Cardyn makes eye contact with Brohn, and Brohn nods, backing off from his annoyance with Manthy but still striding angrily along toward the truck, his boots kicking up puffs of chalky red dust.

Manthy lets Cardyn put his arm around her.

"Our abilities," she says to no one in particular, choking on the word "abilities" like it's a swear word, "All these special things we can do…"

Cardyn pulls her a little closer, and I expect Manthy to object or push him away or hit him, but she does none of that.

"It's just…how can we ever expect to help all the people who need it? Especially if they won't let us?"

"It's not our job to save everyone we encounter," Cardyn says softly as we walk on. "Let alone everyone in the world. I don't care what Naomi says."

Manthy looks up at him. "Then what good are we?"

"We're good," Cardyn says. "We're *good*. That's all we need to know, and it's all we have control over. We're not saviors. All we can do is tell the truth and give the people we come across the freedom to believe it or not as they see fit."

"But we didn't tell them the truth about the Order," I remind him.

"No. We provide opportunity not answers. We fight to enhance life, not to restrict it or bring it under our own personal control. That's the difference between us and a heinous anus like Krug."

Manthy snuffles over a fragile smile, and this time, she does tip her head to let it rest on Cardyn's shoulder as we walk back up to the truck.

After we're all aboard and with Cardyn taking a turn at the wheel, I call up to the Pod to give Olivia the all-clear.

With assistance from Brohn who reaches up the access ladder, Amani and Sheridyn come back down and make a slow bee-line for one of the pull-out cots.

Neither one of them asks us what happened, and we don't offer to tell them. They seem shell-shocked enough without having to know a bunch of details about what's become of this small pocket of the country.

Sobbing a muffled cry, Amani sits on the edge of his cot with his head down. Sheridyn drapes an arm over her eyes and rolls over onto her side, quiet and still as a roughly human-shaped pile of bones.

Taking his turn at the driver's seat, Cardyn flicks at the holo-display, calls up the truck's instrument panel, activates the biometric ignition scanner, and gets us on our way.

After about an hour of weaving between derelict vehicles and around the split and splintered asphalt of the decimated highway, Amani rolls out of his cot and goes over to sit in one of the mag-chairs by the small slit of a window. Leaning against the chair's arm-rest for support, he's riveted as we pass two more towns, just as badly burned out as Odell.

We don't stop this time as the truck bucks and heaves over the wreckage and rubbish littering the road on the highway skirting the annihilated towns.

"I didn't know it was like this," Amani says. It's one of the first things he's said since we left the Processor. "I thought...I mean, we thought President Krug had everything under control."

"He did," Manthy says from where she's slouched in one of the mag-chairs, her eyes glossy. "Only it was under *his* control. All of it. The Eastern Order. The Patriot Army. Everything."

We're all quiet for a few minutes as the truck lurches on. Cardyn calls out to us from over his shoulder and asks if we're all okay back here.

"Fine," I shout over the grumble of the truck's engines, accidentally breaking us out of our collective reverie.

"I heard about you," Amani says. He struggles to sit up and is finally able to with a hand from Rain.

From her cot and without sitting up or turning to face us, Sheridyn says weakly, "We all heard about you."

"How?"

Amani also doesn't turn to face us and is instead mesmerized by the dead world flitting by outside the window.

"There was a man who came to the Processor sometimes," he says in a soft monotone. "He and a team of soldiers brought supplies every couple of weeks. I never talked to him, but he would sometimes pull my friend Xander aside before he left. Then Xander would pass along whatever he got from their conversations. Usually, it wasn't much. Sometimes it was nothing. A few times, he mentioned others like us, including a girl and her raven, and said how they could help put things right."

"Did you tell them?" Sheridyn asks me.

"Did I tell who what?"

Sheridyn squirms on her cot, looking annoyed and impatient. "Did you tell the people back in that town about the Eastern Order?"

"No."

"Why not? Aren't you supposed to be out here spreading the truth?"

She sounds oddly accusatory, especially for someone who hasn't totally gotten clear yet from the bony finger on the outstretched arm of Death.

"I guess...I mean...I don't really..."

"Truth is like a blanket," Brohn says, bailing me out. "It can comfort. Or it can smother. Those people back there...well, let's just say that sometimes breath is more important than truth."

Glancing over, Sheridyn seems to ponder this but doesn't look remotely satisfied with Brohn's answer.

Before anyone can respond one way or the other, Render *kraas* and unfurls his wings.

"He needs to fly," I say needlessly. Sometimes his intentions are far too clear to need me as a translator.

"We've got what must be Chicago dead ahead," Cardyn calls out from behind the wheel.

Brohn stands up and goes over to one of the weapons lockers where he starts reloading our guns. "Might as well get some recon work done."

Giving him a thumb's up, I sit back in my seat and let the connection take over.

I slip into Render's consciousness with relative ease this time, and I'm grateful for the absence of the vice-grip headaches I sometimes get.

From up above, what looks like a hundred-mile expanse of railroad boxcars and shipping containers appears on the horizon. Some of the freight cars have been stacked three or four high, most of them with their once-bright colors now washed-out from weather and age.

Rolling along in the alleyways formed by the endless rows of the rail cars are industrial marina-forklifts, giant payloaders, and huge rusted yellow swing-loaders, their mammoth rotating boom-arms curled up like a flexed arm or stretched skyward like a bellowing elephant trunk. The machines grumble along the intersecting grid of roads formed by the rows and columns of stacked freight cars.

In the distance, beyond the unending metropolis of ridged steel boxes and barely visible through the low-hanging pink cloud suspended over it all, are a handful of taller towers. Some are in various stages of construction with one black tower—vastly taller than the rest—extending high into the clouds, its top disappearing into the swirling fog of the upper atmosphere.

I barely have a chance to register it and pass along the basics to the others when an explosion sends the truck—and us—reeling.

14

OUR EARS RINGING, the seven of us are slammed around inside the vehicle, bouncing off all four walls, the floor, and the ceiling before eventually crashing against the side of the truck, which is now tilted on two wheels at a forty-five-degree angle.

Everything not stored away, hung up, or nailed down—first-aid supplies, boxes of protein cubes, silver tubes of purified rain water—comes sliding and clattering down on top of us in a heap.

Shouts and the crack of gunfire outside reverberate throughout the truck's interior.

Amani, blood gushing from a gash under his eye and a dark bruise already forming on his forehead, clambers to sit up.

Sheridyn, moaning quietly and bleeding from where the IV-drip ripped from her arm, has been tossed on top of me, and I scramble to extricate myself without hurting her in the process. She's light and frail, and I'll be surprised if the impact we just sustained hasn't broken half the bones in her body.

Dragging himself from the cab and into the truck's slanted and chaotic cabin, Cardyn asks what happened, but I can only answer him with a weak groan.

Thrashing herself free from the deepest part of the corner

where she's been wedged, Rain barks at us to get Amani and Sheridyn up into the Pod with Olivia.

Scrambling into action, Brohn starts helping Amani over to the Pod's access ladder. With his arm locked around Amani's waist, it's an angled climb, but he manages to latch onto the long edge of the worktable countertop attached to the kitchenette and haul himself and Amani safely over to the ladder leading up to the Pod.

At the same time, Cardyn slides down the sloped floor and peels Sheridyn off of me and, together, we help her over to the ladder and up into the Pod as well.

Olivia, still attached to her mag-chair, has been thrown sideways, her head and torso pressed up against one of her comm-panels. Brohn and Cardyn leap back down into the cabin while I tend to Olivia.

"What happened?" she asks, squirming to get herself oriented and upright.

"Not sure," I pant, doing my best to sit her up without stepping on her tendrils, which are splayed out in limp colorful bunches on the arms of her chair and sagging down across the inclined floor. "I think we just got attacked."

"You should all be up here," Olivia says, her head and one of her shoulders twitching in some kind of short-circuit spasm. "You'll be safe."

"If there's no one in the truck, it won't take them long to find this Pod. Trust me. Stay here with Amani and Sheridyn. Take care of them. We'll handle it. I'll come up to get you as soon as I can."

With that, I get Olivia as propped up as possible before I go sliding down the access ladder to join Brohn and the others in the cabin.

Slipping past me, Rain waves her hand in front of a security input panel, which is thankfully still working. She skims her fingers along the projected holo-display. At her command, the ladder withdraws into the Pod, and a synth-steel concealment panel slides seamlessly into place, sealing Amani and Sheridyn with Olivia in the Pod where there'll be safe, I hope anyway, from whatever's about to happen.

In the same second, the side door of the truck disappears under a flurry of hot orange sparks.

We're barely on our feet when the door, its edges sizzling and crackling hot, crashes into the rig, and four armed men, decked out in cobbled-together body armor and sporting some old but lethal-looking pistols, rifles, and knives, begin shouldering their way into the truck.

The men aren't especially huge or strong. But they take up a lot of space in these cramped and angled quarters, and they're relentless, charging in and piling on us faster than we can throw them off.

Two of them grab Manthy by her arms as she thrashes and screams. She kicks one of the men into the small kitchenette. His lower back cracks against the edge of the slanted counter, and he rolls in a cringing ball to the side.

Cardyn sidesteps an arcing knife strike and bounds over to deliver a devastating punch to the exposed lower back of one of the men. The guy, burly and bald, flies away from Manthy and tumbles out of the truck, hitting the ground hard. Cardyn leaps out after him, and I follow, weaving my way through, around, and in-between our attackers in the narrow confines of the truck's crowded interior.

Leaping down to the ground, I see there are more of these ferocious-looking men gathered in a menacing semi-circle outside the truck.

Ignoring them for the moment, I dash over to help Cardyn out, but it's not necessary.

Outside of the truck now and with space to maneuver, he delivers a deadly side-kick that catches one of our attackers just below the metal chest-protector, and I can hear his ribs break from here. As he falls, he fires his weapon at Cardyn, but the man's aim is off, and the bullets ping off the side of the truck like little metal bugs.

Cardyn closes in on the man, who pulls the trigger of his gun again only to be greeted by an empty metallic click and another ferocious kick from Cardyn to the side of his head.

Cardyn has his playful side, but when it comes to his protective instinct, he can be as relentless on the attack as he is with the jokes.

The attacker now at Cardyn's feet tries to get up as he reaches for his gun, which has clattered to the ground just a few feet away.

Cardyn locks eyes with the man and says, "Stop. Sleep."

The man's eyes flutter and go white as he slumps over, his tongue lolling out from his slack mouth.

"Got him?" I call out.

"No problem!" Cardyn shouts back.

"Not sure how you do that."

"Me, neither."

"Could use some help here if you have time in your busy schedule!"

Two men step toward me from the semi-circle, their thick fists round and heavy as bowling balls. One of the men takes a swing at me, but I duck, while the other man leaps onto Cardyn from behind. First, he drags Cardyn down and then spins his carbine rifle around, far too big of a weapon for close-quarters hand-to-hand fighting and tries to hit me with the butt end. I dodge the blow and square off to face the man, his round belly sloshing as he moves, his mangy orange beard in a dreadlocked tangle.

I deliver a kick to his exposed knee and am about to close in to finish him off when one of his buddies goes sailing by me, whipping right past my face and skidding through the dirt and landing in a heap at the feet of his compatriots gathered in the clearing. He's followed by another man who comes flying head-first out of the truck and slides to an abrupt and unconscious stop next to his equally unconscious partner.

Brohn and Rain bound out of the truck with more of the armed men shouting and jumping down behind them, grabbing and grappling as they go.

Manthy follows them, and now there's the five of us standing outside the tilted truck with the eight men left, forming a loose but narrowing circle around us.

"Was that you?" I ask Brohn, panting and pointing at the two unmoving men on the ground.

Brohn nods but doesn't take his eyes off of the men around us. "I think I'm getting stronger."

"Well, your penchant for understatement is, anyway," Rain says from over on his other side.

One of the men in front of us, I'm not sure which one, gives a shrill whistle, and in an instant, they all surge forward.

With the men in a circle, their hand-guns, oversized rifles, and artillery-launchers won't do them any good, so they attack with lengths of pipe, slabs of wood, and wildly swinging fists.

Across from me, Rain has been separated out by a thick bear of a man who's got her cornered against the exposed underside of our tipped-over truck. He's four times her size but less than half her speed, and he has nowhere close to her intelligence. He swings a hairy-knuckled fist at her head, but she ducks the attack and steps around the burly man to deliver a flurry of punches to his floating ribs on either side. He cries out and staggers sideways, his head slamming into the thick tread of one of the truck's tires.

"Someone's going to be pissing blood tonight," Cardyn calls out, congratulating Rain with a breathy laugh.

And then he disappears under four of the men, their fists pummeling him down to the ground.

Even Brohn, with all his ever-increasing physical strength and bullet-proof skin, is no match for their ruthless and underhanded fighting techniques. One of the men slugs him with a thick length of rebar. To the guy's obvious, open-mouthed shock, Brohn shrugs off the blow, but it's distracted him long enough for another man to sneak around him and spray some kind of green mist into his face out of a thumb-sized white cannister.

Coughing, Brohn staggers back then pitches forward, collapsing in a gagging heap onto the ground.

I shout out Brohn's name and try to get over to him, but one of the men, taller than the others and with a rusted, broken-handled 18-inch machete in his grip advances on me.

He swings for my head, but I easily evade the strike. He's as surprised as I am when his follow-up attack is met by a clang of metal on metal and a tiny shower of sparks.

Disengaging from her own attacker, Manthy has slid over and blocked the man's machete with one of her two tomahawk axes, which she spins with expert precision. She whips the other axe in a backhand arc, the razor-sharp blade slicing a deep gash the full breadth of the man's chest. A couple inches higher, it would have cut his head off, but I know that's not Manthy's style.

Right about now, though, I kind of wish it were.

I stumble back, startled, as a shoulder-lowered bull-rush from our blind-side sends Manthy flying. She absorbs the blow and rolls to a knee where she's clutched tightly in a powerful bearhug from behind, her arms pinned against her sides. She kicks at the man with her heels, but the metal apron he has lashed to his waist and covering his legs absorbs the impact, and he thrashes Manthy from side to side like a Pitbull with a chew-toy.

At the same time, the man kneeling on the ground in front of Rain whips out an old-style nine-millimeter 2020 before she can react, and he stands, towering over her, with the barrel of the weapon an inch away from her face.

In a flash, she strikes out at the man's wrist in an attempt to dislodge the gun, but he barely budges. Instead, he grabs her by the front of the vest with his free hand and lifts her clean off the ground, this time pressing the open end of the gun barrel hard against her forehead.

Before Cardyn can disengage from his attackers and come to her aid, he's surrounded by four of the men, each with an old but lethal-looking gun trained on him.

We survived the Processor, the desert, General Ekker, and the Patriot Army. Now, we're losing to a bunch of grungy, snaggle-toothed sub-humans.

It's the last thought I have before a crack to the back of my head sends me reeling, and I black out.

15

I don't know how much time has passed when I wake up with blurred vision and a hazy brain. The world is a swirl of washed out colors, and I've got the acid stench of vomit burbling in my throat.

The first thing that comes into focus is my Conspiracy: Brohn, Cardyn, Rain, and Manthy. They're lined up next to me—Brohn and Manthy on one side, Rain and Cardyn on the other—and we're all sitting in metal folding chairs, our hands bound behind our backs. The walls of the rectangular room are corrugated steel, so I figure we must be inside one of the freight cars I saw earlier through Render's eyes. It's hot and mostly dark in here with thin lines of light seeping in from the edges of a large steel door on horizontal rails across from us.

To my left, Brohn's head is down, his chin nearly touching his chest. On my right, Rain is just coming to, her eyes fluttering open, strands of black hair clinging to her face. Next to her, Cardyn is struggling against the ties on his wrist and looks ready to dislocate both shoulders in the process. At the end of our line-up on the other side of Brohn is Manthy. I lean forward to see that she's conscious and is sitting oddly still and quietly calm. Her whorls of burnt-auburn and sun-kissed, chestnut-hued hair hang down in a dusky curtain over most of her face.

Out of a natural but also long-cultivated protective instinct, I scan the room for Render and breathe a sigh of relief when I don't see him. He must still be flying around somewhere, and I can only hope he finds somewhere safe to be until I can get my bearings and connect with him again.

Olivia, Amani, and Sheridyn aren't here either, which means they must still be hiding inside the Pod. If Rain is right, they should be safe there, although I'm not sure for how long.

With Rain now fully awake and on high alert, she clears her throat and turns to me.

"Any guesses who those guys were?"

"No. But Granden wasn't kidding when he said Chicago would be a challenge."

"Understatement. And not the most hospitable introduction to the city." Rain flicks her head past me to where Brohn is just starting to come to. "How is he?"

"He's alive."

"They sprayed him with something," Cardyn calls over from where he's still twisting and wrenching around in an effort to free himself.

"Brohn?" Rain calls out, leaning forward to see past me. "Brohn?"

His head twitches, and a frightening spasm rips through his shoulder as his eyes flutter open.

"I'm okay."

I find that impossible to believe, but now's not the time to argue.

Brohn makes a scratchy noise in the back of his throat and spits on the floor.

"Can you get us out of here?" I ask.

At first, he gives me a vacant, bleary-eyed stare of unfamiliarity. Then, he nods almost absently and strains against the black zip-cuffs bound around his wrists, but nothing happens.

"Give me a second," he says. He shakes his head and tenses up his shoulders before trying again but with the same unsuccessful result.

"I'm okay," he insists. "I don't know why—"

"The stuff they sprayed you with," I say. "The green stuff."

Rain nods her agreement. "It must've done something to you."

Brohn smacks his lips, clears his throat, and spits again.

"The inside of my mouth tastes like the bottoms of my feet."

"How would you know that?" Cardyn asks.

Brohn shoots him a glare.

"Amani," Cardyn starts to say, leaning forward. "And Sheridyn. Do you think—"

"I'm sure they're fine," Rain assures us. She reminds us that the Pod is sealed up, self-contained, and practically invisible from inside or outside the truck. "They'll be okay as long as—"

She doesn't get to finish as she's interrupted by the grinding crank of a metal handle and a blast of light pouring into the room as the big steel door across from us grumbles slowly open with a jarring series of strident stops and starts.

With the door fully open, a dozen giant figures, thick and lumbering as a herd of sauropods, step into the room as we all blink our eyes to adjust to the sudden dissipation of the dark.

Squinting into the light and against the throbbing pain in my temples, I take inventory of our attackers:

Twelve men. Most of them large, but a few who, on closer inspection, are actually on the small side but are draped in thick scraps of metal tied on and held together with an array of frayed ropes, galvanized carbon steel wire, and even lengths of old-style electrical extension cords.

They're all armed with weapons as cobbled together as their makeshift body armor. Interspersed with their Gen-2030 rifles and their Sig Sauer and Desert Eagle handguns are long-handled scythes, tine-hoes, four-pronged compost pitchforks, sharp-toothed cultivators, root-grubbers, and trench shovels.

I know the weapons from our lessons in the Processsor. I recognize the agricultural tools from surviving in the Valta.

Armed with their mixed arsenal, the men are either preparing to hack us to pieces, light torches and go after an ogre, or else they're getting ready to do some serious gardening. I hope it's not the latter. After all we've been through, I'd hate to wind up as fertilizer.

The bald man in front, the largest of the group and wide across as he is tall, introduces himself as "War."

"And this is Lynch," he growls, pointing with a kielbasa-sized finger to the slightly thinner but equally sinister-looking man at his side. "My top lieutenant."

The heads of both men are bald and ghastly pale but streaked with dirt, like someone drizzled sewer water over a couple of underripe honeydews.

Scratching at one of the two raised scars that curves over either ear like seams on a baseball, the man called War gestures around the muggy room at the other men whose red leather jackets, military-style green and beige cargo pants, and flaking skin are in various states of decay.

"These are the men who are going to kill you. I thought you might want to get acquainted."

"Who are you?" Cardyn asks from down at the end of our line.

The men look at each other, puzzled.

When War starts laughing, the others laugh along with him.

"Not sure which New Town you straggled in from, but everyone knows us. We're Survivalists. Garfield Boulevard Syndicate. We own Englewood and everything in it. Do the math. You're in Englewood, *e.g.*: we own you."

"Ergo," Rain snarls from her seat next to me.

War pivots his neckless head around to face her. "What?"

"You said, 'e.g.' That means 'for example.' You meant to say, 'ergo.' It means 'therefore.'"

If my mouth weren't hanging open in shock, I'd yell at Rain to wait until we were a little less tied up in front of a slightly less dangerous-looking assembly of men before she started correcting people's grammar.

Nonplussed, the men mutter and mill around, looking at each other and then at War for guidance about how to react to this strange and unexpected response from the tiny, black-haired, and oddly unafraid spitfire of a girl in front of them.

But their confusion lasts only a second.

When he realizes he's being mocked, War clomps over to the chair where Rain is tied and punches her hard in the face. Her chair spills over right between mine and Cardyn's with an earsplitting clatter, and the side of Rain's head cracks in a sickening clang against the steel floor. At first, I think she must be dead from such a blow, but she glares up at War, her cheek bright red from the punch, blood pouring from her nose and pooling at the corner of her lip.

Brohn barks at the man to leave her alone, as I exchange a corner-of-the-eye look with Cardyn across the space where Rain had been sitting, before War nearly knocked her head off.

Cardyn nods, inhales a relaxing breath, and zeroes in on a square-headed, stubble-cheeked man toward the back of the group. The man blinks in a weird, asymmetrical way as Cardyn makes eye contact with him and talks to him across the space between us as casually as if he were inviting him to sit for afternoon tea.

"Following blind is as bad as flying blind," Cardyn calls out past the milling and agitated men. His voice is loud enough to hear, but it sounds just out of phase, like he's talking through gauze. "If you don't open your eyes, you'll hit a wall and die."

At the back of the crowd, the man's eyes glaze over. He slides a dented aluminum baseball bat from an improvised canvas sheath tied to his waist with a frayed and graying rope. He takes five strides through the crowd of his fellow Survivalists, his arm raised high with the bat clenched in his fat, pink fist.

Out of instinct, I think it looks like he's coming for us, and I wince involuntarily, but instead, he gurgles a guttural groan and swings the bat at the back of War's head.

War's lieutenant Lynch is fast, though, and hyper-alert. He shoulders War aside and raises his forearm to protect himself from the blow now directed at him. With a church-bell clang, the bat bounces off the steel cylindrical plates strapped to Lynch's arm.

The other men leap into action, grabbing the square-headed man by the arms as Lynch pulls out a rust-speckled handgun. Clearly offended and without debating or assessing the situation, he just says, "I don't think so" and shoots the man once in the chest and, as he pitches forward, twice in the head.

I'm stunned practically catatonic as the three gun blasts become a sustained high-pitched ringing sound shrieking through my ears.

Ignoring or else immune to the deafening shock of the sudden discharge of a gun being fired in this enclosed space, War thunders toward us.

"What'd you do to him?" he demands, leaning down into Cardyn's face and pointing with that sausage-thick finger at the dead man.

Cardyn smirks but doesn't answer, and I can tell he's scared. He's right to be. These men aren't normal.

War's rumpled forehead crunches into a furious scowl.

"I asked you a question, Fledge."

Cardyn looks at me, but I've got nothing to say and no way to help him.

With a wave of his hand, War summons three of his men forward. Striding up, his steel-toed boots banging on the metal floor, the first of the three men draws an old Sig P266 from his side holster and presses the barrel so hard to Cardyn's head that Cardyn's chair winds up tilted on its back legs up against the wall. Cardyn tries to turn his head away from the deadly weapon only to have the man swing a forearm into the side of his head. He crashes to the ground next to Rain, who is rolling onto her side and trying to stand up, her hands still tied behind her back.

Rolling free from the chair but with his hands also still bound behind him at the wrist, Cardyn tries to rise to his feet only to be met with a huge black boot to the chest.

War stands over him, the edge of his boot now pressed hard into Cardyn's neck as he squirms, gurgles, and gasps for air.

Brohn, Manthy, and I all cry out, but the men ignore us as two of them seize Cardyn by either arm and drag him out of the room as the rest of us continue to scream out for them to leave him alone.

War steps over Rain and wipes his furrowed and dirty forehead with an equally dirty rag before walking over to stand in front of Brohn.

"You look like a pretty strong boy," he says, his hand under Brohn's chin.

"That's fair," Brohn snaps back, wrenching his head away from War's grimy grip. "And you look like a toothless, cross-eyed lump of animal shit."

Amused, War balls up his fist, which is as big as my whole head, and slugs Brohn full-force in the face.

Brohn's head jerks to the side but otherwise, to War's clear surprise, Brohn barely flinches. War's eyes go wide, and he looks at Lynch who shrugs and nods for him to hit Brohn again. He does, and this time Brohn crashes to the ground, rolls out of his chair, and rises to his feet, hands still tied behind his back.

He's not bleeding, but his eyes are unfocused, his head is down, and his legs look like they're one shake away from collapsing under him.

I shout out his name, but he shakes me off and, eyes in a squint, refocuses on War.

Although we've been trained to survive in situations like this where we may be tied up, injured, or otherwise at a disadvantage, no one prepared me for the helplessness of watching the boy I've grown to love enduring this kind of relentlessly savage assault.

Manthy and I both scream out for War to leave Brohn alone, but War ignores us, advancing instead on Brohn and striking him again and again. Each booming punch snaps Brohn's head to one side, but Brohn refuses to fall.

From the floor, Rain, kneeling now and with her face streaked with blood, cries out for War to stop even as he's egged on by the crowd of men behind him. Rain looks ready to lunge at War, but Lynch anticipates her move and seizes her by the collar, dragging her over to his feet and pressing her face to the floor like he's punishing a disobedient dog.

After absorbing another flurry of crushing blows, Brohn stumbles up against the freight car's wall and drops to one knee as War winces and tries to shake the pain out of his gnarled hand. With Brohn still bound but now down on his knees on the floor in front of him, War rears back and blasts a kick to his head. Brohn smashes up against the wall and tries to get up, but one of the men slides over and sprays that green mist in his face again, and Brohn slumps down while I scream and cry until the lining of my throat goes blistering raw.

The way Ekker explained it when he had me and Brohn captive back in San Francisco, Brohn is like the rest of us: vulnerable, limited, and soft inside. His skin just happens to have a more enhanced molecular density. We're not sure to what degree. I've seen bullets ping off of him, but everything else: his muscles, blood, bones, and his feelings and his fears are, for the most part, the same as everyone else's.

Tilting his head toward the ridged steel door his men just dragged Cardyn out of, War limps toward me and Manthy—the only ones left bound in our chairs—muttering about how he thinks Brohn broke his foot.

"Good," Rain growls from where Lynch is still holding her down with his boot on her neck.

War turns and drops to one knee, gripping Rain's face hard in his hand. "What did your little Compat do to Bovie?"

"Compat?" Rain mumbles, a single tear dripping quietly down her cheek.

"Compatriot. Your friend. Your Flame."

"He didn't do anything," Manthy snaps defensively from her chair.

War turns his attention to her.

"Seems like he did plenty." He stands and points to the square-headed man, now being dragged away to the side of the room while he leaks a trail of blood onto the steel floor. "Bovie's been loyal to me since he was a boy. No way he'd come at me like that."

Manthy hangs her head. Stomping over, War reaches out and runs his fingers through her hair, but she doesn't look up or react.

"Something about you…" he says as he lets her hair fall back down over her face.

"Leave her alone," I growl.

He turns and scans me up and down before walking around behind me. He grips my forearms one at a time in his meaty fist and twists them around as much as my restraints will allow. He leans in close to look at my tattoos, and I can feel his hot breath on my skin.

"Something about all of you," he says, circling back around in front of me. "Not sure what it is, but I've got an idea. Yeah. You'll do."

"We'll do what?" I sob, now fully in the throes of anguished hyperventilation.

"Glad you asked, Chippie. You're about to join us for a Survival Revival. Consider it a test. If you fail, you die."

"And if we pass?"

"You won't."

"We won't what?" I cry. "We won't pass, or we won't die?"

War, his fat bloody fists on his hips, throws his scarred, bald head back and laughs.

"What's life without a little mystery, eh?"

16

WAR FILES OUT, followed by most of his crew. He leaves two men behind to keep an eye on us.

First, they pick up Brohn and Rain and slam them back down into the metal folding chairs. They throw Brohn down so hard I think the chair might collapse underneath him, but it holds, and he casts a frosty glare up at the two guards.

Although she's rumpled and dirty from being knocked down and dragged across the floor, Rain, too, looks more angry than hurt or afraid.

I've got the same rage running through me, although mine is accompanied by plenty of uncertainty, searing pain in my wrists, and by a surplus of, well, abject terror.

It doesn't help that Manthy is sitting quietly on the other side of Brohn or that Cardyn's chair is down there on the other side at the end of the line, ominously empty. I have no idea where War's men took him, why they took him, or what they're planning on doing with him.

"Are you okay?" I whisper over to Manthy.

She looks at me, her eyes clear, her face blank.

"I'll take that as a 'Yes,'" I say.

"How about you guys?" I ask, turning toward Brohn and then Rain.

One of the guards gives me a surly growl, but he doesn't tell me not to talk, so I decide to press my luck.

"Rain. Are you okay?"

Next to me, Rain licks the corner of her lip where a bit of blood continues to trickle down. "I'll live."

"I'll live, too," Brohn says, plenty loud enough for our captors to hear him. "Long enough to make these guys sorry they ever met us."

One of the guards scoffs and adjusts his dented rifle against his shoulder but otherwise doesn't move or respond to Brohn's threat, which I know is also a genuine promise.

"What do you want with us?" Rain asks the two guards.

"That's for War to say," one of the men says.

Staring straight ahead, the second man elbows him. "Guard," he says. "Don't talk."

The first man's cheeks go red, but he straightens himself up and grips his rifle a little tighter.

"I don't think we're going to get much out of these two idiots," Rain says, testing the waters in a dangerous gamble to see what she can get away with.

When the men continue to stare straight ahead at a spot on the wall just above our heads, Rain thrashes around for a second but then stops.

"Old versions of immobilizer cuffs," she says, turning her head to glance around behind her. "I don't think we can break them."

I give her a *shut-up* look, but the guards don't seem to care one way or another.

"What did you do with Cardyn?" I ask the guards, but I'm met with the same detached, icy stare into nothing.

"How long are you planning on keeping us here?" Rain asks.

Again, nothing.

"You won't get anything out of them," Brohn says quietly from his seat next to me. "They're tunnel-trained. No distractions. One task and one task only: Guard us."

"So we can't trick these idiots into letting us in on their plans?"

Brohn tells Rain, "No," and I look over at the guards who continue to stand expressionless and statue-still.

"Or into maybe loosening these ties enough to let us escape?"

"I don't think so."

"Great. Now what?"

Brohn's voice is still labored when he says, "Now, we wait."

So we do.

Hours pass. I try connecting with Render, but I'm too weak and distracted to do it purely through my mind, and, with my hands tied, I can't properly swipe in any of the patterns that might be more effective at activating our connection.

We all know he's out there just as we know Olivia, Amani, and Sheridyn are still hidden in the truck, but we can't say any of that without giving away a strategic advantage or putting our friends in danger.

Instead, we use the time to re-center ourselves. To focus. To get ourselves into survival mode like we were forced to do in the Valta, like we were taught to do in the Processor, and like we've had to do so many times since then.

I'm finally easing into a good run of meditative breathing when the big metal door grinds open again. Two men enter, and our two guards, who haven't budged or blinked in hours, spring to life, and the four of them march toward us.

Beaten up, weakened, and caught off guard, we offer no resistance as the men circle around behind us and haul Brohn and Manthy out of their chairs.

Seizing us roughly by the arms, two other men lift me and Rain to our feet and push us all along.

Depleted and defeated, our legs weak and our hands still bound behind our backs, we're a far cry from the energized

Conspiracy who were celebrating our great victory over the Patriot Army barely a week ago.

A few days. Is that all it's been?

I feel like I've lived too many lives for a girl my age.

Before I can process the reality of this feeling and all of its attendant implications, Brohn, Rain, Manthy, and I are shoved out into the scarlet-tinted daylight, where we blink hard under the hot sun and are marched on wobbly legs between a grid of freight cars—some stacked three-high, and in a few cases, even four-high—lined up in endless rows on either side of us.

Most of the metal cars are covered in graffiti or else painted in a slather of garish colors: electric blue, rose-petal pink, deep-sea green, none of which hides the fractures, dents, or scabby patches of rust. Some of the boxcars have extra doors and windows cut out of their sides and seem to serve as residences. Others are missing one entire side altogether and are set up in a long line as open-faced markets with rickety tables heaped with withered, weedy vegetables, plastic jugs of cloudy water, long racks of dirty syringes, mountainous mounds of grubby fabrics, and shelves piled high with old guns and wooden crates of ammo, fuzzy blue and damp with mold.

From many of the window cut-outs, eyes peek out from behind tattered pieces of canvas curtains. Doors screech shut on rusted rails as we pass. Women—many of them, skin exposed and barely-dressed in an odd blend of skimpy underwear and dark, heavy head-coverings—pull children out of the laneways, ushering them out of the way with urgent whispers as we're pushed by.

The men we pass, many of them pale and skeletal but all armed with holstered guns or shouldered rifles, also step aside, some of them offering nods and low, pumped-fist salutes to War's men, who ignore them as we tramp along.

Vendors, pedestrians, and assorted on-lookers also step aside, duck into alleyways, or avert their eyes as War's men escort us down the laneways and around head-high piles of trash and debris until we arrive at a clearing formed by a ring of railcars, all painted in chipped hues of purples and black.

Under the crushing heat and barely-breathable air, we're forced into the middle of the clearing.

Spinning us around one at a time, one of the Survivalists, bare-chested and caveman-hairy, pulls a pair of wire-snips from a holster on his belt and cuts off our zip-cuffs. Anticipating resistance, the rest of the guards keep their guns, knives, and long-handled, bladed weapons trained on us as we rub the circulation back into the bloody grooves carved into our wrists.

Other than us, War's men, a cranking mechanism of some kind, and more stacks of garbage pushed up against the side of the circle of rail cars forming the outer perimeter, the clearing is relatively empty. The ground is worn down and hard-packed, a victim like so much else around here, of the oppressive, relentless heat and radiation streaming down through what is, at the moment, a cloudless, red-hued sky.

"Feels like the Colosseum," I say to Brohn out of the side of my mouth. "Like we're about to be fed to the lions."

Brohn nods but otherwise doesn't respond.

I've never been to the Colosseum, of course. But Geography and Historical Landmarks was one of the courses we took as Juvens back in the Valta. It made me want to see the world. Now that I'm out in the world, I'm not sure I want to see any more of it.

As much as I'd like us to fight our way out of this, Cardyn is missing, Brohn and Rain can barely stand up, Manthy looks disturbingly unconcerned, and I've got a flitter of painful tingles running down my arms. My brain is too scattered to initiate even a simple connection with Render, and, for the first time in a very long time, I feel like I'm on my own.

"Nice brand," one of the soldiers says almost pleasantly,

looping his huge hand around my forearm and raising it up close to his eyes. "Who's your Syndicate?"

"My what? I'm not—"

The man next to him punches him hard in the shoulder.

"They're not initiated, you chaffer."

A man on his other side pushes him as well for good measure.

"War says to just bottle 'em up, so keep your gropers to yourself."

Towering over me, the three men shove each other a few more times as I cringe under them, relieved to have some shade but terrified I might get crushed to death if their arguing turns into a full-on fight.

A bunch of children peek around a corner of one of the rail cars at the edge of the clearing to have a look at the commotion. They're met with a hail of gunfire from another one of War's men. A spray of bullets plinks holes in the side of a rail car, and the startled gang of kids goes scurrying off the way they came.

I can't tell if the guy fired at them as a warning or if he was actually trying to hit them. Or maybe it's worse than that, and he honestly didn't care what happened after he pulled the trigger.

One of the guards, a human, no-necked sweat factory, steps up to the large cast-iron contraption in the middle of the clearing. As he cranks the handle on the mechanism, a thick slab of stone tilts up several feet into the air like the mouth of a toothless, gaping gator, exposing some kind of dark opening in the ground like a well.

War's men push us forward to the edge of a bleak, damp, fungus-filled underground dungeon. Before we can resist, protest, or assess the situation, they toss us like bags of sand down what must be twenty feet into the subterranean cell.

17

We land hard. Even me.

No easing gently to the ground this time. Without any connection to Render, I'm just a girl in a freefall along with three of my friends.

Rain squeals when we hit the ground. Brohn grunts, and Manthy lets out a low moan as we work to disentangle ourselves and scramble to our feet.

Over our heads, we hear the metallic sound of a crank and a grinding of gears as the massive stone slab thunders down over the opening above us, sealing us in near total darkness. A half-dozen small holes drilled into the thick stone lid offer only weak smatterings of light and nearly nothing in terms of the circulation of air.

"We're safe," Brohn wheezes, climbing to his feet, "and out of the sun."

"For now, at least," Rain says, reaching down with Manthy to help me up.

Stepping back against the wall of the pit, I stumble over something soft on the floor.

"Watch where you're going," a weak voice mumbles from out

of the dark. "I've been through enough without getting walked all over by my best friend."

"Cardyn!" I shriek.

The others gather around us in the gloom with me and Manthy kneeling down to offer Cardyn help getting to his feet, which he accepts with a long, low moan.

"About time you got here," he says through a strained chuckle. "I was getting pretty lonely down here. You'll have to forgive me for not offering you a chair or a cold beverage. I've been busy bleeding and trying not to lose consciousness."

"You're forgiven," I giggle as I give him a tight hug, which I know must hurt, but I don't care.

Even in the dim light from the pinholes high up by the ceiling, I can tell Cardyn's pretty beaten up. But his knuckles look like raw meat, so I'm guessing he gave as good as he got before War's men managed to get him down here.

"What'd they want with you?" I ask. "What did they do?"

Cardyn shakes his head. "I slipped away for a second after they dragged me out of that freight car. Not much I could do with my hands tied up, though. I tried using my persuasion thing, but they hit me with that green gas."

"Like they did with Brohn."

"Yeah. Same stuff, I figure. I lasted a few minutes. Took a few of them with me. But I couldn't stop them all. They got a hold of me, dragged me off to some underground bunker. They threw me into a kind of a cell. A glass box, really. There were three other kids in there. Two girls and a boy. About our age."

"In the cell?"

"No. That was the funny thing. They were outside of it. With a tall woman and a short man. They looked as out of place here as we do."

"Who were they?"

"I didn't get a chance to ask. I wasn't in there for more than a minute before that big guy War came into the cube and asked me some more about who we are and about what I did to his buddy."

"And?"

"And I told him to go piss up a rope." Cardyn grunts a painful half-laugh. "I don't remember much after that. Other than waking up down here."

"Well, we're glad you're okay," Brohn says.

"I'm mildly damaged. I'll let you know when I get to 'Okay.' Hey, did you find out anything after they took me out of there?"

"Only that War's guards are dumb but dangerous, disciplined, and pretty well-trained. Other than that, not much."

"Well," Cardyn sighs, "let's see if we can get out of here and maybe get to know our hosts a little better."

Inching my way along the edge of the pit, I feel the walls, looking for a hatch, a door, a seam, a vent—anything to indicate a possible way out. I even try to dig my fingernails into the rough surface, hoping maybe I can peel off a chunk of rock to use as a foothold to climb up or as a weapon when the opportunity comes, but the walls and the floor are a single cylinder of pebbly poured concrete.

"Anything?" Brohn asks, his voice regaining some of the old strength and confidence.

"Nothing."

"I've already tried," Cardyn says. "We're in some kind of well or old weapons silo. Can't even climb the walls to check out the stone lid up there. But there's always a way out of everything, right?"

"Suggestions?" I ask Rain.

"I'm going to sit down."

Rain plops down, and, with no better options, we all do the same, facing each other in a circle, our backs against the rounded wall, and our feet clustered together in the center of our cylindrical prison cell.

Brohn rests his head on my shoulder.

"You sure you're okay?" I ask into the murky darkness.

"I'll be fine," he says, but he doesn't make a move to sit up, and I don't know if it's the beating he took, general fatigue, an after effect of the green gas, or the brutality of the world around us that's keeping him down.

Even with all his physical strength and relentless determination, Brohn is hardly indestructible. For all the years I've known him, he's carried the weight of leadership and responsibility on his broad shoulders—always without complaint—and it's nice to know he's willing to let me be strong for him from time to time.

"We've got to get out of here," he says, patting my leg and sitting up straight.

"Although I still have some great interior design ideas for this place," Cardyn says grandly, "I think I'm going to have to agree with you on this one."

"Can Render help?" Manthy asks.

"If I can get some rest, focus a little, I can connect with him. Maybe. But even if I can, I'm not sure what good that'll do. He can't exactly lift up the stone hatch or dig us out."

Rain, streaks of dried blood on her face, inhales a deep breath with visible effort and takes another look around at our underground cell.

"There's no tech for Manthy to tap into. And without our comm-links, we can't contact Olivia. Not that she'd be able to do much anyway."

"Olivia," I say. "She's got Amani and Sheridyn with her."

"I told you," Rain says, feeling her nose and wiggling it to make sure it's not broken. "They'll be fine."

"You said they'd be okay 'as long as—'"

"As long as they don't try to get out and provided no one decides to slice the truck apart for scrap."

I tell Rain this new information is hardly reassuring.

"I can't be *re*assuring when I'm not sure myself," Rain responds.

"I see your point."

Pressing the toe of his boot against mine, Cardyn asks what I think War really wants with us.

"Probably what every evil warlord wants: the chance to flex his muscle, consolidate power, secure his territory, send a message to his enemies, and make himself feel big by making someone else feel small."

Cardyn nods. "Or maybe he just needs a hug."

"I volunteer you."

"I think I'm all hugged out."

Our laughs echo weakly in the dim dungeon, and we settle back against the walls to talk strategy and to await our fate.

At one point, Brohn and I fall asleep leaning against each other, my arm hooked into his. When I wake up from a quick but pleasant dream, my back and neck are sore, my wrists are still tender, and this thumping headache has apparently decided to keep me company for the long haul.

But there's a strange energy in this pit, which Rain theorizes has something to do with our proximity to each other.

"Ekker did tell us our abilities are enhanced by being close together," Brohn reminds us, his arm around my shoulders. "It's why they isolated us like that for so long in the Valta."

"We were all together in the truck," I remind him. "I didn't feel any special enhancement then."

"Maybe it only works when we're together in times of distress," Rain muses. "Like an adrenalin rush. Or a collective consciousness kind of thing. Do you guys feel it?"

"Feel what?" Cardyn yawns.

"The boost. The vitality. I don't know what to call it."

"I know what you mean," Brohn says, raising his hands and forearms in front of his face and pivoting them around. "It feels like I'm getting recharged somehow."

"Yeah," I confess. "Me, too. For all the good it does us, though.

For a group that's supposed to be so special and advanced, we're pretty powerless at the moment."

Cardyn rolls over onto his side, his legs tucked up against his chest.

"I hope no one plans on us being superheroes. Because we kind of suck at it."

Sitting cross-legged, her back straight, her hands resting loosely on her knees, Manthy tells us not to worry.

"With patience, all things are possible."

"How about that stone slab up there," Cardyn sneers. "Will patience lift that thing?"

Manthy shoots him a dirty look before returning to what I assume is her meditation.

The hours drag on.

We sit, talk, stand, stretch, plan, sleep, and repeat.

We've gone for long times before without food or water, so, even though it's not ideal, it's not a matter of life or death. For now, at least.

Still, a bathroom break would be nice.

Cardyn squints up at the dust-filled shafts of light struggling through the air holes.

"Maybe they forgot about us."

"Maybe they think we're dead," I suggest.

"They're testing us," Rain says quietly. "They're testing us to see if we are what they think we are."

"Emergents?"

"I think so."

"How do you know?"

"I don't. It's a hypothesis. But it's where the facts lead. If they wanted us dead, there wouldn't be air holes at the top of this thing. If they wanted us gone, they would have gotten rid of us. Tossed us into one of the landfills we saw piled up throughout the city. If they just wanted us weak, they'd beat the sand out of us but wouldn't leave us down here to recover. Eventually, they'll need to feed us and give us water, so we're going to wind up being a drain on their resources, which seem to be pretty limited, which means that whatever they plan to do with us should be happening soon. We just need to wait and stay alive until then. Trust me."

Of all the things we've ever done, trusting Rain is something that's never been a problem. As someone who seems able to process countless possible scenarios and see a dozen moves ahead, Rain is definitely someone we can and have often relied on to help us believe in escape when there's no apparent way out. Even with all our training, experience, and emerging abilities, faith in each other has always been our real source of strength and our most reliable path to survival.

For most people, I'm sure being entombed alive like this would be too much to bear. The dim light, the stifling heat, the lack of food and water, the fact of captivity. I've read stories about how the mind can give out even before the body.

But these Survivalists didn't count on the experience and stubbornness we bring to the table.

For over ten years, we survived drone strikes. We had to struggle for the basic necessities of life. After we were recruited at the age of seventeen, we lived in an underground bunker for our entire time at the Processor. We were even trapped down there once for several days before we got out. We've lived in the desert and in the mountains while we were on the run. And we trained and helped lead the Insubordinates in their victory over the Patriot Army in San Francisco.

Being buried alive isn't exactly high on my to-do list, but I've experienced worse. We all have.

If the Survivalists want to break us down and use us somehow for their own purposes as Rain suspects, they're going to have to get much more creative and a lot nastier than this.

Besides, my head has cleared up enough to allow me to

initiate the swipe patterns on my arm implants that help connect me with Render.

It's not exactly freedom—we're still stuck down here—but it's a start.

"And a good start," Rain says. "It's the first move in a long sequence, but it ends with us getting out of here."

"Soon, I hope," Cardyn says, rubbing his hands together in mock glee.

"Did the guards tell you anything?" I ask.

Cardyn gives a snort of disbelief when he tells us they said it could be weeks or even months.

"They said they take more skeletons out of these pits than people. Typical scare tactics."

"It'll be a few more days," Rain says evenly.

Letting his hands fall to his sides, Cardyn says, "Days?"

"Why?" Rain asks. "Did you have something else to do?"

"Lots."

"How do you know?" Brohn asks Rain.

"It's where the facts lead. Card's right. The skeleton threat was just a scare tactic. A way to keep us weak with ignorance. It won't be that long. It'll be another three days. Besides, a few more days of confinement will give us a chance to get our bearings through Kress and Render. And isn't putting up with a few more days down here worth staying alive and getting out in the end? Three days," Rain promises. "Four, tops."

Cardyn pouts and crosses his arms.

Manthy looks around for a second, then closes her eyes and relaxes into a series of slow, even breaths.

Brohn pulls me close to him and suggests we trust Rain's calculations and settle in for a few days of patient surviving.

"No one I'd rather spend time surviving with," I say as I lean my head against his chest.

Even in the dark and with my head facing away from him, I can still feel the comforting warmth of his smile.

18

THERE HAVE BEEN plenty of times when my connection with Render and the abilities he shares with me have been convenient. Life-saving, even.

This isn't one of those times.

Separated like this and still not at one hundred percent, I get information ranging from spotty to crystal clear about the world outside our crypt-like prison, but I'm unable to do anything about our situation.

So I spend my time seeing what Render sees while I remain trapped in this dark, underground tomb with my Conspiracy.

It's been four days. I know this because of Render. When I connect with him, his awareness becomes mine. So, I can feel the passing of time. While we've been sitting here, imprisoned, cramped, and helpless, I've seen four sunsets and four sunrises through his eyes. From two-hundred feet above, I've gotten a literal bird's eye view of the area where we're being held.

In the past, Render has performed as a feathered spy-drone. But that type of function relies on my ability to communicate my intentions, and right now, I'm limited to seeing what he sees. Anything else I've wanted to try—spying on War and his men or getting more detailed information about how Olivia, Amani, and Sheridyn are holding up—has eluded me.

"This is turning into real torture," I complain.

His eyes closed, Brohn smiles and reaches over to give me a flirtatious poke in the ribs.

"This is nothing we haven't lived through before."

"True. But only being able to half-connect with Render...well, it's like being able to see and smell great food that's just out of reach."

We're quiet for a minute as I lean my head against Brohn's chest. His arm is draped cloak-like around my shoulders, and, considering our current dilemma, the weight and nearness of him makes me feel unusually free. Brohn's body is warm, and he brushes wisps of loose hair away from my face. He gives my shoulder a comforting squeeze with one hand while the fingers of our other hand interlock and rest lightly on my lap.

Except for being in a deep pit with unclimbable cement walls, this is where I want to be.

"That's from a Greek myth, right?" Cardyn asks sleepily from out of the dark.

Without taking my head away from Brohn's chest, I raise my eyes to meet Cardyn's across the small, shadowy space of our cell.

"What's from a Greek myth?"

"The thing about not being able to reach the food."

"Tantalus."

"Right. Tantalus."

"He was tormented forever by not being able to eat the fruit from the tree above him or drink the water from the stream below him."

"So why did he keep trying?"

"I don't know. I guess that's the point, isn't it?"

"What? That trying is its own torture? That's a pretty bleak point."

"No. That trying, never giving up in the face of obstacles, is the key to immortality."

"That's not the key to immortality," Cardyn says.

"Oh," Rain answers. "*You* know the key to immortality?"

"Sure. If you want to live forever, wake up every morning..."

"And?" Rain asks.

Cardyn giggles. "Nothing. Just wake up every morning, and you'll live forever."

"You're such a looner," Rain groans.

Cardyn sighs and sounds sleepy again.

"I don't think I'd want to live forever if it meant I couldn't eat or drink the things I want. And can we please stop talking about food? I think my stomach might actually collapse in on itself like a black hole before we manage to find a way out of here."

"You're the one who brought it up," Manthy says, her voice accusatory and laced with judgement. "It wouldn't bother you so much if you concentrated on your meditation."

"Some of us aren't as good at shutting our minds down."

"Your mind seems pretty shut down to me," Manthy scoffs, turning her back to him.

"Knock it off," Brohn says, his voice light and even. "Can you two save the bickering for when we get out of here?"

"She started it," Cardyn says.

Manthy doesn't respond, but, even through the dark and humid air, I see her turn back around to stick her tongue out at Cardyn before she closes her eyes and returns to her meditation.

"Stone walls do not a prison make," Rain mumbles, trying to keep our spirits up.

"Nor iron bars a cage," I say, finishing the line from Richard Lovelace's poem, "To Althea from Prison."

"I don't know how you remember things like that," Cardyn says.

"It *is* impressive," Brohn boasts on my behalf.

"If anyone's interested," I say, "that poem ends, 'If I have freedom in my love, and in my soul am free, angels alone, that soar above, enjoy such liberty.'"

"See?" Cardyn exclaims with far too much enthusiasm for someone who hasn't had a shower in nearly a week. "There's always hope. As long as we have love in our hearts, our souls will continue to soar free."

"It's a platitude," Brohn grumbles. "It doesn't have to be an either-or proposition. I'd rather have love in my heart and a soaring soul *and* not be buried alive."

"Speaking of angels soaring above," Rain says. "Anything else from Render?"

"It's dangerous out there, but he's staying as safe as possible. He knows where we are and that we're in trouble. But he's frustrated about not being able to do anything about it."

"Tell him to join the club," Brohn grumbles.

"He's also worried about being seen and getting shot at."

"Another great club to join," Brohn teases. "Hey. What about the truck?"

I know this is his way of asking about Olivia, Amani, and Sheridyn who, as far as we know, are still hiding out in the Pod.

"No sign anyone's left the truck," I tell him.

Sounding especially worried, Cardyn predicts our captors will find the Pod.

"It's just a matter of time. You think in a place like this they won't carve that truck up and use every bit of scrap they can?"

"I would've thought the same," I say. "But the truck is still in the same spot. Still tilted up against that same embankment, bottom exposed and everything. War and his men have been inside it. They've looted it. Took the rest of the weapons, first-aid kids, and provisions from the supply lockers. But they haven't made any effort to get it back on its wheels or running again. And they definitely haven't torn it apart. It's almost like they respect it too much to defile it."

"Maybe because it's a government truck?" Brohn suggests.

"Maybe."

"Or they just don't have the means to maneuver a truck that big?"

"Possibly."

"Or it could have something to do with us."

"Interesting. Creepy, but interesting."

"They wouldn't be able to start it anyway," Rain says. "It's keyed to our genetic markers. If they try to circumvent the ignition protocols, the bolt-bypass will engage, and they'll be left with nothing but a big metal box on a very locked transmission."

"Well, for what it's worth and from what I can get from Render, I don't think they've found the Pod."

"Great," Cardyn says. "Then Olivia, Amani, and Sheridyn can look forward to suffocating or starving to death."

"I don't think so," I say after a moment's contemplation. "Not yet anyway."

"It's true," Rain adds. "The Pod is fully stocked and designed to survive way more than this. It's radiation-proof, impact resistant, and it can even be detached and sent underwater like a little submarine if needed."

"All so Krug can survive the apocalypse while everyone else suffers and dies," I say.

"Well," Cardyn drawls, "it'd serve him right if that thing keeps Olivia, Amani, and Sheridyn safe long enough for them to join us in taking him down."

"What about up there?" Brohn asks, flicking his thumb skyward. "What do we have to look forward to when we get out of here?"

When he says "when" instead of "if," I note some of the old optimism creeping back into his voice. It's refreshing.

"Remember the tent-city in Oakland?"

"Sure."

"This is a hundred times as big. But instead of tents, it's

almost all those railroad cars. At least on the outskirts of the city core. They run forever. I can't tell the exact distance, but it's a lot.

"Rail cars. Like the ones they dragged us past to get here?" Cardyn asks.

"Yes. Same as the ones we saw. Only there must be millions of them. They've been converted into living quarters. Apartments. Shops. Markets. Things like that. Then shoved together and stacked to make bigger buildings. There must be at least a hundred distinct neighborhoods up there."

"How can you tell?"

"The colors mostly."

"War mentioned Chicago is divided into territories."

"I see what he means. From Render's point of view, it looks like a rainbow-colored jigsaw puzzle that doesn't actually form a picture of anything."

Cardyn stands, stretches his back, and presses his hands against the cold wall of rock.

"I'm guessing they're not neighborhoods with fancy gardens and lots of landscaped greenspace."

I shake my head. "It's just railcars, then a ring of open land, kind of like a barrier. It's got houses like in San Francisco. More rundown, maybe. But a lot of them are pretty big. No trees or grass or anything like that. After that, there's a core of towers. Lots of skyscrapers. Some are being torn down. I think others are being built up. Like those arcologies we saw."

"The ones that look like they're under construction?" Cardyn asks.

"Yes. With Krug Tower in the middle."

"So all we have to do is get out of here, make our way through—how big did you say the city is?"

"Not sure. Looks like it's got to be at least fifty or sixty miles north to south and another thirty or forty miles west away from the water. At least."

"How many square miles is that, Rain?"

"Twenty-four hundred."

"So twenty-four-hundred square miles of...what?"

"Hell, basically," I sigh.

"Great. And we need to get through what you think are probably gang territories?"

"Yes."

"Then past this barrier area."

"With the old houses. Yes."

"Great. Past the barrier area, through the city core, and right up to the front door of Krug Tower, which is probably the most well-guarded structure in the country."

"From what Wisp's intel says," Rain reminds us, "technically the White House has more guards."

"Thanks, Rain," I say. "That's remarkably unhelpful."

Rain shrugs as Cardyn continues his worried summary of our situation.

"And then we do...what? Knock on the door and say, 'Hey in there. Can you please release any and all kids you may be torturing in your insane mad-scientist attempt to govern the future trajectory of all of humanity?'"

"You make it sound like it'll be a challenge."

"No. Piece of cake."

I'm about ready to ask Rain to do her trick where she magically comes up with an optimal strategy for our eventual infiltration of Krug Tower and liberation of its Emergent inhabitants when I'm interrupted by the grind of the huge slab of stone above our heads. It creaks open with a crunch of gears and a raspy screech like a rusted nail being pried out of a hunk of petrified wood. Light pours down into our subterranean prison, and we all look up, shielding our burning eyes with our hands.

"See," Rain says, standing and brushing her hands on her pants. "Like I told you. Four days. Tops."

Cardyn groans and stretches his arms one at a time across his chest.

"I don't suppose you can predict what we're having for dinner?"

The silhouettes above drop a braided rope ladder down into the pit and bark at us to climb up.

"And don't try anything clever," a voice calls down. "Or I'll shoot you in the legs and leave you up in West Garfield Park for the Violators to have their way with."

The faceless man beckons us up, his gun glinting in the harsh light as if to emphasize his point.

Not that we need any extra motivation. I don't know who or what a Violator is, but it doesn't sound friendly, and it I'm not interested in finding out one way or the other.

Brohn takes the lead, and, one by one, we ascend the frayed and shaking rope ladder until we're all standing in the clearing facing a small platoon of War's men lined up in front of us like a firing squad.

19

ONE OF THE MEN, his jacket hanging loosely open to reveal his thicket of matted chest hair, approaches us to clamp a thick band of steel around each of our waists.

A thin man with a greasy goatee threads a heavy chain through manacles on the steel bands until my Conspiracy and I are bound together single-file like a five-piece human charm bracelet.

"You're not going to kill us, are you?" Cardyn asks from the front of the line.

Lynch, War's right-hand man, steps forward and holsters his weapon.

"Not for me to say. That's up to War. Right now, our job is to take you to the Basilica."

The "Basilica," we discover after a long march through more rows of rail cars, turns out to be another open-air space, only this one is enclosed on all sides by a high wall of corrugated metal, ringed at the top with a combination of nail-filled posts and looping coils of razor wire. The dirt under us is packed down hard with most of the space in the clearing being taken up by rows of long wooden church pews and a stage at the front made from a wheel-less upside-down car with an old-style blue mailbox standing on top.

Amplified by the surrounding metal walls, the heat is even worse here than it was out in the desert.

"Think we could get a little water?" Cardyn asks one of our armed escorts who responds with a canine growl and a dry, hacking cough before spitting a greenish-yellow lump of phlegm onto the ground at Cardyn's feet.

"I'll take that as a 'No.'"

Still chained together at the waist, we're shoved down onto a pew.

The hard-packed, reddish-gray dirt beneath our feet combined with the oppressive heat and the hordes of sweaty, barrel-chested men all around give this all the feel of a Roman coliseum combined with an outdoor rock concert.

It's actually, as it turns out, a church.

Dressed in military fatigues, Lynch climbs a small set of wooden steps onto the overturned car and introduces War.

With the sun setting behind him, War lumbers up to the mailbox, which seems to serve as a lectern. I have no idea where he managed to scrounge his purple army vest or his matching glossy black and purple camo cargo pants, but he looks flamboyantly round and regal, like something that should be off floating in a parade somewhere.

He's got one of the newer versions of the HK MP7A9 rifles tied with a strip of leather and slung across his chest. I can tell from here that his weapon has all the perks: suppressor, pic rail, extended magazine, night-vision scope, and a parallax-removal sight. On top of that, he's got a two-gun holster stretched impossibly tight around his waist and a belt full of assorted knives and sharpened screwdrivers to complete the ensemble. His scarred scalp glistens with sweat under the yellow light from the bank of incandescent bulbs screwed into fixtures along a series of tall wooden poles arranged in a semi-circle behind him.

SURVIVAL

Also behind him, perched on a thick wooden stand, is a gray and purple vulture. It's hunched over and shaggy, its pink head lolling back and forth as it looks out over the crowd with its squinting dead eyes. Shrouded at the base by a tuft of dirty feathers, its pimply neck is curved like the world's ugliest question mark.

Burned into the face of the blue mailbox is a circle and an arrow superimposed over the silhouetted image of a bird.

When War turns to the side to consult with Lynch, his bare meaty shoulder is revealed to have the same image branded onto his skin.

"What is it?" Cardyn asks me from the corner of his mouth. "A raven?"

I shake my head, and Rain leans across me and Brohn toward Cardyn.

"It's a vulture. You can tell by the wings. Wide and split into those long fingers at the ends. The arrow is the male symbol."

The man behind us growls for us to shut up.

"They're symbols of Ares," Rain whispers in passive-aggressive defiance of the guard, her voice barely a breath. "The god of war."

I'm reminded of Wisp, Brohn's kid sister who organized the San Francisco rebellion and who gave an impassioned and inspirational speech right before leading us all into battle.

War stands like Wisp did, before a throng of adoring fans, the agitated masses waiting for just the right leader to come along at just the right time and tell them everything they want to hear.

That's about as far as the comparison goes, though. Wisp was a true visionary, a tireless revolutionary who practiced what she preached and who wanted nothing more than the end of bullying and the true beginnings of a world based on empathy, humility, self-discipline, and unconditional respect. In that regard, if Wisp has an opposite, the thick-necked, bare-armed man in the purple and black fatigues standing before us is it.

War puts both fists under his chin, his forearms pressed together, and the rowdy, armed, and unwashed congregation goes dead quiet.

One at a time, War points to Rain, Manthy, and me, jabbing his finger toward us like a dagger. He gives us a disappointed frown and shakes his head, although, without a neck to speak of, it's more like a full body-swivel.

"Welcome, Survivors," War begins, turning his attention to the crowd.

"Welcome, War!" the crowd responds.

War lowers his eyes for a second, his hands gripping the edge of the mailbox. Behind him, the vulture swings its neck from side to side and ruffles its mangled array of matted and molting feathers. The reddish haze from the setting sun combines with the hot waves of yellow from the lights on the posts around the clearing to cast sinister-looking shadows like demons' fingers along the ground, across the crowd, and up the walls of the surrounding rail cars.

"In Exodus 22:18," War preaches into a clunky microphone clamped to the top of the mailbox, "Moses himself warns us we must never allow a witch to live. And now there are three among us! Among us and very much alive!"

He waves his hand at me, Rain, and Manthy like we're prizes on a game show. His voice clacks and cracks in deep, thunderous booms, his words like river stones toppling down an embankment.

"We know from Adam the dangers of female temptation. We know from Samson the dangers of a retributive woman. The saint in Timothy proclaims, 'I do not permit a woman to teach or to have authority over a man. She must be silent.'"

War gestures at us again and shouts out to his congregation,

"Do these *females* look prepared to submit to our authority?" He sneers when he says, "females," like it's a curse word.

The congregation grumbles a unified, "No!" in answer.

"Ephesians 5:22," War continues, "governs that wives must submit to their husbands as to the Lord. Do these *females* look prepared to submit?"

Again, the congregation exclaims, "No!" in unison.

"Colossians 3:18. 'Wives, submit yourselves unto your own husbands, as it is fit in the Lord.' In Corinthians we are reminded that women must keep silent in the churches. They must speak only at home as their husbands allow. And women must keep their heads covered as a reminder of man's authority over her. Do they speak under the supervising authority of a guiding voice?"

"No, War!"

"Do these women have their heads covered?"

"No, War!"

War grumbles into the microphone and coughs to clear his throat.

"'So the man took his concubine and sent her outside to them, and they raped her and abused her throughout the night, and at dawn they let her go. At daybreak the woman went back to the house where her master was staying, fell down at the door and lay there until daylight. When her master got up in the morning and opened the door of the house and stepped out to continue on his way, there lay his concubine, fallen in the doorway of the house, with her hands on the threshold. He said to her, "Get up. Let's go." But there was no answer. Then the man put her on his donkey and set out for home.' Judges 19:25-28."

As one and as though the rambling, pointless story somehow made the most sense in the world, the congregation shouts out, "Long live War!"

Rain nudges me in the ribs and whispers, "What the hell does that mean?" out of the corner of her mouth.

I raise my shoulders and whisper back that I don't know. I remember the words, of course. My memory has been that good lately. But some of those biblical stories are beyond baffling.

"And the betrayers," War continues, pointing now at Brohn and Cardyn, "The betrayers must also be brought low. Loving thy neighbor only gets you stabbed in the back. Strangers want what you have. They want to bring you down so they may lord over you. They must be stopped before they start. An eye for an eye means you must blind them before they get a chance to blind you."

"Long live War!"

"Finally, my brothers, we survive. Look no further than Jeremiah 31:2. 'Thus says the Lord, 'The people who survived the sword found grace in the wilderness.' And have we survived the sword?"

"We have, War!"

"And have we found grace in the wilderness?"

"We have, War!"

War is sweating now and seems to be in some kind of trance. He absently dabs at his greasy face with a frayed piece of gray-brown fabric before going on.

"Deuteronomy 6:24 says, 'So the Lord commanded us to observe all these rules, to fear the Lord our God for our own good and for our survival, as it is today.'"

"We survive today, War!"

"Exodus 32:27. And he said unto them: 'Thus saith the Lord, the God of Israel: Put ye every man his sword upon his thigh, and go to and from gate to gate throughout the camp, and slay every man his brother, and every man his companion, and every man his neighbour.' Exodus 32:28. 'And the sons of Levi did according to the word of Moses, and there fell of the people that day three-thousand men.' Do you hear me, Survivors?"

"We hear you, War!"

"I say again. There fell of the people that day *three-thousand men*! Moses commands half his followers to kill the other half! They obey. They kill. They kill friends and kin. They survive! Can we do any less?"

"We survive today, War!"

"The Template justifies violence to preserve ourselves. Lest we forget and as Noah will always remember, God—the hero, the survivor, the first mass murderer—drowned nearly every living thing on the planet. How can we do any less?"

"We survive today, War!"

War pumps his fat fists in the air. "This, my brothers, is the Survival Revival!"

"We survive today, War!"

"We have witches and betrayers among us."

"Yes, we have, War!"

"They will be our slayers or our saviors."

"Death and salvation in War!"

War reaches into a leather satchel tucked into his vest and withdraws a hunk of grayish-blue meat that I realize in horror is the remnant of a human hand. He tosses it over his shoulder to the vulture, which unfurls its blotched and bumpy neck and opens its mouth to gobble down the gruesome treat. A slippery skinless finger hangs out the side of its yellow beak. The vulture tilts its head sideways, the fleshy wattle wriggling above its nostrils, and sucks down the decaying digit.

Cardyn says, "Ugh" and turns his head.

The crowd goes even more rowdy and breaks into a chant of "Who thrives? Who survives?" over and over.

War signals to five bald and burly men, each furrow-browed, scorched red by the sun, and the size of a small tank. They march up behind the pew where my Conspiracy and I are still chained together at the waist and drenched in sweat in the unrelenting evening heat.

"And Abner said to Joab," War bellows from the dais, "let the young men arise and compete before us."

War points to a cluster of his men off to the side.

"Transport Team. Take them to the Theater."

Then he swings around to face us, his voice peppered by the buzz of the microphone, and does a dramatically slow count to three on his fingers.

"You have three choices, witches and betrayers: survive, arise, or demise."

20

"Theater?" I ask out loud over the chanting and cheering crowd.

"Why do I get the feeling they're not taking us to see a lavish Broadway musical?" Cardyn asks us from his position at the front of our little chain-gang.

"You've never seen a musical," Manthy calls over to him from her position at the end.

"Neither have you," Cardyn fires back.

She sticks her tongue out at him, and he returns the gesture while Brohn barks at them to stay focused. Twitching his head and looking absently skyward, he turns to me.

"Why must we be the meat in the middle of an imbecile sandwich?"

My laugh is cut off by one of War's henchmen, a guy roughly the size and shape of an aircraft carrier, who loops the end of our chain around his immense forearm and hauls us all at once to our feet.

I'm starting to feel less like a person and more like a piece of beat-up old luggage. We've been dragged from our truck. Dragged to the pit where we spent four torturous days. Dragged into War's twisted sermon.

Now, we're being dragged through a hot maze of interconnected rail cars and finally outside to where hundreds, no—*thousands*, of people are milling along both sides of the road in wait. There are no cheers or jeers as we're violently escorted past the crowd. Instead, the onlookers—rugged, ragged, and with the deep trenches of poverty and oppression creasing their faces—part way for us.

The smell of the place is overwhelmingly awful, and Rain, who's just behind me in our forced march, says she's sure she's going to throw up.

I can't say I blame her, although I ask her to at least aim to the side if she has to spew.

On either side of us, gelatinous mounds of suppurated garbage line nearly every laneway and ooze a practically tangible stench. Large, open pits drop down a full foot into gurgling underground sewers where a soup of human waste and marinated garbage chugs along in a burbling brown river.

I'm trying to stay as close to Brohn as possible, my feet bumping his heels as the men behind us shout at us to keep moving.

Brohn looks over and whispers for me not to worry.

"Worry is about all I've got right now," I quiver back.

The man behind me rams the butt of his rifle into my back right between my shoulder blades. I cry out, and my legs buckle, but Brohn shoots back a hand and supports me as we continue to march forward. He makes a move like he might turn around and slug the guy, but I reach up and stop him with a hand to his forearm.

"Not yet," I say under my breath.

Brohn shoots the man a nasty, curled-lip scowl, but we follow his instructions and keep shuffling our way, single-file, through the bleak mass of onlookers.

Finally, the crowd ends and opens up at the edge of what looks like it might be a dry river bed or the remnants of an old canal or sewer system. Huge mountains of rubble, broken building materials, sheets of steel, and long-scrapped skeletons of old vehicles block off one of the open ends of the deep trench with a huge steel door sealing off the other side, to form a kind of half-pipe, hundred-foot wide mosquito-infested arena with yellow puddles of brackish water interspersed along the rough and rocky red ground.

Thousands of spectators, hundreds-deep, have gathered on both sides of the amphitheater. Although I'd normally expect a cacophony of hoots and hollers in a situation like this, the bleak crowd is eerily quiet.

"Why don't they make any noise?" I ask Brohn, who is still just in front of me in our little five-person convoy.

"I don't know. But it's creeping me out."

"Would you like it better if they were swearing and throwing things at us?" Rain asks from behind me.

"At least we'd know they were alive," I tell her over my shoulder. "This is too much like the calm before a very catastrophic zombie storm."

"There's no such thing as zombies," Manthy informs us all from the end of the line.

At that moment, on our side of the ravine-arena, six men roll War out on a broken mag-chair that's been fitted with two makeshift loops of tank tread, rusted coppery-green and kicking up dust as they grind over the splintered and bramble-infested concrete walkway.

Rocking back and forth, the vulture from church is perched on a post fixed to the back of War's jolting throne. The evil-looking bird lets out a creepy gurgle-hiss like a blender grinding ball-bearings underwater.

The crowd parts for War's procession. I'm sure it's all supposed to look very regal and intimidating, and, to a certain degree, it does. But it's also clear that War is the ruler of a fragile, decimated kingdom of pseudo-worshippers who follow him out of fear and, most likely, out of a lack of alternatives.

His guards position the five of us in a line on the edge of the arena. At the top of the embankment on the far side of the river bed, ten feral-looking women are pushed forward where they glower at us across the distance through hate-filled eyes.

Like most of the other people in the throng of onlookers, the women are dressed in form-fitting but ratty brown canvas coveralls cinched at the waist with what appears to be a belt of barbed wire. From here, I can see that each woman has a number carved onto her exposed forearms and a brand, red and raised, burned into the side of her neck. It's the same bird and arrow symbol we saw burned into War's shoulder and into the mailbox lectern at his so-called church.

Unlocking our manacles and sliding the heavy chain out, its linked length falling heavily to the ground, War's men separate Brohn and Cardyn from the rest of us. The heavy steel bands around our waists slide to the ground with a muted clatter. Brohn and Cardyn try to move back toward me, Rain, and Manthy, but they're stopped before they can take more than a single step.

My protests—verbal and physical—are met with a fist to the side of my head that sends me crashing into Rain and Manthy, who catch me before I hit the ground.

I manage to shake off the blinding flash of white, but I can't get rid of the high-pitched ringing in my ears or the excruciating thrum in my temples.

Before I can process what's going on, three other men standing behind us lock onto our shoulders and push us down to our knees. The man behind me clamps my head in his huge hand and forces me to watch as his fellow Survivalists push Brohn and Cardyn down into the arena.

As Manthy, Rain, and I watch, the weight of the guards' hands holding us down, our two friends tumble down the steep, curved side of the river bed and crash to a stop below in a cloud of red dust.

On the far side, the ten branded women also leap into the arena, kicking up huge clouds of dirt and dust of their own as they slide down the embankment and land in an animal crouch at the bottom.

Staring with furious eyes across at Brohn and Cardyn, the women mill around, taking a few steps forward and then a few steps back, predators preparing themselves to take down this fresh prey.

Behind us, War rises up in his chair and bellows into a telecomm voice-booster.

"Witness the challenge of the rivals to survival!"

Down in the pit, the women are savage. And I don't mean savage in the sense of aggressive or ruthless, although they're both of those things. No, these women are sub-human somehow. It's in their look, the matted and disheveled hair, the long craggy fingernails, the thick eyebrows. Their eyes burn golden-orange like a cat's in a dimly lit corner.

And yet there is also something enchanting about them. Maybe it's the way they move, panther-like. Or it could be in the sleek ripple of muscles in their forearms and calves that peek out from beneath their undersized and dirty canvas outfits.

The women outnumber Brohn and Cardyn, but that appears to be their only advantage. That and their uncaring ruthlessness. Neither is enough.

In less than a minute, with the stone-still crowd suddenly exploded into a cheering frenzy, Brohn and Cardyn are standing in the arena below us, their chests heaving from exertion, the bodies of the women lying in an overlap at their feet like wet sacks of sand.

I risk a head turn and a relieved smile in Rain's direction, but she and Manthy are both still staring open-mouthed at the carnage below.

On the far side of the arena, hundreds of women—all dressed like the ones Brohn and Cardyn just dispatched—are being held back by a line of armed and armored men.

"We have fighters on our hands!" War's voice thunders out in a hail of static from the system of clunky, gun-metal gray speakers posted along either side of the arena. "Combat is easy. Victory is as inevitable for one side as defeat is for the other. Survivors are worthy. Only survival, itself, is sacred."

With that, War orders me, Rain, and Manthy down into the arena to join Brohn and Cardyn. When we hesitate, War's guards lunge toward us, and we leap—half out of instinct, half out of fear, but entirely because we don't have a choice—down into the pit.

21

ON THE FAR SIDE, five of the men—shirtless, barefoot, and clothed only in tight, knee-length gray shorts—slide down from the opposite bank to face us.

Like many of these Survivalists, the five combatants are large. Unlike the others, though, they are large in a different, leaner, and, frankly, more terrifying way.

They each must be nearly seven-feet tall and look alike enough to be brothers or even clones. Shirtless and lacking body hair, their muscles glisten and ripple in the hot, stagnant air of the open arena. With no body fat, their abs look carved out of stone. Their arms tense and flex as hard and unforgiving as braids of steel cables. On the left side of their chests, each man has War's vulture and male emblem, raised and rubbery, branded onto their skin. Despite the generally battered and disheveled look of this place, the men's hair is surprisingly well-groomed, slicked back and blond like a team of Nazi warrior-bankers.

Accompanying them are twenty thinner men, gangly and clearly a far cry from this warrior class. This latter group hauls the moaning, twitching, and unconscious bodies of the defeated women over to a platform hooked up to a pulley on the far wall.

They load the women onto the lift and signal up to another group of men who start winding up a wagon-wheel shaped crank that lifts the platform and the women up and out of the arena.

While this is going on, Brohn and Cardyn backpedal to join me, Rain, and Manthy.

"That was quite a performance," I say to Brohn and Cardyn.

Brohn winks. "Two of us against the ten of them."

"And they were outnumbered," Cardyn beams.

"All we had to do was fight five times as hard."

I smile up at Brohn, who is sweat-soaked and panting but clearly reinvigorated.

"Glad to see you're feeling better."

"I'd rather not have to fight our way out of this," he nods, "but as long as we don't have a choice, we might as well win."

"At least they're not armed," Cardyn notes with a flick of a thumb in the direction of the five giants across the way. "Nice to see that some people in this world can still be civilized in their voyeuristic clashes to the death."

Manthy mumbles, "Give me a break," under her breath as Rain shouts at us to get ready as our new opponents get a signal from War and suddenly sprint toward us.

We're good fighters, but these men are better.

They attack us with a combination of accuracy, speed, and strength we just can't match. Before I know it, one of them has me in a choke-hold, with Brohn reeling under a flurry of precision strikes to the neck and solar plexus. Such an attack usually wouldn't faze him, but he's obviously exhausted, and I'm not sure how long his skin can stay indestructible under these conditions. One of the men catches Rain's leg mid-kick and hurls her into Cardyn who goes reeling, limbs splayed and bleeding from his nose and mouth, backwards onto the ground. Rain and Cardyn don't even have time to untangle themselves and get up before their attacker is on them again, raining a flurry of unpulled punches to their heads as they try to cover up.

One of the men manages to evade a series of quick jabs from Manthy. Locking one hand onto her wrist, he spins her around and pins her to a line of rusty oil drums lining one side of the arena. With his hand around the back of her neck, her hair clumped in his fist, he slams her head down onto the top of the drum, and her body goes limp. He raises his fist high into the air, ready to bring it down in a crushing, fatal arc onto the back of Manthy's head.

That's when a switch clicks in my own head, and I go from prey to predator.

I can't say how it happens or why it happens now, but I know my mind's been accessed. From somewhere high overhead, Render has connected with me. And, unlike the past few days of partial and limited telempathy, this is a beyond-complete connection.

In an instant, his thoughts, memories, emotions, and consciousness are my own. And so are his abilities.

All of them.

In the wild, ravens are known for their ferocity, for their incredible agility, their uncanny intelligence, and for their gift of mimicry. In mythology, they're known for their gift of prophecy and for being shamanic tricksters.

In the space of a single beat of powerfully flapped wings, I'm imbued with all of it. The reality. The mythology. I am instantly transformed into *Kakari Isutse*, the Girl Who Dreams in Raven. I'm only vaguely aware of what happens after that. The next thirty seconds pass like a flitting dream mixed with a hallucination mixed with a déjà vu all wrapped up in a mosaic of compressed time.

In my own mind, everything is slow, a bead of honey crawling down the outside of a cold glass jar. At the same time, I feel like I'm a blur, a flurry of action. I see what all five men are going to do before they do it, before they even know themselves what they are going to do. They're moving in slow-motion, backwards even, and I'm in overdrive.

I distract Man One with a sound I'm somehow able to project off the steep wall of the riverbed. He whips his head around, thinking there's an attacker behind him. He's got my forearm blasting into the base of his skull before he knows what's happening. Dancing past the falling man, I duck Man Two's slow-motion punch, circle around behind him before he's finished the action, and reach up to deliver a double blade-hand strike to the side of his neck. The impact to his carotid artery sends his eyes back into his head and his body sagging to the ground.

I anticipate the reaction of Man Three before he does. I see him lunge at me before he lunges, and I counter with a straight kick to the middle of his chest that has him gasping for air on the ground next to his two partners before he even knows he's been hit.

Man Four and Man Five dig their boots into the ground, preparing to advance toward me, but a spinning back-heel to the floating rib of one man and a well-placed straight kick to the groin of the other, and I've got them down before they finish taking their first step. With the last two men on their knees and a little closer to my height, I press my advantage with an elbow to the jaw of Man Four and an upward heel-thrust under the chin of Man Five.

Whatever was left holding them up evaporates, and they shift out of slow-motion, slamming face first at full speed into the hard-packed earth.

When I'm done, the five men are strewn at my feet in a twisted pile of broken limbs, empty lungs, and bloodied bodies.

Render is still wafting around inside me, a vapor of his consciousness mingling with my own. Everything he and his kind have stood for and symbolized over thousands of years snakes through my mind and permeates my body. The spirit of war and violence, the creator of the world, the Nordic notions of thought and memory—in this single moment, they're all me.

According to some accounts of the bible, ravens were released by Noah after the flood but didn't return because they were out feasting on the dead. I look down at the men's blood soaking into the hard rust-colored dirt and breathe a sigh of relief that this whole thing hasn't made me hungry.

Without questioning the supernatural event that's just happened, Brohn, Cardyn, Rain, and Manthy gather themselves up and huddle around me, and we stand in a protective circle, our eyes on the ring of potential assailants lining the two edges of the arena above us.

War looks down, furious, but then he laughs and gives a half-wave and a clenched fist to Lynch who nods his understanding. The tall steel door sealing off one side of the arena opens on warped and rusted rails, screeching a sound into the hot air like an animal in agony. The ground trembles as the sound of impact tremors rolls over us in waves.

"The two boys have defeated the women. The five of you together have overcome our five Custodians of Combat. You have therefore proven yourselves worthy enough to meet Press-and-Die, the best of us, the ultimate Man," War calls down to us. "It was nice knowing you."

22

"Press-and-Die?" Cardyn asks as the towering steel door, as high up as the entire arena, grinds open on rusted rails.

What lumbers out is a Modified.

But this isn't one of the shrunken, near-catatonic Modifieds we encountered in Caldwell's lab in San Francisco.

This Modified is a flesh and blood tank. He's part human, part industrial machine press. His exposed muscles on one arm and one leg are wrapped in thick coils of orange wire. His forearms flex with spring-loaded industrial hydraulics. Whatever power source he has in the clunky steel box affixed to his chest must be radioactive because even the metallic parts of him are covered in sizzling blisters.

Clearly a slave of the Survivalists, he stomps toward us, an inhibitor collar clamped on his neck, War's vulture symbol burned deep into the part of his mammoth skull that's still covered in human skin just above the asymmetrical ocular sensors passing for his eyes.

Without hesitating, the titanic Modified charges across the pit. The ground literally splits under him, a fault-line forming between his massive steel boots.

"Survival," War shouts down to us from his mobile throne, "is its own test, its own result. Survival is its own reward!"

After looking up at War, the giant machine-man swings around to face us.

"Press-and-Die?" Cardyn pseudo-smiles. "That thing's name is Press-and-Die? Talk about on-the-nose."

"The Modifieds aren't 'things,'" I remind him. "They're people."

"Either way, I don't think it, I mean *he*, is much of a people person."

Launching into battle mode and guided by our training, we form a loose circle around the behemoth.

Cardyn calls out to him. "Slow down, Big Guy, or you might blow a gasket."

That seems to disorient the giant machine-man but only for a second. He shakes off Cardyn's persuasion and takes a swing with his arm of gears, pulleys, and pistons. For someone and something so large, he moves fast, and Cardyn rolls to the ground, barely dodging the mighty blow.

Wobbly from the intensity of my connection to Render and the equally intense after-effects of separation, I've got nothing to offer.

Emergent or not, I'm still just a hundred-and-twenty-pound girl squaring off against a very angry industrial engine of tunnel-visioned destruction.

I try anyway. Because, after all, what choice do I have?

I manage to evade his first strike, but he clips me on the follow-through with one of the synth-steel rods making up his forearm. The impact, even though it's the smallest fraction of his strength, drives me into the ground and forces my arm to get twisted under me.

I'm trying to be strong and get back to the fight, but my arm is swollen, and I can hear the radius and ulna bones crunching against each other as I try to roll away.

Press-and-Die pivots his head around on a pair of screeching cam-shafts and looks down at me with an expression that I swear is apologetic. He pauses for a second, seemingly unsure if he should continue his attack now that I'm wounded, or else back off at my all-too evident pain.

Taking advantage of his hesitation, Rain distracts our opponent while Manthy slips around behind him.

Brohn gathers his legs under him and charges full-tilt at the monstrous machine-man. He must know it's a pointless attack, but I see now that he's not going for the knockout. Just a blow to distract Press-and-Die long enough for Manthy to leap from a pile of wooden skids, up onto the row of rusted oil drums, and onto the Modified's back where she locks her legs around his gear-filled torso and slaps her hands onto either side of his contorted half-human head.

Manthy's eyes go black, and Press-and-Die's go blank.

Short-circuited, he collapses face first into the dirt sending up a cloud of Mt. Vesuvius level debris as Manthy leaps off of him and rolls to a sliding stop ten feet away.

When the dust and smoke settle and the echo of Press-and-Die's collapse fades into a receding hum, there's a very long moment of silence from the crowd lined up and pressed forward above us. Then one cheer goes up, one word shouted from deep in the otherwise stunned-silent throng:

"Emergents!"

From his palatial chair and under the shadow of the ominous vulture perched just behind his shoulder, War scowls but then his features lighten, and he stands up. The vulture raises its head on its curved and scabby neck and follows War with its eyes as War leans down over the riverbed arena.

"Maybe you are who we thought you were," he calls down. "No one has ever survived all three trials."

"That's us," Brohn calls back, his voice laced with snark. "Survivors."

War runs his gloved hand along his thick jaw and his meaty, whiskery chin. "So it would seem."

"Does this mean you'll let us go?" I call up. My voice sounds hollow and shaky in my ears. My arm is killing me, my heart hasn't stopped racing, and I feel furious enough to kill or cry, although at the moment, I can't tell which.

War gives me a long look before his eyes go sad, and he gives us all a shrug of resignation.

"I can't do that," he says, pounding his fist to his chest and then glancing out toward the huge black tower jutting up into the low-hanging reddish-gray evening clouds. "You're weapons. This is war. I'd be foolish to give you up."

"But we can help you!" Rain shouts. She points to the same black tower. "We want Krug as much as you do. If you let us go, we can get in there, free the others, and take him down for good!"

Lynch steps forward and whispers something to War, who shakes his head at first but then scowls and nods.

"I'll consider it," he calls down, his voice rumbling in baritone waves into the curved riverbed. "In the meantime, I won't take any chances."

War taps his temple and then makes a series of circle motions in the air with his finger. The vulture behind him raises its head and bellows a horrific raspy hiss, and, in unison, dozens of War's armed and armored men slide down into the arena and encircle us, their guns old and weathered, but still deadly.

Exhausted and outnumbered, we raise our hands in surrender. Well, *I* raise one hand. The other feels like it'll fall off if I even *think* about moving it.

Our surrender isn't enough for War's men, however, and they blast a gas-filled canister at our feet. The green vapor puffs out as gentle as a summer cloud, and the next thing I know, my eyes roll back, the world goes dark, and, after our successive victories in combat, I feel myself being dragged away, yet again, by the heels of my boots.

23

When I blink myself awake, I take in our new accommodations. It seems I've spent far too much of my life as a captive. We were isolated in the Valta, controlled in the Processor, hidden in the Style, and confined to War's prison pit.

For better or worse, at least this prison appears to be nothing more than another one of the millions of freight cars, only this one's been converted into a more typical jail cell. It's complete with ridged iron bars over an opening carved out of the corrugated ceiling above our heads and a sliding steel door with no discernible latches, handle, or lock on this side.

It's other-worldly hot with a universe of dust specks hovering lazily in the column of blazing light beaming down into the freight car.

At least we're not underground this time.

The others are already awake, and I'm embarrassed about being the last one to regain consciousness. I try to wave my greetings to my Conspiracy when an excruciating lightning-strike of pain sears through my forearm.

"Oh, frack," I say, wincing in agony and trying hard to stop myself from throwing up. "I think my arm's...broken."

Cardyn slides over, slipping out of his vest and shirt as he does.

War's men took our weapons after our first encounter, but at least they left us with our cargo pants, boots, and compression tops. Cardyn and Rain even managed to keep their gray short-sleeve button-ups and their tactical vests.

Cardyn cradles my forearm in his hands with the tenderness of a child holding a baby bird. It doesn't matter how gentle he is, though. It still hurts.

He leans his ear to my arm, listening for the sound of unnatural movement and gazes at the ceiling like a safe-cracker immersed in the deepest concentration.

"Well?" Brohn asks. "What's your diagnosis, Doctor?"

"Definitely broken," he sighs. "Radius is broken clean through. The ulna is just cracked."

"How refreshing," I moan.

Cardyn fashions his button shirt into a sling, tying it around the back of my neck with a nimble flourish.

"That'll have to do until we come up with something better."

I offer him a weak, "Thanks."

The pain is intense, and even the motion of my body in mid-breath puts my pain receptors into a frenetic bout of hyper-activity.

"I doubt they have the best medical facilities around here," Rain says.

Brohn sits down next to me and puts his arm around my shoulders, careful not to jar me. I lean my head against his, and he asks how I'm doing.

"Not sure what hurts more," I grumble. "The arm or winning all of War's challenges but still being locked in here anyway."

"Doesn't seem fair, does it?" Brohn asks. He runs his hand along my hair and tidies the sweaty runaway bits clinging to my cheeks.

"You know," Cardyn says with a sarcastic drawl, "it'd be nice to get *rewarded* instead of punished for one of these victories for a change."

"What were you thinking?" Rain asks. "A medal? A ribbon? A ceremonial parade?"

Cardyn brushes her off with a wave of his hand but then gives a sheepish grin.

"A parade would be nice."

"What you did out there," Brohn says to me, "that was some serious next level combat."

"Talk about deserving a parade," Cardyn gushes. "How'd you do it anyway?"

"Not sure. And not much to show for it," I sigh and then wince as I try to raise my arm. "Except for another prison cell and a broken wing."

Cardyn is up and pacing now, but Rain and Manthy are sitting against the far wall with their knees pulled up to their chests.

Without lifting her eyes, Rain asks Manthy how she's feeling.

Manthy doesn't say anything at first, and we all look over at her. Even at her most expressive, Manthy can be hard to read.

Then, unexpectedly, she starts crying and laughing at the same time. Cardyn stops mid-pace, and we're all staring at Manthy, open mouthed. For as long as I've known her, she's been the kind of girl who would probably do great things someday if given the opportunity, although I never knew if it would be as a heroic savior or as an evil genius, and now I'm wondering if she's finally tipped over the wrong edge.

Rain is looking at her like her hair's on fire, but Cardyn leans over and asks if she's okay.

"That's exactly it," Manthy says, offering up a half-smile and wiping tears from her eyes with the heels of her hands. "I'm not okay."

"Then what—?" I start to ask from across the column of light between us, but Manthy stops me with a raised hand.

"I think I might be *better* than okay."

"Um...That's great," Brohn says. "Isn't it?"

Manthy shakes her head and stares up at a spot on the ceiling. "It's scary." She pushes herself to her feet and paces in small steps back and forth in front of the wall at the far side of the rail car, the heels of her boots pinging in steady metallic beats.

"When we were out there...fighting for our lives...when I linked up with that Modified—"

"Which was marvie, by the way!" Cardyn gushes, but Manthy ignores him.

"I felt connected. But in a different way than before."

We're all quiet, looking from one to the other and waiting for Manthy to go on, but she stops and stares at us like she's already explained everything.

"I can't say I know exactly what you mean," I tell Manthy at last. "But I have an idea. My connection with Render keeps evolving. Every new level is scarier than the one before."

Manthy nods. "That's kind of it. Only I don't think I'm afraid anymore."

"Of being an Emergent?" Rain ventures.

Manthy nods again and leans against the cold steel wall, her arms crossed defiantly in front of her, even though no one has said anything to challenge her.

"Well," Brohn says. "I think I speak for all of us when I say I'm glad you are whatever you are."

"And glad you're not afraid," I add.

"I was plenty afraid for all of us," Cardyn says, his suddenly peppy voice almost a song. "If it wasn't for you, we'd be pretty dead right now instead of only being scared incontinent."

"Um, I'm not incontinent," I say.

Brohn and Rain both say, "Me, neither."

Cardyn pauses. "Right. Me, neither."

Simultaneously, we burst into peals of laughter. The shudder running through me causes a searing pain in my arm, but I grit my teeth and bear it for the sake of our rare moment of levity.

We're all just catching our breath when the sound of someone outside the cell door startles us, and I instinctively whip around, which causes another streak of pain to go pulsing through my arm. I can't will this one away, though.

Brohn puts one hand on my shoulder and tells me to keep still as he climbs to his feet to stand in the middle of the cell along with Cardyn and Rain. Manthy steps forward as well, and the four of them take on a defensive, counter-incursion position like we were taught back in the Processor with Brohn at the point, Cardyn and Rain in flanking positions, and Manthy standing behind them and off to one side as situation evaluator and support combatant.

I'd love to leap up and help them, but it feels like the lower half of my arm might slough off if I move.

The clang of metal on metal rings into the cell, and the door slides open with an ancient groan. Light floods the room, and we shield our eyes at the figure in silhouette standing in the open doorway.

The man steps forward, a gold-plated Sig Sauer leveled at us from his hip.

Brohn drops his hands and takes a step back. "Lynch."

Lynch doesn't say anything, although he does lower his gun. From the back of the room, Manthy takes a quick glance out into the dirt and rubbish-strewn alleyway behind him. "Nice gun," she says. "Converted from nine-mil to .357. Night insert. Auto-reflex sight."

Lynch doesn't say anything.

"Semi-automatic. Fourteen rounds."

Lynch continues his odd, silent stare.

"You're alone," Manthy says, sounding matter-of-fact.

Still, Lynch doesn't respond.

"No guards?" Manthy asks as casually as if she's asking if he'd be kind enough to pass the pepper.

She's saying this for our benefit. Brohn is holding eye contact with Lynch, which makes Manthy the person with the best view of the space outside the cell, and she's cleverly passing along information we can use to assess our situation and optimize our chances for escape.

The only problem is, Lynch isn't responding. He looks confused, not himself somehow. He's edgy, shifting his weight awkwardly from foot to foot.

Brohn and I exchange a look as Rain takes a small, almost imperceptible step toward Lynch.

It's now or never.

Brohn's forearm flexes, and he raises discreetly onto the balls of his feet, prepared to go on the attack.

Then, one of the most amazing things I've ever seen happens before my eyes. And I've seen a lot of amazing things.

I blink, and Lynch is Amani.

I blink again, and he's Lynch. Kind of.

And then, finally, his features settle into the gaunt, worried, handsome face of the boy we rescued from the Processor.

"What's happening?" Cardyn asks, dumbfounded as the rest of us. "How'd you...?"

"How'd you find us?" Rain asks.

Amani flicks his head skyward. "Kress's bird—"

"His name is Render," Manthy says, stepping forward. "And he's not her bird."

Amani looks confused, but we don't have time to get into the semantics of ownership or the psychology behind Manthy's protective instinct toward me.

Instead, Brohn says, "Let's go!"

He lifts me up, his hands hooked under my arms.

We bolt along the litter-filled alleyway, past a small cluster of kids who scamper away as we sprint by, and under one of the huge yellow swing-loaders, its enormous lift-arms stacking one rail car onto another as it belches churning smoke into the midnight air.

Dashing at top speed ourselves and practically trampling each other in the process, we follow Amani—who now looks like an Amani-Lynch hybrid—on a frantic zig-zag through the corridors and laneways of sharp right angles that make up the endless slum of a city.

"Come on!" he urges.

Not that we need any extra incentive.

I'm breathing hard, and my arm is swelling up in its sling and turning various shades of purple when we slide to a stop in a dank, closet-sized entryway with a massive wooden door riveted on rusty hinges to a cutout in the side of a rail car.

"This is how I got in," Amani explains.

Brohn reaches for the door handle, but Amani stops him and points down at the floor.

"Not there. Down *there.*"

Amani steps aside as Brohn seizes the metal latch and pulls up what turns out to be a trap door.

"Come on," Amani urges.

He turns and clambers down a chipped yellow access ladder into the darkness below.

"No choice," Brohn says and leads the rest of us down the cold metal ladder.

At the bottom, it takes my eyes a second to adjust to the dark.

"It's an old wine cellar," Amani explains. "And a series of basements and sewer lines running under this whole line of rail cars. Once Render pinpointed your location, Olivia was able to call up schematics on the area. The specs are over twenty years old, but it was enough for us to figure out how to get in."

"And hopefully how to get out," Rain adds.

Amani huffs a light laugh and says, "That's the idea. There's a small set of stairs going up and another door at the end of the basement under a rail car down this way. A storm door. It empties out to an old tire yard where your truck is. There are no guards on it right now. At least there weren't when I left."

"Olivia and Sheridyn?" I ask. "Are they—?"

"They're fine. When I left they were fine. Olivia didn't want me to leave, but I had to help you. I owed you that much. Me and Sheridyn, both."

"Um…How…?" Cardyn stammers. "How did you manage to look like Lynch back there?"

Amani, who looks like himself again, gives him a knowing smile.

"Did you ever meet someone who seemed familiar, but you just couldn't place them?"

"Sure. I guess."

"Well, that might have been someone like me."

"Do you change your appearance?" Cardyn whispers, clearly as fascinated as the rest of us as we jog along the oppressively humid subterranean corridor.

"That would be remarkie. But no. I can't change anything about myself. I can only sometimes alter how someone sees me. Think of it as me slipping a pair of hazy glasses over their eyes while they're not looking. When they see me, they see someone who might look a little like me but isn't."

"Then you're an Emergent," Cardyn says. "Like us."

"I guess I'm an Emergent. But not like you. It hurts a lot, and I can't do it all the time. And I can't always control how it works."

"You're more like us than you realize," Brohn tells him. "We're new at this, too."

Amani smiles as we run, apparently reassured, and says he's sorry for what we've gone through. "Still," he huffs, "it's nice to know we're all pretty much in the same boat."

I don't have the heart to tell him how many holes this particular boat comes with.

With the doors missing at the end of each section of this

underground tunnel, it's a straight shot for another few minutes until we screech to a halt at another set of concrete stairs, this one leading up to a pair of large wooden doors, which Brohn pushes open with little trouble.

Out of breath and heads reeling, we follow Amani across a clearing and back to our truck, which is still like we left it, lying tilted on its side against an embankment of packed earth and broken concrete slabs.

A blast of black out of the corner of my eye startles me until I realize it's Render. He alights with a black flurry of gold-trimmed feathers on my shoulder and gives me a peck with his beak to the side of my head.

"Hey! What was that for?"

You were gone too long.

I cup his head in my palm and press his face to my cheek.

"I'm okay. We're all okay. We just need to get out of here, okay Pal?"

Render gives me a series of clacking purrs–his version of a satisfied sigh of relief—and flutters up to the top of the truck.

"I'll go in," I offer.

Brohn stops me with a hand on my shoulder.

"Your arm—"

"Hurts, but I'm okay," I assure him. "Really."

"Okay. I'll go with you. Rain, are you okay keeping an eye on things out here?"

Rain says, "No problem. Just hurry," and Brohn lifts me up and helps me clamber into the truck and then follows along behind me.

Grabbing anything I can for balance, I climb with my good hand up to the back where I scan open the access ladder to the Pod. Inside, Olivia and Sheridyn are startled and then relieved to see me.

"Obviously Amani found you," Olivia says, her tendrils flicking with what I assume is happiness.

"He did. Are you okay?"

"We've been in here for over four days. It's been...disorienting to say the least."

Turning to Sheridyn, I ask if she's okay, although I can see very clearly she's not.

She puts her hands to her face and bursts into tears.

I kneel down in front of her on the slanted floor. "Don't worry. We're going to get out of here. All of us."

Snuffling, she slumps back into her angled seat.

"I was scared."

"Us, too," Brohn admits. "But we're going to be out of here before you know it."

Sheridyn gives a weak glance around at the interior of the rakishly tilted truck.

"What happened?"

"We were captured. But don't worry. We're out. We're free. And, as soon as we get this thing straightened up and on its wheels, we'll get nice and far away from here."

Sheridyn wipes her eyes and nods.

"Wait here," Brohn instructs her. "We'll be right back."

Holding my broken arm close to my body, I slide back down into the cabin with Brohn and out of the truck to where the others are still pondering the problem of how to right the massive vehicle so we can get out here before War's men figure out what's happened and come running.

Manthy puts her arm out, and Render glides down to her from his perch on top of the truck.

Cardyn is clearly frustrated at having escaped only to be stuck without the transportation we need to actually get away.

"Now what?"

"At least there aren't any guards," I say.

"Sure. Why bother guarding a truck that can't move?"

"Time to do your thing, Brohn," I say.

Together, we go around to the back of the vehicle and slide

into the dark space between the truck's side and the head-high ridge of earth it's leaning against.

Brohn takes a breath and steps forward, placing his hands on the frame and the side wall of the big rig. Filling with blood, his biceps look ready to pop under his compression t-shirt as he puts his weight and his strength into righting the lopsided vehicle.

The truck trembles, as if eager to get right-side up, and, his back pressed hard against the mound of dirt and debris behind him, Brohn digs his boots into the unforgiving dirt and grunts with another push.

We're all anxious and jittery, glancing around for War's men and desperate beyond measure to get the truck upright and get out of this hell-hole.

"They're going to find out we're gone," Cardyn says, dancing in place like he has to pee.

Rain puts a motherly hand on his shoulder.

"Wetting yourself isn't going to get us out of here any faster."

"It won't hurt."

Telling the two of them to quiet down so he can concentrate, Brohn steels himself, repositions his feet, and pushes even harder than before, but the truck doesn't move.

In the stunned silence of disappointment, Brohn hangs his head, defeated.

"I…can't. It's too heavy. I don't have…there's just nothing left."

"Now what?" I ask.

We're answered by the ground shaking beneath our feet. Like a nest of startled bugs, we scurry out from under the truck, but Cardyn is the only one of us who can make his voice work. Although the only thing he says as he sees the tank-sized Modified machine-man thundering toward us is, "Uh oh."

Kicking up clouds of rust-red dust as he charges forward across the clearing, Press-and-Die lowers his shoulder like he's going to drive into us and kill us all at once. We scatter to the side, but he makes a bee-line for the truck. He clamps his steel-plated hands of muscle and gears onto its top edge and, with one swift motion, pulls it back onto its wheels.

The huge, treaded tires of the monstrous vehicle bounce onto the ground with a series of earth-shattering thuds before the truck rocks itself still.

Press-and-Die's jaw quakes out something that sounds like, "Go," but it's such a garbled mess of a voice that he could be saying almost anything. Either way, no one is interested in sticking around to translate, and we pile into the truck, practically stepping over each other in the process.

Brohn slides into the driver's seat, activates the mag-starter with his thumb in the biometric prick-pad, and we roar down the road, leaving a cloud of red dust and a band of running Survivalists firing their guns impotently in our wake.

The viz-screen in the cabin shows us what's happening behind us.

With us safely out of range, the Survivalists turn their weapons on our giant liberator who has nearly disappeared in a haze of muzzle fire and blue smoke.

Press-and-Die raises his formidable flesh and steel arms against the onslaught and crumbles to the ground.

"We can't leave him!" Manthy shouts.

But even she's got to know there's no way we're going back.

With slavery behind us and freedom in front of us, it's not even a choice.

So I have to wonder, as we hurtle away down the path so clearly right: why does leaving this Modified behind—this machine-man we barely know—feel so wrong?

24

WITH OUR TIRES grinding up a huge cloud of dust behind us, we whip along through old partially-paved streets, around unmanned payloaders, under the greasy bellies of more of the towering yellow swing-loaders, and through the litter-strewn, right-angled corridors formed by the unending rows and columns of rail cars.

At first, it's a white-knuckled, stomach-churning race to get to anywhere other than where we were.

The seven of us are crammed into the cab with Cardyn standing and swaying, his hands gripped hard on the back of the seat in front of him as he does his best not to get tossed while the truck slams left and right through the congested labyrinth.

I'm clamped onto the edge of my seat with one hand while I hold my broken arm across my body and try not to pass out.

We don't have anything resembling a road map and no destination in mind. Brohn has us going in the general direction of Krug Tower, our ultimate goal.

Meanwhile, we just keep slamming around against each other as Brohn coaxes the truck through the laneways that grow narrower and more crowded and cluttered as we go until I think we might get stuck or least slowed down enough for War and his men to track us down.

"I didn't see any motorized vehicles in War's camp," Cardyn shouts over the grind of the engine and the constant, bone-jarring thump of the tires on the mounds of buckled asphalt that pass for roads.

"Doesn't mean they don't have them," I point out.

Cardyn keeps glancing back like he expects War and his men to be on board and surging at us through the cabin.

"Can you give us a rear-view?" I ask Rain.

From the navigator's seat next to Brohn's, she shouts back "Sure" over her shoulder and scans a series of codes on the input panel up front. A rear-view display, shadowy red, appears in the air above the center console. There are plenty of people behind us, many of them just stepping into the road from where they were pressed up against the sides of rail cars as we motored through.

Finally, and clearly with no one in pursuit, Brohn eases off the accelerator, and we chug along with throngs of pedestrians and drivers on gas-powered scooters zipping by on either side of us, all apparently content to go about their business as our massive government truck rumbles along through their neighborhoods.

Even at this slower speed, wind whips through the gaping hole in the side of the truck and carries with it the putrid stench of pollution, body odor, and human waste.

Although the laneways are crowded with people, lined with open sewer trenches, and packed with mountain ranges of derelict vehicles—many of them doubling as residences—everyone in our path gives our truck a wide berth.

"They think we're the Patriot Army," Cardyn guesses.

"Or possibly even President Krug," I suggest.

Brohn doesn't take his eyes off the road.

"Understandable. Technically, even with all the markings sand-blasted off, it's his truck. Personally, I can't wait to drive it up to his front lawn and return it to him…"

"Along with a few dozen boot stomps to his lying face," Cardyn adds.

As we continue along, we see groups of people, mostly kids, stopping to try to catch a glimpse inside the truck where the door used to be.

Some of the kids smile and wave. Some run along next to us, craning their necks to get a better look at either us in the cab or at the posh interior of the cabin. I can't tell which.

I get the feeling they're used to seeing a Patriot Army presence but usually in some kind of convoy or, if Krug is involved and happens to be in town—Chicago, we've come to learn, is his second home—an abundance of celebratory fanfare.

I seriously doubt it's every day that a monstrous rig like this rolls unannounced and unescorted through such dangerous and poverty-stricken neighborhoods.

I tell this to Brohn, who points out that the two go hand in hand.

"We've gotten used to the idea that violence and poverty are just two conditions so-called inferior people wind up living under as a result of their own bad luck or else their inherent inferiority. But that's just another one of Krug's lies. He does everything he can to keep people poor, knowing the violence will soon follow."

"Right," I agree. "Then he can justify any tyranny in the name of combatting the violence…"

"…which he brought about."

"Nothing like growing up in a no-win situation," Cardyn groans.

Amani says, "Tell me about it," as he crosses his arms and slumps down in his seat with a pouting frown.

Up ahead, a low cloud of dark debris whirls and undulates over the expansive slum of steel boxes stretching out for miles with dozens of tall buildings rising up over the miasma. Lording over it all is Krug Tower, practically on top of us now, with its countless reflecting obsidian windows and a spire at the top like a scorpion's stinger piercing the sky.

"Where are we?" Amani asks.

Sheridyn's head is on a swivel as she glances back and forth through the cab's small front and side windows.

"What is all this?"

She's gripping the arms of her seat for stability as Brohn continues his more cautious navigation of the pitted, crowded, and litter-strewn roadway, and we creep ever closer to the tower.

"This is all Chicago," Rain tells Sheridyn.

Chicago is half impoverished, half wealth. From what we can tell, there are only two types of building left: the enormous, interconnected skyscrapers stretching skyward up ahead and the boxy steel shacks of the shantytowns where we are down below.

"What's that building?" Sheridyn asks, pointing through the narrow slit of a front window.

"Krug Tower," I explain. "It's the one we've been talking about. The place we're headed."

"We're going there?"

"That's the plan."

"Inside?"

"Can't break anyone out without getting inside, ourselves."

Sheridyn goes dormouse quiet.

"It's where the Wealthies live," Rain says, breaking the silence. "We suspect the top floors are a Processor."

Now, Sheridyn's voice shakes. "A Processor?"

"Mm-hm. Same as ours. Only it's at the top of a tower instead of in the middle of the woods. Either way, it serves the same purpose."

"Slavery," Cardyn says, and Rain nods.

Olivia's voice pings through the commcaster.

"I've been scanning the interfaces around the city core. There's a fleet of drones on constant patrol around the arcology construction sites and the other residential towers with the bulk of them programmed to run a security and surveillance circuit around Krug Tower."

Olivia calls up a satellite feed showing a partial projection of the city. The image floats in front of us in the cab, radically incomplete and with poor resolution.

"It's the best I can manage," Olivia apologizes. "The local comm-grid is too secure. If I try to infiltrate it any deeper, the Patriots will track me and trace us."

"Don't worry," I say, leaning over the instrument panel. "As usual, you've already gone above and beyond the call of duty."

Olivia's voice pings back a "Thanks," and I imagine her smiling up in her pod, tendrils waggling at being recognized for a job well done.

As we tool along, we pass a small Patriot Army foot-patrol. They look at our truck grumbling by, lines of confusion furrowed into their stark, always-angry faces. I see one of them tap his ear and say something into his comm-link while the two others with him draw their guns.

"Whatever connections you've made will have to do," Brohn calls out to Olivia. "We need to get off the road."

"That I can help with," Olivia says.

She highlights a route in red on the holo-projection in front of Rain.

"It looks like you want us to drive clean off the end of the earth," Cardyn says, leaning over her shoulder.

"It's an abandoned airplane hangar," Olivia informs us.

"There are heat signatures."

"Probably squatters," Rain guesses.

"Not Patriots?"

Rain squints at the image. "I don't think so."

"I'm not sure I'm ready to deal with another one of these Syndicates," Cardyn sighs. "Don't get me wrong. Being beaten up and imprisoned makes for a nice break in the day, but I think I'd rather keep my blood on the inside for a while."

"Agreed," Olivia says. "That's why we're not going to the hangar."

"Then where—?"

"Behind the hangar is an old water reservoir. It's the one spot in the area that doesn't appear overly populated. That's where we need to go."

"Can you get us there?" I ask Brohn.

He leans over for a glimpse at the image projected in the air in front of the main console and gives a slow nod.

"I think so."

Although it's less than a minute's drive from the congested bustle of the Chicago neighborhoods we just left, the area by the hangar is relatively empty with a few fires from oil drums over by a line of campers and makeshift tents as the only sign of life.

Steering clear of that area, Brohn loops around the hangar and drives through a wall of dried, entangled vegetation.

"Are you sure this is right?" Cardyn shouts into the commcaster.

Olivia assures us it is, so, trusting her, Brohn steers the truck down a rocky embankment, over a short field of debris, and into a large, concrete water run-off tunnel just big enough for us to fit the truck into.

"Feels like we're driving into the mouth of a whale," Brohn says, his eyes flicking between the windows and the holo-monitors as he eases the rig into the tunnel's dark opening.

He flicks off the truck's ignition, and, for the first time in a long time, we breathe in a moment of dark, peaceful silence.

"I guess we better head out," I suggest. "See if we can find supplies. War's crew really wiped us out."

"Good thing the doors slide," Cardyn says. "If they opened out, we'd be in trouble."

"Do you think the truck'll be okay?" Manthy asks almost sorrowfully. It's like this huge rig is a new puppy, and she's worried about it peeing on the rug or something.

"We don't really have a choice," Brohn says as he climbs out of the driver's seat and starts to make his way back into the cabin. "We can't risk spending any more time out in the open than we already have."

"Besides," Cardyn adds, ducking down as he follows Brohn out of the cab and into the main body of the rig, "it's not like we're going to find valet parking around here."

In the cabin, we fling open the storage lockers to find them empty, and I'm about to get sulky about it when Rain reminds us of the extra supplies hidden in Olivia's Pod.

We all share a sigh of relief and a big group smile as Rain summons the ladder and clambers up into the Pod. As we stand below, Rain tosses down fresh sets of cargo pants, compression tops, and tactical combat vests. After that, she drops down a synth-steel box packed with ten-millimeter supermag glocks.

"And here!" she calls down to Manthy. "Look what I found!"

Manthy beams as Rain drops two Tomahawk axes down, handle first for safety, into her waiting arms.

Manthy barely suppresses a squeal of delight.

It's a rare sight these days, seeing all of us clean, locked, and loaded.

Even Amani and Sheridyn are showing revitalized signs of life. I hate to say, it but the four days of being confined in the Pod with Olivia seem to have done them some good. They're not one-hundred percent, but they're both more energetic and relatively alert than any other time since we found them.

"I think we should be armed, too," Amani suggests. "If we're really going out there, I mean."

We all agree, and I take responsibility for slipping clips into two of the guns and handing them over as Manthy stands in front of a weapons locker, twirling her two new Tomahawk axes until she looks like a prop plane priming for take-off.

"How'd you learn how to do that, anyway?" Cardyn asks, backing up against the side of the cabin and clearly trying hard to hide how impressed he is.

"I've never liked guns," Manthy says without looking at him. "Too easy."

Fully outfitted now with handguns and combat knives, we leave Olivia in the Pod and make our way on foot, with Render perched on my shoulder, toward the dark cloud up ahead.

"I wish she could come with us," Manthy says, looking back at the truck, which is barely visible in the near total darkness of the abandoned water tunnel.

"She'll be just fine," I tell Manthy. "Besides, she seems to like the time alone. At this rate, she'll be patched into the whole global grid before we get back. And just imagine the advantage we'll have then."

Manthy seems satisfied by this, and she even reaches over to give my hand a gentle squeeze. It's an unexpected and unnecessary gesture from a girl who doesn't make unexpected or unnecessary gestures. Maybe that's why I feel tears well up in my eyes.

"Remember," Brohn calls back from his position at the point, "reconnaissance only. This is just to get our bearings and plan out our next moves. Stay invisible. Don't engage. We need intel now, not action."

Render flies ahead, disappearing into the shadows, and I lose my connection with him. The air is barely breathable. He's still recovering from his injuries, and I'm not able to be much help at the moment. Fortunately, the mass of smog and floating debris clears a bit as we walk on. The thick wooded area of dead trees and vines we find ourselves hacking our way through is bleak and dark, even now in the middle of the afternoon.

The seven of us walk down an old access road behind the airplane hangar. The road is as cratered and neglected as the highway we drove in on with a forest of vines, brambles, and undergrowth pressing in on us from all sides.

"Watch out for the thorns," Rain says, flicking her head toward one of the masses of purple vines with the splayed abundance of long, translucent spines. "They're dangerous."

"They contain an alkaloid toxin," I explain to Amani and Sheridyn, who both look like they're having second thoughts about coming along. "It's a paralytic agent. A nicotinic receptor inhibitor. Causes the diaphragm to seize up so you can't breathe and die. This species looks like a mutated version of the ones originally found in South America. Apparently, they found their way north."

"Don't mind Miss Encyclopedia here," Cardyn says with a dismissive wave of his hand. "She can't help herself." He puts his arm out to nudge Amani and Sheridyn toward the center of the barely-visible path and away from the legion of deadly thorns. "Stay away from them, though," he whispers, thinking incorrectly that I can't hear him. "If Kress is right, I'm not prepared to carry the two of you back to the truck."

Walking ahead a few paces, I can't help but smile.

A rustle from the tops of the brittle black trees catches our attention, and we all look up to see Render darting his way through the gnarled branches until he finds one he likes up ahead. He alights on it and ticks his head around, skimming the area for danger.

I scan my tattoos, but I'm still having trouble accessing our connection. Without it, I feel like I'm flying blind. His senses are so sharp they make mine seem pointless and weak by comparison.

Even though my Conspiracy is battle trained, battle tested,

and on high alert, we don't have much experience living out here in the real world. I lived in Boston with my parents until I was six. Then I spent the next decade isolated in the Valta where I was pumped full of the president's endless barrage of fake news. Then a couple months on the run, a week of training and combat in San Francisco, and then back out on the road on a quest to build an army to help take back our country. So we're a tough bunch. Strong, smart, but woefully inexperienced when it comes to walking through the reality of the world.

Slipping through another layer in the jumble of vegetation, we continue to make our way on foot toward Krug Tower, which is close enough now to block out the last shreds of daylight and leave us shivering in its shadow.

"Um," Cardyn begins, "shouldn't we maybe have a plan?"

"I'm open to suggestions," Brohn grumbles.

"It's too dangerous for Render to go scouting," I explain to Cardyn, who already knows all this anyway. "And Olivia can't access the local comm-grid any more than she already has."

"Can't Manthy do her...you know...her 'Manthy' thing?"

"If you keep bugging me," Manthy says, "I'm going to kick you in your 'Cardyn' thing."

"Consider this a simple scouting mission," Rain snaps. "If we can at least figure out how many guards we're dealing with on the perimeter, we can figure out the rest once we're inside."

Over to our right, on the far side of the tangled mass of vines, the tops of a series of houses poke up into the sky. The roofs are strong and pointed. From here, we can just make out the columns and multi-pane windows. Some of the houses have cracked and partial pediments and porticoes with broken or missing columns. At least one of the houses has a porch with a railing wrapping around the entire second floor. Several look like they've had bombs dropped on them, which Rain guesses is exactly what happened.

"Do you think anyone lives over there?" I ask.

"If so," Cardyn says, "I'd rather not meet them."

"Why not?" Manthy says, a hint of teasing in her voice. "It looks nice."

I suggest we at least check it out. "We're on a recon mission, after all, right?"

The others agree, although Brohn seems to hesitate. When I ask him what's wrong, he shakes his head, but I press him until he tells me what's on his mind.

"I'd just feel better if you had your full connection with Render."

I know he doesn't mean it as an insult. In fact, I'd feel the same. But it stings knowing I can't control the one thing I bring to the table.

As we round a bend in the path, we emerge onto a small alley running behind the big houses. Most of the houses are missing all their windows and have partial walls and collapsed rooftops with what looks like entire jungles of creepers and scrub-brush bursting out of them.

It's here that we slam face-first into one of the Patriot Patrollers. He seems as stunned to see us as we are to see him. He reaches for his gun, but he's distracted by the dust storm Render kicks up as he swoops down out of nowhere and beats his powerful wings in the small alleyway.

With her hand shielding her eyes, Rain sweeps the man's legs out from under him with a spinning back-kick. His head cracks hard against the ground, but his helmet protects him from any serious damage. There's not much in the world that could protect him, however, from Rain's follow-up double-punch to the bridge of his nose followed by a well-placed knee-drop to his solar plexus and a plunging forearm to his exposed throat. The air whooshes out of him, and his eyelids flutter before he gives up his futile attempt to hang onto consciousness.

Render, apparently satisfied that his work here is done, flies away as Brohn restrains the Patriot soldier with his own zip-cuffs.

"Where's Render off to?" Rain asks me.

"I don't know. Has he seemed kind of, I don't know…edgy to you lately?"

"Honestly," she shrugs, "I can't tell the difference between an edgy bird and a relaxed one."

"What do we do with him?" Cardyn asks, pointing to the downed soldier.

I point to a big square door in the ground.

"It's an old delivery chute. Looks like it leads to a basement."

"Let's toss him down there."

"Shouldn't we kill him?" Sheridyn asks, and it's such an unsettling question coming from this frail girl.

"We don't kill if we don't have to," I explain. "And we've had to more times than I care to count."

"She's right," Cardyn explains to Amani and Sheridyn. He points to the looming black tower rising to a dizzying height practically a stone's throw from where we are. "There's going to be more than enough killing to come. Let's hope we're not on the wrong end of it."

"For now," Brohn says, grabbing the limp soldier by the back of his jacket and dragging him over to the wooden door, "let's make sure he's out of commission long enough to not get in our way. We'll toss him down there. He'll live at least. And someone'll find him, eventually."

Manthy leans over as Brohn drags the man past her and pulls the communication patch off his shoulder and the comm-link from behind his ear. She holds up a finger, and Brohn pauses as she also takes the unconscious soldier's gun, ammo packs, maglight, and combat knife.

Once she's stripped him of his gear, Cardyn and Rain lift the heavy wooden double-doors, and Brohn hurls the Patriot soldier down into the dark cellar below.

Cardyn and Rain let the doors crash down with a heavy thud, and Brohn grabs a length of discarded rebar from the ground, slips it through the big metal-hooped handles, and twists it like only he can.

"There," he says, brushing his hands on his pants. "That ought to keep him out of our hair for a while."

Behind us, a voice that doesn't belong to any of us says, "Nice job."

25

HAPPY TO HAVE ESCAPED from War and his goons, made it safely through miles of Chicago slums, and now having gotten rid of that pesky Patriot patroller, we find ourselves the subject of another round of unwanted attention.

This time, though, it's in the form of three women.

We spin around to face them, me and Brohn whipping out our guns in one motion, with Manthy slipping her Tomahawk axes out of their sheaths as we prepare for battle.

Instinctively, we all step in front of Amani and Sheridyn. They're not little kids. In fact, they're less than a year younger than us. But having seen what they went through in the Processor, I know we all feel especially protective of them.

We saved them. We brought them with us and promised to keep them safe even as we hope they'll join us in a major battle against impossible odds. Whatever else happens, we owe it to them to put their lives before our own.

Squaring off against our three new adversaries, Rain asks them what they want with us.

Unlike most of our previous encounters, which have usually involved fighting for our lives, this time we're met with toothy smiles and open arms instead of with gunshots and punches to the face.

It's a refreshing change.

"It's not a trick," the woman in front says, her hands open, palms facing us. She's on the short side and has an enormous truss of dreadlocked hair tied back in thick bundles and hanging nearly to her feet. "We're not going to hurt you."

"Aren't you afraid we might hurt *you*?" Cardyn calls to her from behind me.

The woman—colorfully-clad in an ornately-patterned dress, her face smooth but contemplative—looks like she's giving this some serious thought before shaking her head and then reaching out in an offer to shake Brohn's hand.

Brohn raises his hand without seeming to realize he's doing it while his other arm hangs loosely by his side, gun at the ready, finger on the trigger just in case.

"We've learned to live with a healthy dose of caution around here," the woman says as Brohn stares blankly. She releases his hand and takes mine. Her hands are small, but her grip is firm, and her skin is tough as the bark on a black locust tree. "But we gave up on being afraid a long time ago."

"The only thing we've ever given up on," the woman behind her adds.

"Or ever will," says the third.

One at a time, the three women dip their heads in greeting while we offer up stiff smiles and try to process this potentially positive but still uncertain turn of events.

All three of the women have glossy, burnished skin, eyes as dark and glistening as wet walnuts. And that hair. It must have taken decades to grow. It hangs heavily from their heads in ropes of blacks and browns, coppers and oranges, and a spectrum of grays and silvers all adorned with strips of yellow and red fabric and a rainbow array of glistening metal clips. With all that hair and with all those embellishments, it's a wonder these women can even move around.

Yet, there is a lightness about them. Like they've absorbed the sunlight here but not the skin-chafing radiation. Like the burden of poverty and the proximity of death haven't been weighing them down. Like if they wanted to, heavy hair and all, they could fly.

"Mayla," the lead woman says.

I'm the first one to shake off the hypnosis.

"I'm Kress. This is Brohn. Cardyn. Rain. Manthy. Our two new friends here are Amani and Sheridyn."

"It's nice to meet all of you," Mayla says sweetly. "And my friends here are Suffolk and Dura."

The two women next to Mayla bow their heads and hold their hands out toward us, palms up, as if they're offering us invisible bowls of soup.

When we all shuffle around looking confused, Mayla laughs and explains it's their way of starting off every new encounter with an offer of peace and hospitality.

Awkwardly, we return the gesture, which elicits another pleasant laugh from Mayla, who points over to one of the big houses we saw poking up above the jungle and asks if we'd like to join them for some food, shelter, and safety.

"Peace and hospitality seem like pretty rare commodities around here," Cardyn mumbles, and I elbow him and tell him not to be rude.

"It's okay," Mayla assures us. "He's right. There's plenty here in short supply. A lukewarm meal and a roof are about all we can offer, but they're yours if you like."

Brohn turns toward me on one side and then to Cardyn on the other, as if searching for confirmation or else a rejection of this offer. When no one says anything one way or the other, he steps forward, gives Mayla the faintest of bows, and says we gladly accept.

"I'm happy to hear it. Frankly, I haven't seen a group in this much need of peace and hospitality in a very long time."

At first, I think it's an insult, but her tight-lipped smile bursts into a hearty, explosive laugh, which envelops all of us like a cool breeze, and we laugh along with the three women at our own expense.

Dabbing happy tears from her eyes, Mayla scans us up and down from the bottoms of our dirt-caked boots to the tops of our mangy, sweat-and-blood encrusted heads.

"You didn't come here on foot?"

"No," Sheridyn says, pointing back the way we just came. "We have a truck. It's a few hundred yards that way. In a tunnel."

Brohn holds up his hand and gives her a sharp look over his shoulder. He's right to cut her off. Until we know more about these women, we can't afford to be too generous with our personal information. They could be well-meaning and sincere, or they could be waiting for us to lower our guard, waiting for the right moment to take us down.

If Render were here, he'd signal me with his instinctive gut feeling one way or another, but he's out there somewhere, and I can't even sense his presence at the moment. And, frankly, that scares me more than the cloud of uncertainty we currently find ourselves under.

"We're just happy to run into someone who isn't trying to kill us," I say.

"Hospitality is hard to come by," Mayla says. "Which is why we offer it when we can and hope it's appreciated and passed along when it's accepted in the spirit it's given."

"Hospitality can be every bit as contagious as violence," Suffolk adds. "An open hand can get a lot more done than a closed fist."

"And with fewer broken bones as a result," I suggest, holding up my purplish swollen arm, still throbbing inside the sling Cardyn made for me.

Suffolk steps forward and peers at my arm. She makes a series of "tsk" noises with her tongue and glares over at two curious men in army green camouflage, who have just materialized out from the jungle, rifles at the ready with backup handguns slung low on their hips.

I'm already reaching for my gun, but Suffolk shoos the two men away before turning back to Mayla.

The men, nearly invisible now, retreat backwards into the edge of the strange snarl of urban jungle.

"Our escort," Mayla explains. "Most folks around here respect us enough to leave us alone."

"The ones who don't," Dura adds, "wind up regretting it for the few minutes of life they have left."

Although I don't respond out loud to that, I find it hard to believe. From what I've seen of this expanse of a city so far, three women out alone like this are hardly in a position to be smug about their safety. On the other hand, some people might say the same thing about Rain, but I wouldn't bet against her when the chips are down, as my father used to say.

Suffolk finishes inspecting my arm and turns back to Mayla and Dura.

"She needs medical attention. If she wants to keep that arm, anyway."

I gulp at this, surprised the injury is that bad and horrified about the prospect of losing a limb.

Mayla shoots a cautionary glare at Suffolk. "Don't panic the girl."

Suffolk apologizes, and Mayla returns her attention to me. "We'll take you back to the Crib. We can fix you up before you get on your way to wherever it is you need to get to."

"Thank you," I say.

Brohn and the rest of our Conspiracy echo my appreciation, and Mayla spins around, her long, whip-like hair snapping along with her, and leads us down a nearly-hidden path, through the dense mesh of brittle vines, and along a series of broken and buckled sidewalks in what was probably once a nice, residential neighborhood.

Now, though, it's boarded up house after boarded up house with the lawns overgrown into a single ten-foot-high impenetrable mass of gnarled vegetation punctuated by starbursts of those deadly-looking translucent thorns.

"Radiation," Mayla says with a tilt of her head toward a long row of derelict houses.

"No one can live there," Suffolk explains.

"Not to say folks don't try," Dura adds. "But they don't live there for long."

"They don't live long at all," Mayla says, still marching ahead with the rest of us trundling along behind her.

The roadway we're on, cratered and knee-deep with debris, is filled with people shuffling in small groups in every direction.

Still, there's an eerie quiet to it all. The people here don't talk except in muffled whispers. There's nothing motorized to be seen. Nothing working, anyway. There's no shortage of doorless, rusted husks of old gas and electric cars, most of which appear to serve as housing for the hunched and huddled men and women who occupy them.

A few people approach Mayla as we walk, asking her for supplies, advice, or permission to travel from one zone to the next, but Mayla dismisses them—politely but firmly and with a flick of her head at us—and insists she has other matters to attend to first.

The Crib, as Mayla calls it, turns out to be one of the huge mansions we saw before with towering once-white columns covered with a latticework of crispy brown vines. The external stairs up to the front door are shattered to near impassability, but Mayla and her two friends weave their way around the holes and hop up onto the debris-strewn wrap-around porch.

Mayla apologizes to us for the condition of the stairs and says she has a labor crew on a supply run as we speak.

"Strong building materials are hard to come by," she informs us.

At the top of the stairs, Mayla leads us across the wide porch. She pushes open the big wooden door and welcomes us across the threshold.

Inside, the three women escort us through a foyer of checkerboard marble and past a set of patched-together stairs curving up in a graceful swoop to a second-floor landing. Up above, their small faces squished between the white railings, a group of children eye us warily, their hands gripped around the vertical struts of the balustrade like little prisoners watching the arrival of a batch of new inmates.

"Our daughters," Dura explains.

"And sons," Suffolk adds.

Dura nods, but I think I detect a hint of hostility in her quiet agreement.

With Mayla still in the lead, we continue down a dusty hallway and through a set of near ten-foot high double-doors into what seems to have been a ballroom or maybe a dining room for a thousand people at some point in the long-ago, obliterated past. The cavernous, opulent room is deep, high, and huge. Its floor, Mayla explains, is refurbished cherrywood coated in a type of linseed oil, "to give it that 'dance on me' kind of glow."

Adding to the out-of-place opulence, a row of six chandeliers, their many thin arms curling in smooth arcs like a family of big silver squids, hangs in a straight line down from the ceiling along the middle of the room. The wallpaper is peeled in some places and faded to near nothingness in others. Parts of the walls and the ceiling are obscured by what looks to be two-hundred-years' worth of dust, grease, and grime. Other parts are newly painted and polished to a high shine.

"We're a work in progress," Suffolk explains, a note of apology in her voice.

"It's marvie," Cardyn exclaims, turning in a slow circle, his chin up, as he takes in the overwhelming space.

The entire room is rimmed by a type of beadboard wainscoting, four-feet high and running along the entire perimeter of the giant space.

The opposite side of the room is a series of tall, partially boarded-up windows. At the far end of the room is a fireplace the size of a small garage.

Multiple sets of couches, chairs, settees, and ottomans are sprinkled in clusters throughout the room. Their upholstery is a matching pattern of pink and white stripes with yellow flowers, all very old but also relatively clean.

Suffolk and Dura drag one of the sofas, a cushioned footstool, and a matching love-seat around to form a squarish seating area under one of the boarded-up windows.

Mayla sits down on one of the loveseats with Suffolk next to her and Dura, a hint of a scowl on her face, standing behind them like a protective sentry.

Mayla offers us seats, which we gratefully accept.

Although the mag-chairs in the truck are very comfortable, we've unfortunately spent most of the last week, thanks to War and his Syndicate of Survivalists, sitting on the cold, unforgiving floors of an assortment of prisons and detention cells.

Plopping down into the soft, marshmallow-y couch cushions, we all let out a smorgasbord of happy sighs. The cushions may be frayed and stained, but they're plush and, more important, they're in the house of a group of women who haven't made any attempts on our lives.

For now, at least.

26

Mayla tilts her head toward a woman across the room, who signals her understanding and bustles over with a tray of empty aluminum cans surrounding a fat-bottomed glass pitcher of brown water.

As she pours the water, the woman introduces herself as Eralia, and Brohn points one at a time at our Conspiracy, offering up each of our names in turn.

Cardyn sniffs at his cup, and Mayla smiles at our cautious reaction to the unusual water.

"Don't worry," she says. "It's filtered and flavored and very much *not* poisoned."

I'm the first one to take a sip. The water looks like thick iced tea, but it tastes like acidic sewer water and yet is still somehow refreshing, invigorating even.

"It's a bit of lemongrass, pennyroyal, and redroot pigweed."

Cardyn freezes with the cup poised near his lip. "Pigweed?"

"Amaranthus retroflexus," Mayla says. "It's an edible weed. The name is Greek. It means 'the immortal, unfading flower.'"

"Hey!" Cardyn says to Manthy. "Amaranthine. That's like you!"

He reaches over me and puts up his hand as if to high-five her, but she stares at him and then turns back to Mayla, who looks confused.

"Manthy's full name is Amaranthine," I tell her.

"Our very own never-fading flower," Cardyn gushes, and for a second, I think Manthy might leap over me and slug him, but she takes a breath and seems content to let her annoyed scowl speak for itself.

"You'll need to take these, too," Eralia says, holding out a handful of cylindrical white pills. "If they plan on staying any length of time," she adds with a glance over at Mayla.

Brohn holds his hand up, palm out.

"Um, I don't think we should…"

"It's potassium iodide and pentetic acid," Mayla coos as if she's offering butterscotch to a bunch of five-year-old Neos.

"It's okay," I say to Brohn. "It's a treatment for radiation sickness."

Brohn plucks one of the pills from Eralia's open palm and inspects it under the light and then sniffs it before turning back to me.

I give him a go-ahead nod as I take one of the pills and swallow it down with a gulp of the tepid brown water.

One of the side-effects I'm finding from my relationship with Render is that some of my senses, including smell but also an instinct for what's healthy and what's potentially toxic, have become nicely sharpened. It's not a perfect skill, so there's still a risk we're about to be drugged and dragged into a dungeon somewhere, but trust has become a kind of useful commodity on our adventures. We don't trust a lot of people out here, but when we do let our guard down, it's always after careful consideration, and good things tend to follow.

"Don't mind our suspicion," I tell the women. "We've been through a lot."

Mayla tells us she totally understands and relaxes as the rest of us swallow the pills we're offered.

"Not to be rude or unappreciative," Brohn says with a long look around, "but who are you? What is this place?"

"This is our Crib," Mayla says. "Our sanctuary. Our home. It's from here we keep as many people alive as possible. We're the Unkindness."

Cardyn scratches his head. "The Unkindness?"

Mayla gives him a slightly mocking laugh.

"We help people who are too tired or scared or inexperienced to help themselves."

"Sounds like we're in the same business," Brohn replies.

"The thing is," Mayla says, her elbows draped over her knees, the longer this war goes on, the more people there are who need our help."

"Speaking of which," Rain pipes in. "Anything you can do to help Kress's arm?"

"Of course," Suffolk says, her voice as warm and soft as sand.

She slides from the couch to kneel in front of me. Grabbing a black satchel from the floor next to the couch along the way, she removes the makeshift sling on my arm and draws a silver cannister from her bag. She shakes the can and then applies a kind of glossy blue spray-gel that feels cool against my skin and hardens before my eyes.

"How'd this happen?" she asks.

"We ran into a group of Survivalists."

"War?"

At first, I think she's offering to engage us in combat, but then I realize she's saying the name of our previous captor.

"Yes. His name is War."

A murmur goes through a huddle of women who have appeared over by the swinging door leading to what looks from here like a kitchen, but Mayla waves them quiet.

"We heard a rumor he got his hands on some strays last week.

I guess you're the strays. He's not someone you really want to run into."

"Now you tell us."

"He's also not someone who lets people go."

"He didn't let us go," Cardyn brags through a gulp of water. "We escaped."

"Really? Interesting."

"How so?"

Mayla shrugs and leans forward to inspect my arm and the gelatinous blue cast. Suffolk reaches back into the satchel and hands her a glass V-shaped device, which Mayla proceeds to glide along the cast.

"It should take a few weeks to heal up," Maya says. "Wait? When did you get this break?"

"A few hours ago. Escaping from War."

"Hm."

"What?"

"Suffolk's tomographer here must be as broken as your arm. According to this, the bone's already nearly healed. And you say it's only been a few hours?"

"It still hurts."

"I don't doubt it."

With her two friends and the curious cluster of onlookers watching our every move, Mayla continues to inspect us as if we were specimens of rare insects sealed up in glass jars.

"So," she says, her voice drawn out in a light-hearted drawl. "Let's start with the obvious: Seven teenagers alone in the Chicago New Town who've managed to avoid the Patriots, escape from War—something no one ever does—navigate through at least four Syndicate-controlled zones in a decked-out military escort truck, and make it to a stone's throw from Krug Tower and the city center. Does that sound about right?"

Brohn and I look back and forth at each other, neither of us knowing how to respond to this succinct, almost dismissive, but still very accurate assessment of our situation.

Mayla breaks the conversational stalemate for us.

"You don't happen to have a raven?"

I don't need to look around at my Conspiracy this time to know all of our jaws just dropped in unison.

"And you know this, how?"

"The Unkindness has resources the Patriots don't know about." Mayla points over to the woman who served us the water. "Before the war, Eralia was an aerospace engineer. Celestia is upstairs. She was a military logistical analyst and communications specialist. Dura here was a software designer. Suffolk and I were both radiation technologists. Six of our members worked in Krug's Real-News Department before they started asking too many questions and got arrested."

"Arrested?"

"Krug can't have people knowing things. Facts are his kryptonite, so he criminalized the truth. Speak it, and you'd find yourself out of a job, discredited, a social media pariah...the works."

"Do you know what it's like to have your life ripped apart on social media?" Dura snarls.

We look around at each other before Rain answers for us.

"We've never had social media," she explains, a hint of apology in her voice. "We know what it was. We know it connected people over a global network."

Dura grunts a half-laugh. "It was definitely a global network. As for connecting people, that was an illusion. In the wrong hands and with all the wrong people in charge, it became weaponized as a means to keep people *dis*connected."

"Krug turned divide and conquer into an art," Suffolk sighs.

Mayla nods her agreement and swallows one of the white pills, herself. "Defund the schools, keep minority communities poor, promote unhealthy living, build those arcology monstrosities to keep the Wealthies safe, and let the Eastern Order come in and wipe the rest of us out. It's almost beautiful in its simplicity. Well, it would be if it didn't cause so much ugliness for so many."

"About the war…," I begin.

"What about it?"

I take a deep breath, hesitant as always to reveal such an enormous truth. I look over to Brohn and Rain, both of whom nod their heads for me to go on. Manthy stares at me. Cardyn gives me a brotherly nudge and says, "It's what we're here for."

"You, see," I begin. "The thing about the war…"

"Yes?"

"It's not real."

Mayla's voice drops down as her eyebrows go up, her words spaced out in a suspicious, molasses crawl. "How do you mean?"

"The secret about the Eastern Order is one of the truths Krug criminalized," Brohn says, gesturing around at our expansive accommodations and then pointing to the partially-boarded window out at Krug Tower. "The Order. The war. It's a hoax. A set-up. A way to keep control over everyone. A way to keep you living like this while he lives like that."

There's a long silence, and for a second, I think time may have actually come to a stand-still. But then Mayla's eyes go bright and wide, and a toothy smile takes over her face.

"See!" she squeals with girlish glee and a series of stabbing finger-points at Suffolk and Dura. "I told them, but they didn't believe me!"

The other two women blush, their attention suddenly on everything in the room but us.

Mayla leaps up and paces over to the window and then back over to us like she's got more energy than she knows what to do with.

"The attacks. The explosions. The battles broadcast on the viz-screens. All the evidence of war was there," she says at last. "Except that it wasn't. What did we have? Images on a network of monitors we couldn't access or control. The words of a greedy, paranoid liar."

"We were all duped," Cardyn says.

"But that's not the scary part," Rain says. "It's how easy it was. It's like we *wanted* to be fooled into having an enemy to hate."

"And Krug rode our fear all the way to unlimited wealth and unchecked power," Brohn finishes.

Mayla settles back onto the couch, her triumphant smile fading as the reality of what she knew all along but couldn't dare believe begins to sink in.

"I had a feeling…" she says, biting the inside of her cheek and staring at the ceiling. Eventually, her gaze settles back on me. "All fake, right?"

I nod.

"No Eastern Order?"

"No."

"No invasion?"

"No."

"No enemy?"

"No. Well, yes. The enemy was Krug all along."

"Not just Krug," Brohn adds. "Ignorance and fear are enemies, too. And deadly as any weapon or invading army."

Mayla sits back in the plush sofa, her sandaled feet barely touching the floor. She gives us a long once-over.

"You're a clever bunch, aren't you?" she beams appreciatively.

"We have our moments," Brohn says.

"Talented, too. I can tell."

We all kind of shrug.

"Listen," she says after a few seconds of quiet, introspective smiling, "In 1864, Baudelaire wrote in a story that 'la plus belle des ruses du Diable est de vous persuader qu'il n'existe pas.'"

"The most elegant of the Devil's cons is to persuade you that he doesn't exist," I translate, recalling my language lessons from when I was a Neo being taught French and Latin by a precocious Juven named Merrick Michael.

"Very good," Mayla says. "But now I'm starting to think he's topped himself. Seems like now the best con this particular devil pulled is persuading us that we *need* him to exist, that he's one of us, and that despite all evidence to the contrary, he has our best interests at heart."

"Shame on him for fooling us," Dura says. "And shame on us for letting ourselves be fooled."

"Most of us want to be fooled in one way or another," Suffolk says. "And Krug knew it. I don't want to give him too much credit. But he's not stupid. Just ignorant."

"Isn't that the same thing?" I ask.

Mayla shakes her head. "'Stupid' is a lack of knowledge. 'Ignorance' is a lack of wisdom."

"I always figured Krug was deficient in both."

Mayla gives us a rich, happy laugh.

"You'd think so. But no. He's a vile, soulless, morally bankrupt, and paranoid pool of diarrheal pus. But when it comes to accumulating power, pitting his enemies—which is everyone who doesn't worship him—against each other, he knows exactly what he's doing. You said it yourself. The last twenty years have been a huge, manipulative lie."

Rain pulls her feet up onto the couch and crosses her legs as she undoes her ponytail.

"Adolf Hitler once said that to conquer a nation, first, you had to disarm its citizens. Krug figured out a better way. To conquer your *own* nation, make sure your enemies are unhealthy, uneducated, and heavily armed. Then, fill them with lies and fear and sit back and let them kill each other."

Mayla says, "It's a strategy that's been working for a long time. Very few have figured it out or had the courage or, frankly, the ability to do anything it about it. Which leads us to you. So, who are you, really?"

I look at my Conspiracy before turning back to Mayla. "As you've probably already figured out, we're the Emergents."

"Emergents."

"It's what Krug and his scientists call us, anyway."

"We know something about Emergents. You have abilities?"

"Nothing world-changing."

"We can do a few things everyone can do," Rain says. "Just a little better in one area or another."

Dura leans over the back of the couch, her bare arms shiny and smooth as partially-browned butter.

"We never really thought you were real."

"There's a lot of that going around," Cardyn says. "Sometimes I wonder it myself."

"Trust me," I say. "We're as real as it gets."

"And the things you can do…?"

"I've got tough skin," Brohn says with a blush and a knuckle-tap to his temple. "Cardyn can be unusually…convincing. Rain has a gift for strategy and logistics. Manthy—"

But Manthy cuts Brohn off with an obnoxiously loud clearing of her throat.

"Manthy is a person," she says, "not a show pony."

Brohn gives her a stunned look before turning back to Mayla and whispering behind his hand, "Manthy can talk to tech."

"I see." Mayla nods and tilts her chin toward Amani and Sheridyn. "And these two?"

"I can disguise myself kind of," Amani says, beaming like a little kid who just learned how to ride a two-wheeler.

"Really?"

"Kind of," Amani blushes. "It doesn't work all the time."

Mayla nods and turns to Sheridyn.

"And you?"

"I'm just a girl," Sheridyn says, her head down. "I wasn't…I couldn't be what they wanted to make me. Like Amani. Or like our friends…"

"They killed the others," Amani explains to our hosts. "Back in the Processor. It's what they do when you're supposed to have abilities but don't."

"They secluded us in small towns," I add. "They killed off the adults."

"Usually through targeted drone strikes," Brohn says. "Making it look like the work of the Eastern Order."

"Which doesn't exist," Mayla says by way of confirmation.

"Right. A discovery that cost the lives of millions, including two of our friends."

"Then they'd take a batch of us every year to a Processor where we'd get tested and trained."

"But it was all a trick to find out who was an Emergent, who wasn't, who they could use, and who they could kill off."

"They killed your friends?" Suffolk asks, her voice hushed, her eyes rimmed pink with tears of distress.

Amani and Sheridyn both lower their eyes. Amani turns toward Rain who is sitting next to him, and she offers him her hand, which he takes in his. She pats his forearm and tells him how sorry she is, how sorry we all are. "We'll keep you safe," she assures him and Sheridyn who both offer up their mumbled thanks.

"So that's kind of our story," Brohn says. "And you seem to already know Kress and Render, although I'm not sure how."

"Word gets around. When the word is important enough, that is. And this thing you do. The way they say you dream in raven…"

"I'm not entirely sure where that came from. Some of the Insubordinates in San Francisco came up with that one. As far as I know, I dream like everybody else."

"And the raven?"

"Okay," I admit. "I can think and feel what Render feels. As long as I'm not too distracted or stressed."

"So your dreams are real. The magic happens when you're awake."

"That's one way to put it, I guess."

"Do we get a demonstration?"

"It's not really a parlor trick," I say with a sudden awareness of why Manthy tends to shy away from talking about us as Emergents.

Mayla, Suffolk, and Dura turn toward Rain as Rain comes to my defense.

"When you can do something special," she says, "as we're learning, you stop being you and start becoming known as the thing you can do."

"I get that," Mayla says, turning back to me. "It's part of who and what you are."

"Exactly," I say, relieved that Mayla seems to get it.

"So…do we get a demonstration?"

"Right now?"

"Sure."

"I don't know—"

Brohn nudges me, and I sigh a hollow, "Okay. I need to check in on Render, anyway. He disappeared back in those woods right before you first found us."

"You don't control him?" Dura asks.

I chuckle at this. "What Render and I have is the opposite of control."

I wince as I scan the implants on my unbroken arm and explain how I can sometimes connect without my dad's tech.

"But our week with War and the pain of this broken arm make it harder. Anyway, here goes."

I hear the women gasp as my eyes go black.

27

AMANI AND SHERIDYN offer up a little inhalation of their own, and I realize they've never actually seen me do this before.

After another few seconds, I disconnect, and my eyes go back to normal.

"Did you do it?" Dura asks, her eyes darting around the grand room like she expects Render to come bursting in, which, to everyone's surprise but my own, is exactly what happens.

The room is lined with boarded up windows. But there's a gap in many of them, including an empty space at the top of the window just above Dura's head. It's through here that Render slices into the room in an explosion of dust and jet-black feathers to startled jumps and a chorus of amazed gasps and wide-eyed shock from pretty much everyone.

Cardyn gives an exaggerated, pseudo nonchalant yawn with his arms stretched wide like he's bored of seeing this little summoning trick, but I know he's as impressed as anyone. In the Valta, he was the only one who I let come along when I would sneak away into the woods to train Render. We made hundreds of those excursions, and Cardyn couldn't get enough. He was popular and liked to socialize, but he always found a way to make sneaking off with me and Render his top priority.

Now, Render perches on my shoulder.

The women, along with Amani and Sheridyn, stare at the two of us.

Mayla and Suffolk leap from the couch and drop to their knees in front of me, looking up at Render and his gilded filaments of armor.

"*Kakari Isutse.*"

I shrug. "So they say."

Still on her knees, Mayla shouts out to the next room, and dozens of women along with several men burst through the swinging kitchen door at the far end and materialize from the four sets of tall doors leading into the ballroom from the hallway.

I lean back in the couch as the men and women of the Unkindness push their way in front of me.

"My daughter is sick," one of the women says, stepping forward.

"Mine has been taken by the Survivalists—the Kenwood Park Syndicate—as a concubine," another adds.

"My sisters, too," another says. "The Bridgeport Syndicate."

A man about my dad's age but stooped and grizzled gray asks if we know people named, "Jevaun, T'shelle, and Ajana."

"I don't think so."

The man starts to cry. "Jevaun is my son. T'shelle and Ajana are his cousins. My sister's twin girls. They were taken," he says, pointing back in the direction of Krug Tower. "Like you were taken."

A woman pleads for us to help them. Like several of the others, she drops to her knees in front of me and takes my arm, pressing her forehead against my hand. Her dreadlocks, firehose thick and filled with glistening metallic clips, drape over my forearms and spill over onto the floor like an intricately decorated waterfall.

"My daughter, too," she says. "Nika. Can you help her?"

"How about if we give Kress and her friends a little space?" Mayla calls out over the buzz of the half-giddy, half-desperate throng.

Reluctantly ushered away by some of the older women, the crowd disappears back into the kitchen and the other rooms of the house, leaving us alone again in the ballroom with Mayla, Suffolk, and Dura.

"We have a mission," I tell them.

Mayla doesn't say anything, just looks me right in the eye and waits for me to finish.

"Our mission," I go on, clearing my throat, "is the kids up in that black tower."

"Krug Tower," Mayla says.

"Right. There may be as many as twenty other Emergents in there."

"If your children are in there..." Brohn starts.

"We'll do our best to find them, get them out," I finish.

"It's why we're here," Cardyn assures our hosts.

"It's what we're...built for," Rain adds, sitting between our two newest members. She pats Amani's knee with one hand and interlocks her fingers and Sheridyn's with the other.

"The tower is heavily guarded," Suffolk points out.

I nod.

"We know."

"The Wealthies...they never leave," Dura says. "It's a world of its own there now."

"We know that, too."

Mayla leans forward, clearly intrigued and squinting as she wraps her mind around the enormity of the moment.

"You're going to break into a tower you can't break into?"

"Yes."

"And free...how many did you say?"

"Twenty. More or less."

"You're not sure."

"No."

"So there could be more. Or none. Our own kids could be in there. Subjects like you were. Or they could be—"

"Our intel is good."

"The intel you got from Brohn's little sister? The one in San Francisco?"

"Yes. She's just short, though. She's hardly little."

"She's fifteen?"

"Yes."

"And she has access to intel no one else has access to? Not even us?"

"With help from Granden. Yes. And Olivia."

"Olivia. The Modified you say is back in your truck?"

"She's gotten us further than we deserve and saved our lives too many times to count."

"And she says there are as many as twenty seventeen-year-olds in there, including the ones we've lost, who may or may not have abilities like yours?"

"Yes."

"Say they don't have any abilities. What then?"

"We free them anyway. They'll die otherwise."

"Everyone dies."

"True. But not everyone is killed."

"Fair enough. Let's say they have abilities. Let's say some of them—maybe even kids like Jevaun, T'shelle, and Ajana—really are Emergents like you."

"Then we see if they're willing to join us. If you're willing to let them join us."

"And to die for your cause?"

"If they think it's worth it."

"And if they don't?"

"We return them to you—the ones who are yours anyway—and you can all live your lives as you see fit. The others...well, you can take care of them, or we can help track down the families they were stolen from before we leave."

"And if they agree to go with you to Washington, D.C…if these kids, our kids, agree to wage a hopeless war against Krug and his Patriot Army right in the middle of the hub of power…?"

"If they agree to come with us, then, by definition, the cause isn't hopeless," Rain says.

Mayla seems to consider this. "In the last few months, we've heard stories about impossible things happening."

Brohn leans forward, his arms draped over his knees, his voice a baritone wave. "Things are only impossible until they happen."

There's a long silence, which Brohn finally breaks as he leans back.

"We're going into that tower one way or another. We're saving who we can, one way or another. And we're taking this country back, one way or another. Some of those kids might be yours. You said it yourself. We really hope you won't stand in our way."

Mayla puts her hands up and smiles into the face of Brohn's skepticism.

"We're not going to stand in your way. In fact, we're going to help you."

"Really?"

"We have nothing to lose but our chains—" Mayla begins.

"And a world to win," I conclude. "*The Communist Manifesto*. Karl Marx and Friedrich Engels. 1848. The Samuel Moore translation."

Mayla raises an eyebrow. "I see it's true what we've heard about your memory."

"What can I say?" I shrug. "I remember things."

Mayla stands up. "Us, too." She waves her hand at the big empty room. "We remember how it came to this. We remember how our mothers made excuses, and how we inherited those excuses. Like giving up more and more little pieces of ourselves was somehow embedded in our DNA. They fought for freedom. They never suspected how aggressively men like Krug would fight back."

"Krug didn't invent oppression," I remind her.

"No. He just fed and watered it. Made it look legitimate to the bullies and bullshitters waiting for someone to tell them their inhumanity made them privileged."

Mayla catches me wincing and asks about my arm.

"It hurts," I admit. "But not as much as before."

"What is that thing you put on her, anyway?" Cardyn asks, reaching out to run a finger along the gelatinous blue cast, which has now turned into swirls of milky white.

"It's a plasticine mold," Suffolk explains. "With a special brand of methyl esters, pain inhibitors, calcium regenerators, and my personal concoction of marigold, emulsifiers, and herbal anti-inflammatories."

"Works like a charm," I say, wriggling my fingers and flexing my arm at the elbow.

"Well, it's been known to work," Suffolk says. "But I think maybe *you're* the charm."

"We've lived very *un*charmed lives," Brohn informs her. "Not everyone's here who is supposed to be here."

We hang our heads at the memory of our friends Karmine and Terk who were killed and of Kella who is alive but will probably never be the same vibrant girl she was.

"We've heard bits and pieces," Mayla says at last. "If it's not too much, are you willing to fill us in on the rest?"

Brohn sighs a reluctant, "Sure" and tells Mayla, Suffolk, and Dura that he'll start at the beginning.

Sitting in the big musty ballroom, we tell Maya and the Unkindness about our experiences, what we went through to get here, and we spend a lot of time looking over our shoulders, wondering if and when War and his Survivalists are going to show up and finish what they started.

"Don't worry," Mayla says as I glance over to the doorways for possibly the hundredth time in the last ten minutes. "War is dangerous. But the Survivalists are also insanely territorial. They'd have to get through a dozen other Syndicates just to get here. Fuller Park. The West Towns. Dearborn. South Loop. Lincoln Park. You're lucky you made it this far alive."

"You don't sound like you believe that," I say, trying not sound too accusatory.

"About it being luck?"

"You know something."

"I'm curious. What makes you think that?"

"I don't think it. I know it. I can tell."

"Are you reading my mind?"

I'm about to protest the absurdity of this when Mayla's mouth stretches into a broad, playful smile.

"I'm kidding. But you are reading something about me, aren't you?"

"Like what?"

"My tone. Body language. Micro-adjustments to my voice, hand position, involuntary ocular reflex."

"I don't know how to do any of that."

"It doesn't mean you're not doing it."

Mayla pauses and gives the seven of us a once-over. "Do you know what 'mushin' is?"

"Sure," Rain volunteers. "It means, 'no mind.' It's the Zen concept that the mind should be liberated from external, distracting forces."

Mayla nods. "It's also a state of mind most of us find hard to achieve and impossible to maintain."

"Okay…"

"I think Kress is on her way to a place no one has been before. A place monks, priests, and prophets have either been trying to get to or else claiming they've been but never really have."

"I'm seventeen," I say, turning the forearm of my unbroken arm around to expose the pattern of tattoos as if that explains everything. "My dad gave me these."

"And?"

"And what?"

Mayla squints at me out of the corner of her eye.

I squirm and finally add, "And it turns out I might not need them."

Mayla leans forward, clearly excited, as if she's just had an epiphany. "Stay with us."

"We can't," Brohn says. "We have a mission. What we're trying to do…it's not on a whim. We were isolated for almost our entire lives, and we're only just now starting to figure out why and what's been going on out here. Our abilities, these things we can do…they aren't free. They come with a price, an obligation. We have to do what we can to set things right. And now that includes finding and freeing your sons and daughters and anyone else who was taken."

"Sounds noble. Heroic, even."

"We're not heroes," I insist.

"Well," Brohn confesses through an adorable blush of embarrassment and fury, "there's a bit of revenge to factor in it as well. Krug and his men tricked and tortured us. We lost two of our best friends. And if I can use my abilities as an Emergent, or whatever I am, to bash Krug's face in, so much the better."

"If you don't stay with us long-term, will you at least stay until Kress's arm is fully healed? I'd love for you to have a look around." Mayla stands up and squints through two of the wooden slats nailed up against the window frame. "You sound like you know who you'll be fighting against. If you're going to fight, though, you might as well get to know some of the folks you'll be fighting *for*."

28

THE NEXT MORNING, after a long, deep sleep with all of us waking up from couches or from various palettes of blankets on the floor, Brohn pulls me aside and suggests we take Mayla up on her idea and go out together, just the two of us.

"Like a date?"

"Sure. Why not? We've done it before."

It's true. In San Francisco, on a break from our battle preparations, we spent a whole afternoon together, wandering around, exploring the city, and reveling in living the lives of normal teenagers for a change.

Of course, that was the same day we got beaten up, shot, kidnapped, and imprisoned. So for us, "normal" tends to be kind of a fleeting and pretty imprecise notion.

"Brohn and I are thinking about going out for a stroll," I inform Mayla, who has come into the room with Suffolk and Dura, each of them carrying trays of brown water, another round of anti-radiation pills, and small metal bowls of white-and-blue speckled protein cubes.

The three women we've quickly come to know as supremely generous hosts are accompanied by a man, also with dreadlocked hair down to his knees. His ropey arms and legs are dark and scarred under his pristine white dress-shirt and khaki shorts.

"This is Zidane," Mayla says almost as an afterthought as she plops down in the armchair across from me and Brohn. "He's one of the Providers."

"I help feed the folks," Zidane says through a lopsided smile. He's missing half his teeth, but the ones he has are square-edged and glossy white.

"I got the week's rations," Zidane informs Mayla through a lisp. "And took care of that little botheration with Ransack," he adds, conspiratorially out of the side of his crooked mouth.

"Ransack is a wanna-be warlord," Suffolk explains. "Five-foot tall little pimply piece o' work with balls too big and a brain too small. Wants to run the Humboldt Park Syndicate, but no one will give him enough weapons. Spends most of his time now trying to recruit followers from the Squatters who live in the old subway tunnels between here and the Loop."

"You don't have a working subway here, do you?" Brohn asks.

"Oh, no. The 'L-trains' are long-gone, too."

"L-trains?"

"Short for 'elevated trains.' Had a whole system running through the city. Over a hundred miles of tracks. Once the Wealthies didn't need the transportation hub anymore, they let it go to shit. Now the 'L' is scrap and a death-trap for kids, and the tunnels are a hang-out for the Tappers, Squatters, the Submitters. Folks like that."

"Tappers?"

"You know. Tappers. Submitters. The drug-addled. The wasted. The ones who've given up."

"Marx said religion is the opiate of the people. Turns out, *opiates* are the opiate of the people," Dura says with an unamused smile.

"Krug did his homework," Suffolk mutters, twisting one of her long locks of hair serpent-like around her forearm. "Got right to the heart of what keeps people in a state of chaos, ignorance, and fear. Ever heard of a revolution being carried off by people who are ignorant and afraid?"

We all shake our heads, "No."

"That's 'cause it's never happened and never will."

Our voices all echo in this large space, and I feel like we might get in trouble if we're overheard somehow. I ask Mayla if the Patriots ever send drones out here.

"They're built for surveillance," I remind her. "Are you ever afraid they're going to find out what you're up to? The things you talk about? Try to take you down?"

"We *think* about it all the time," Mayla says with a sly grin. "But we never worry."

"Why's that?" Brohn asks.

"Not sure. We're careful. That helps. But the truth is, they know we help keep the peace. We provide shelter, supplies. We negotiate truces between Syndicates. As long as there are folks like us, the people will never get desperate enough to revolt."

"So doesn't that mean you're helping the Patriots to stay in charge?" I ask.

Mayla shrugs. "The only options are Patriots in charge with us alive, all of us dying of starvation, or all of us dying in a long-shot revolution."

"Two of those three scenarios," Suffolks interjects, "end up with us and a lot of others dead."

"Don't dismiss the long-shot possibility," Brohn says, his voice low but pleasant as he turns to me and gives me a lighthearted elbow to the ribs. "What is it Card always used to say?"

"What's life without a little impossibility to overcome?"

We all have a good laugh over this, and it's nice to feel optimistic, cared for, and comfortable all at the same time.

While we're talking, Zidane slips back into the kitchen, returns, and sidles around the couch. Like the women, he's carrying a round silver tray, only his is piled high with a weedy assortment of green leaves and tangles of purplish vines, which he promises through another wet lisp, are a lot tastier than they look. He sits down next to Mayla and, with a quick flourish, he begins to wrap the vegetable matter into tidy rolls.

"After what I hear War put you through," Zidane says, "I would'a figured you'd have had enough of Chicag-hole already."

"We survived the Survivalists," Brohn brags.

Zidane seems to appreciate this fact, but Mayla frowns and appears a bit more concerned.

"It's not just the Survivalists," she says. "There's Assault Gangs. Hustlers. Tinkerers. Scroungers. Any one of them could decide that their needs are more important than your lives."

"When did human life become so...disposable?" I ask glumly.

"I look human to you," she says, "but I'm not."

"Oh," I laugh. "What are you?"

Mayla stands and steps over to one of the windows behind the couch and peels back a rag of a curtain. Pink morning light streaks in, and Mayla points up at Krug Tower and at the smaller but still intimidating arcologies being constructed in its shadow. "A few thousand people living in self-powered, self-contained buildings."

Zidane nods and says, "Mm-hm" without looking up from his wraps as Mayla continues.

"They messed up our world, and when we demanded they fix it, they told us to frack off and then they went and built their own world. They're the Wealthies. We're the Baseborn."

"So? It's just labels."

"Right," Mayla agrees. "And the Wealthies label means 'a person with a lot wealth.' Being a Baseborn means 'someone who hasn't risen to the level of being a person.' We're not human to them. Not anymore."

Nodding and mumbling "Amen," Zidane finishes wrapping the rolls and offers two of them to me and Brohn. We say, "Thanks" at the same time, and Zidane beams his black and white piano-keys of a smile before striding off to join Suffolk and Dura, who are still distributing food to Cardyn, Rain, Amani, Sheridyn, and Manthy over on the other side of the room.

I nudge Brohn and point him in the direction of Sheridyn, who is slumped over in one of the armchairs.

"She's still not looking too good. Maybe we should take her with us? Get her some fresh air?"

Before Brohn can respond, Mayla cuts in to remind us that the air around here is hardly fresh.

"Want to do that girl some good, let her stay here and collect herself."

"It's just that we don't really know what's wrong with her," Brohn says. "We got her and Amani out of the Processor. Amani seems to be coming along, but Sheridyn is, well…not."

"I'm thinking maybe it's radiation sickness," Mayla suggests.

When Brohn and I look doubtful, she throws up her hands.

"Just a guess. She's got the symptoms. Some of them, anyway."

"But Amani doesn't."

"All the more reason to keep her inside while you go off and have your date."

"It's not a date," I blush.

Brohn puts his arm around me and plants a big kiss on my cheek.

"The hell, it isn't," he laughs.

"Will we at least be safe?" I ask Mayla. "Out there, I mean?"

Hearing the determination in my voice, she sighs and looks from me to Brohn and back to me again. "As long as you stick together."

"We always do," Brohn announces with pride.

"But don't actually *walk* together," Mayla adds.

Brohn and I stare at her, waiting for the punchline.

"I know it sounds crazy," she continues, "but a woman is expected to walk behind the man she's with."

"You're joking."

"I wish I was. But no."

"And if we decide to walk side by side like regular people?"

"Well, technically, there's no law against it."

"So what's the problem?"

"There's no law. But the legality of the thing might wind up being the least of your worries. There are Patriot soldiers all over the place out there. Some won't care. Others will. And the ones who care, care a lot. They make kills, not arrests."

"They can get away with killing regular citizens who are just taking a walk?"

"Well. Technically, they can face up to three days of leave with pay. But even that's usually overturned on appeal. So, yes."

Mayla calls across the room to Zidane to make sure he's taking proper care of the rest of our Conspiracy before turning back to us.

"The Patriot presence is a funny thing. They patrol. They say they're keeping the peace. But they won't be out here for long."

"Wait. That's good, right?" Brohn asks.

Mayla gives him a motherly smile. "Once they're gone, it means no more pretense. No more acting like we're worth saving. They'll hole up in the arcologies with the Wealthies and leave the rest of us out here to fend for ourselves."

"Which means kill each other and die," I say.

Mayla says, "Absolutely" as Suffolk and Dura walk up to us with the rest of our Conspiracy right behind.

Cardyn is licking his fingers, and he calls out his compliments to Zidane, who gives him a happy salute before disappearing into the kitchen.

"These two want to go out," Mayla informs the others. "I told them about the Patriots."

"Other women might go after you, too," Dura says to me and Brohn as she sits down on the arm of the couch. "There are certain cultural expectations so deeply embedded by now...not everything outside your mountain town operates according to common sense rules of kindness, altruism, and empathy."

"Our town is gone," Brohn reminds her.

"I'm sorry. I know."

"Maybe take the rest of your Conspiracy with you?" Suffolk suggests. "Safety in numbers."

"But also a lot of attention," Rain says. "I'm okay staying here and letting Brohn and Kress have their fun."

"Me, too," Cardyn adds. "Just try not to get kidnapped this time, okay?"

Brohn stands, stretches, and claps Cardyn on the shoulder, telling him not to worry.

"Kress can ask Render to keep an eye out and watch our backs."

"Actually," Suffolk sighs, "I don't recommend letting him fly around too much. Most species of birds around here have either gone away or have gone extinct."

"But he's going to want to fly," I protest. "No offense, but for us, your place is a palace. For him, it's kind of a prison."

Manthy says she has an idea about how he can go for a flight and still stay safe inside Mayla's Crib at the same time.

I laugh at first but then realize Manthy is totally serious. "I'm sorry," I say. "What did you have in mind?"

"Funny you should mention having something 'in mind,'" Manthy says without looking at me. Walking over to the window sill where Render is quietly preening himself, she runs her finger along his glossy black beak, something he usually doesn't care for, but right now, he's purring as softly as a deeply contented cat. Manthy skims her hands over the overlapping golden plates covering some of his flight feathers, and Render quivers and coos like he's being tickled.

"I think I can give him the *sensation* of flight."

Brohn shrugs and says, "Why not?" and those two words strike me suddenly as extraordinarily liberating.

"Why not?" I repeat. "Wait," I add, whipping back around to face Mayla. "You said before that I can get killed for not walking the right distance behind Brohn?"

"No," Mayla says. "Brohn would get killed for not being man enough to keep you in your place."

"And Kress?" Brohn asks.

"If a Patriot did feel like making an arrest, she could get sent to one of the WECs. That's a Weekend Etiquette Course. It's just behavior modification, reconditioning, re-patriotizing. Things like that. Or she could get put on some service crew somewhere. If she's lucky, she might get a month or two as a maid for one of the Wealthies."

"They should wear Concealers," Suffolk advises as she pours a second round of brown water into my metal cup.

"They're like Dissimulators," Mayla explains. "Only they're not military-grade. Scroungers use them all the time. They won't mask your heat signature or alter your body contour or anything like the old-style Beards."

"Beards?"

"Camouflagers. The drones can see through them now. They haven't figured out the Concealers yet. They've got a shifting palette of nano-cells. Those'll bounce a false image back to the surveillance drones. You asked if we worry about getting spied on. The Concealers help us not have to worry about that so much when we go out. The drones'll figure them out, but it takes them a few seconds, and by then, the Concealer will roll over to a new image. It won't work more than a few times before you get tagged, so I suggest staying covered up and on the move as much as possible."

Mayla shouts out across the long room for Zidane to bring in some Concealers, and almost immediately, he returns from the kitchen with a small brown box no bigger than an old eyeglass case.

"Going out?" he asks.

"Going to try," I say.

The whole time all of us have been talking, Amani has been watching quietly from his seat next to Rain, his eyes ping-ponging back and forth between us.

Finally, he raises his hand, and I feel like his teacher instead of his peer or his friend when I call on him.

"I'd like to go with you," he says. "If you have another one of those masks."

Brohn and I look to Mayla for confirmation one way or another, but she just shrugs.

"Makes no difference to me."

"In fact," Mayla says, "it'll probably keep you safer with two males to one female."

"What is wrong with you people?" I practically shout. "Did you all just wind up with so much spare time that you had nothing else to do but go around ranking people and making up these stupid rules about who could do what and who was better than who?"

"It was a slow burn," Mayla concedes. "But even a slow burn eventually gets you cooked."

"You're sure you want to go out there?" Brohn asks.

Amani stands slowly and gives Brohn a halfhearted, "Yes."

"Okay. Just stick close."

Mayla takes the case from Zidane and pops open the lid to reveal a small pile of gossamer sheets like thin, translucent pancakes.

"Here," she says to me. "Give it a try."

The delicate material sticks to my face like a second skin, and I panic for a second thinking it might smother me.

But Suffolk anticipates my anxiety and tells me to relax.

"It won't suffocate you. Breathe normally. The membrane is micro-permeable and practically invisible. It'll fool the drones for a few seconds. To anyone else, it'll just look like you've got a good sheen of sweat going."

Suffolk hands Brohn and Amani one of the floppy Concealer skins, which they slip onto their faces.

Cardyn, Rain, and Manthy tell us to be careful and promise they'll take good care of Sheridyn and Render while we're gone.

Giving Render one last stroke along his wing and a pat to his round, armored head, I slip my hand into Brohn's, and we walk out of the ballroom and down the long hallway leading to the front door. With Amani padding along like a curious little brother, we step out into the hot red morning.

29

It takes us nearly twenty minutes to navigate the few hundred yards of dead jungle surrounding the Unkindness's Crib.

Once we're out in the open again, we step into a neighborhood crammed tight with people and noisy with the din of haggling and bickering shoppers desperate to get as many provisions for as little as possible.

Many of them scramble over or around huge lengths of twisted steel and I-beam supports, the un-scavenged remnants of what Mayla told us was the "L-train."

For the most part, people ignore us. Some have their faces covered with pieces of gauze. Others protect their noses and mouths with twisted strips of soiled fabric. A group of women wearing fogged-up swimming goggles and gritty, charcoal-gray surgical masks scurries past us without acknowledging our presence.

Keeping one's head down and avoiding eye contact seem to be the rules of thumb around here. It's like everyone's a land mine, and no one wants to risk a misstep that sets someone else off.

In Reno, everyone was armed. It's the same here, only there are a lot more people and a lot more weapons. According to

Mayla, Chicago runs for well over twenty miles in every direction. That adds up to a lot of people and a lot of guns.

"How can so many people even afford those weapons?" I ask Brohn as I try not to choke on the particle-filled air. "Those men over there have high-grade military tactical stuff. A lot of it was never meant for civilian use."

With one arm across his nose and mouth, Brohn responds with a single-shoulder shrug. "According to Mayla, guns are the cheapest thing around."

It's true. Last night, with all of us gathered around in the ballroom, Mayla, Suffolk, and Dura filled us in on some of the less savory elements of life in Chicago. According to them, guns, "battery-acid booze," and drugs are easy to come by. Practically free if you were in need and knew where to look. "And pretty much everyone is in need," she told us. "And everyone knows where to look."

She went on to tell us about the drug culture where people gobbled down everything from diversion shots and fentanyl powder to joyrides and tap-outs.

"There's stuff to make you forget. Stuff to make it feel like your wildest fantasies are coming true before your eyes. All imported. All addictive. All mind-numbing and pacifying. And all eventually deadly. Try finding clean water or a competent doctor. Now *those* are expensive. Best way to wipe out your enemies is to give them the tools to do it themselves."

Now, shielding his eyes from the sun with one hand, Brohn points up at Krug Tower with the other.

"Tomorrow. That's where we'll be."

"Then we better get going with enjoying today."

Brohn and I spend the rest of the evening and into the darkening night together with Amani tagging along. He's like a puppy following us loyally from place to place. I get it. We saved his life. We're Emergents, and he dodged a bullet, almost literally, by staying alive as long as he did. Even though he's our age, he comes across as much younger, and it's kind of like he's our kid, and we're his doting parents taking him out for a leisurely afternoon stroll.

Of course, the leisurely strolls I remember from when I was six didn't involve avoiding eye contact with haggard strangers and hoping not to get shot.

As we navigate our way around the neighborhood, all of it under the ominous shadow of Krug Tower and the partially-built arcologies in the city center Loop, Brohn keeps trying to slow his pace so we can walk together, but Mayla's warning has me on edge, and I'm deliberately staying a half-step behind him. Just in case.

Distracted now by everything, Amani keeps falling even farther behind, and I have to keep turning around and telling him to keep up.

The streets are patrolled by Patriot officers, who thankfully don't seem to recognize us. The Concealers aren't meant to obscure us from human vision, but they seem to distort our features just enough, so we don't appear completely as ourselves to any Patriot on the lookout for us.

The real danger is from the surveillance drones buzzing around overhead.

According to Mayla, they're programmed to spot certain infractions: Women with too much skin covered. Women with not *enough* skin covered. Men loitering in groups of four or more. And the stupid rule about a woman having to walk behind a man.

I know how potentially dangerous it is to be out like this. But I need to see this place, and I need to be with Brohn. I love my friends and my Conspiracy, but there are definitely times when I wind up missing Brohn even when he's sitting two feet away from me.

So I'm enjoying this meandering walk through the scariest and most depressing city I've ever been in.

Without currency or tap-coins, we have no choice but to make this a simple walk-around, which is fine with me.

As we navigate the long-neglected roadways, we come across one of the giant yellow industrial loaders in the process of stacking more rail cars on top of each other. The work area is cordoned off with floating orange holo-pylons, and little kids gather around by the hundreds to watch the automated mammoth machine at work.

The loader's powerful mag-turbine engines kick up a terrible cloud of dust, which the kids find amusing, and they scamper and play in the falling ash like it's a gentle winter snowfall.

Brohn and I watch for a few minutes, careful to keep an eye on Amani, who keeps getting distracted by the endless crush of pedestrians and by the long rows of kiosks stacked high with junk all around us.

"We've turned into a species of scavengers," Brohn says to me over the din and rumble of the towering forklift.

"This is what the Wealthies are afraid of," I call back, my arm hovering just above my eyes to keep out the cloud of stinging debris. "It's what they're trying to stop themselves from becoming."

"Then they shouldn't have let all this happen in the first place."

I nod and wave for us to get going, and we continue on our way with Amani scampering to catch up.

A few streets later, we come across a row of open-faced rail cars, all lined with people selling deep-fried plants and animal scraps out of steel barrels bubbling over with sizzling oil.

"They're using ammo as currency," I point out.

Brohn follows my finger in the direction of a crush of people pressing forward toward the vendors, tin plates in their hands, as they haggle for food. The vendors bellow out prices and flash numbers on their fingers, and the eager customers rummage in their pockets for handfuls of bullets, small detonators, pinball grenades, and a range of assorted manufactured and improvised ammunition, which they plunk onto metal scales before receiving their meals.

Brohn pats one of the weapons packs on his belt.

"Think we can afford to sacrifice a few bullets for breakfast?"

I tell him, "Sure. Why not?"

"You and Amani stay here. I'll see what I can scrounge."

Brohn—tall, broad-shouldered, and brimming with confidence—strides right into the middle of the mass of sweaty and desperate customers, who step deferentially to the side, their eyes averted as he passes.

"He's not afraid of anything, is he?" Amani asks.

"He's afraid of a lot of things, actually."

"Brohn is?"

"Sure. He's afraid of doing the wrong thing. He's afraid of letting us down or leading us down the wrong path. And I know he's afraid that nothing we do here will make a difference to any of the people who need us the most."

Across the roadway, Brohn has reached the vendors and their line of boiling barrels. I can almost make out what he's saying as he holds out a handful of nine and ten-millimeter bullets and haggles among the hundreds—maybe thousands of other people in the pressing mob. If Render were around, I could really home in on Brohn, but as it is, I have to be satisfied with picking up a few words here and there as they ride back to me on the cadence of his voice.

"I hope he doesn't get shot," Amani says.

"He won't. Besides, he's kind of bullet-proof."

"Really?"

"Mm-hm."

"Is he your boyfriend?"

"We're not a fan of labels. But sure," I laugh, "if that makes it easier…"

Amani lowers his eyes as Brohn works his way back out of the crowd, three tin plates of scraps in hand.

"It's insane over there," he pants. "I must've got groped a hundred times."

I give him a smack to the shoulder and tell him not to be gross.

Brohn throws his arm around me in total defiance of what's apparently customary around here and says we should get going.

As we walk, we sample the food Brohn managed to procure, and honestly, it's not all that bad. The purple clumps of leaves are crisp and salty. The strips of dark meat, while thin and on the stringy side, at least taste like real meat, although I'm too afraid to guess from what animal.

Brohn says, "Not bad."

"I guess 'not bad' is about as good as we can hope for."

We walk around for another hour or so, careful to keep track of where we are in the jam-packed maze of people and rail cars.

In that short time, we witness three fist-fights, a middle-aged man chasing a group of small boys with a machete, and another scuffle over water rations that ends with a man whipping out a small silver gun from his belt and shooting another man twice in the head and the woman he's with point-blank in the chest.

All this while two Patriot soldiers stand just down the laneway, watching as casually as if they were strolling by a duck pond.

Following Brohn, I grab Amani's elbow and drag him around a corner where we jog as inconspicuously as possible in the opposite direction.

"We'll see plenty of action tomorrow," Brohn reminds me. "Probably best to try to stay alive today."

30

FIGURING it's best not to press our luck, we decide to head back to Mayla's house. We take a slight detour along the way to check in on Olivia back in the truck.

We're all happy to see that she and the truck are just how we left them.

"You're sure you're okay in here?" Brohn asks, his head ducked down in the low-ceilinged Pod. "We'd be happy to keep you company."

Olivia's colorful tendrils flutter as she rotates in her mag-chair, sharing her attention with us and her bank of projected schematics of Krug Tower. Populated by scrolling code, surveillance feeds, and endless images of strategic calculation simulations, the gossamer displays pulse, change, and fluctuate in the air as we look on.

"I'm more connected than any of you," Olivia laughs. "Well, except maybe for Kress and Render. Being alone isn't the same thing as being lonely. I'm just impaired, not incomplete."

"And definitely not incompetent," I add.

"I certainly hope not!"

Amani leans forward to inspect one of the pixilated images.

"Is that from a drone?"

"A surveillance drone," Olivia says, giving us what I think is a wink. "I've been able to piggy-back on some of the tower's security and surveillance protocols. Nothing too sophisticated. But I want to make sure you've got the best chance of success as possible."

"Should we send Rain up here?" I ask through a poorly-stifled yawn. It's been a long day. A long life, actually. "Or Manthy?"

Olivia seems to consider this for a second before shaking her head and turning toward a drone-feed showing a line of Patriot soldiers reporting for guard duty at the foot of the enormous tower.

"No," she says at last. "I can handle this part. We'll have time for more planning tomorrow. For today, let them rest. Let yourselves rest. You push yourselves so hard to help so many. Before you jump back into war, sometimes it's just as important to take a pause to remember what peace feels like. Otherwise, how will you remember what it is you're fighting for?"

"Best advice I've heard all day," Brohn laughs. He points to the holo-image of the black tower rising up above the shimmering lights on Olivia's central console. "We'll leave you to it, but we'll be back tomorrow to make sure we're all on the same page before we try to get into that thing."

Turning back to face her glass screens and projected technographics, Olivia wishes us goodnight, and Amani and I follow Brohn back down the ladder and out of the truck.

Once outside, Brohn takes my hand in his, and, with Amani padding along behind us, we tramp our way back through the jungle, and emerge in the clearing in front of the Crib.

"It really must've been something before all this," I say, looking up at the gigantic mansion of a house.

"I bet a lot of these houses were," Brohn guesses. "Such a waste."

"Anything built can be broken," I remind him.

"And anything broken can be rebuilt," he finishes.

"Come on," Amani says, darting up the front steps and across the porch. "I want to check on Sher."

Brohn and I say, "Okay," and we follow Amani into the house, through the marble-floored foyer, down the main hall, and into the huge ballroom.

Cardyn is lying on one of the couches, his leg stretched out over its back. Manthy is sitting on the floor next to him.

"So, how was the date?" Cardyn calls to us as we drag ourselves across the room.

"It was lovely," I gush, thrusting my arm through Brohn's. "A beautiful stroll with my handsome gentleman caller."

"Give me a break," Cardyn groans, throwing his arm over his eyes.

At the same time, Rain bounces up to greet us, a wooden box cradled in her arms like a sleeping baby.

"It's a chess set," she squeals. "It was in a storage bin in one of the upstairs closets. Mayla says no one here ever learned to play."

"Where is she, anyway?"

"She had to get supplies from somewhere. Suffolk and Dura are upstairs. Zidane and some of the other Unkindness are in the kitchen making dinner."

Brohn and I plop down onto one of the couches and laugh when Amani does the same, imitating our contented sighs and lightly folded arms.

"Actually, we kind of already ate," Brohn says, and he and I recount our walk through the chaos of the city and our successful acquisition of food from one of the vendors.

"We checked in on Olivia, too," I add.

Rain grimaces and shakes her head. "I should be back in the Pod with her. We have so much to do, and we've hardly prepared."

Brohn puts a hand up as Rain starts to head toward the door.

"She says she's got it under control. We'll finish up tomorrow."

Rain pauses. "Really?"

"It's what she says."

"You're sure?" Rain asks, looking from me to Brohn and back to me. "*She's* sure?"

"Sure sounds like it," I smile.

Rain seems to contemplate this before finally allowing her shoulders to relax.

"Hey!" Rain calls out to Amani from where she's walked over and started setting up the chess pieces on a homemade wooden table in front of one of the couches. "Feel like a game?"

"I've never played."

"All the more reason to learn."

Amani looks at me and Brohn as if for permission. Brohn, his arm around me and my leg over his, tells Amani to go ahead and give it a shot.

"Rain's not only brilliant," he says. "She's a great teacher, too."

"She's also deadly in unarmed combat," I add, "so try not to piss her off."

Amani giggles at this and bounds over to join Rain.

Meanwhile, I whistle for Render, who is down at the far end of the room, pacing along the marble mantle above the fireplace. He perks his head up before launching himself into the air. He glides toward me and weaves around the links of chain holding up the giant chandeliers that hang from the ceiling.

He alights on the back of the couch just behind my head and nuzzles my ear with his bulky black beak.

"How was he?" I call out to Manthy.

Manthy looks up from where she's sitting on the floor across from Cardyn and gives me a thumb's up.

"For all he knows, he spent the day flying around in the Valta."

"You can make him think he's in the Valta?"

Manthy says, "Apparently."

"And he was happy?"

"Yes."

Brohn leans over to kiss me, and Render offers him an ear-nuzzle of his own, which makes Brohn laugh.

"Tickles," he says.

Render gives his hackles a shake and flies back the entire length of the room to return to his perch on the fireplace mantle where he goes about giving himself a good preening.

Meanwhile, I let myself melt into Brohn's arms.

Sitting across from each other in wide pink and yellow armchairs, Rain teaches Amani how to play chess, and he turns out to be a quick study. I don't know how to play as well as Rain, but I'm okay, and I'm good enough to know that Amani, by imitating Rain, is picking the game up with extraordinary speed.

In the long shadows cast by an oil lamp on the small wooden table next to them, Rain and Amani flick and slide the pieces around like directors choreographing a ballet.

Meanwhile, on the other side of the room, Cardyn and Manthy appear to be tolerating each other's company. Cardyn has started telling her jokes, which she's been responding to with grim silence.

At one point, as he's returning from the kitchen with two glasses of brown water, he corrects me before I'm finished groaning to Brohn about his lame jokes.

"They're not jokes," he insists. "They're anti-jokes."

"Anti-jokes?"

"It's jokes without a punchline," he explains to me and Brohn.

"A joke without a punchline?" Brohn asks. "Isn't that just—?"

"Stupid?" I finish.

Apparently offended, Cardyn harrumphs at us. "In the right context, 'stupid' is just another word for 'funny.'"

Then, he goes back to the corner where Manthy is sitting cross-legged and straight-backed on a braided throw-rug. Cardyn sets the glasses of water on the floor before plunking himself down across from her, his lazy slouch in stark contrast with her tall, upright posture.

A few minutes later, Mayla arrives and greets me and Brohn with a wide, white smile. She raises two blue plastic bags, overflowing with reddish-brown leaves and the skinny, fur-covered legs of an animal.

"Hungry?" she asks.

Brohn and I exchange a knowing look.

"Sure," he says. "We grabbed a bite while we were out. But we can always eat."

"Great! I'll be right back."

Mayla drops the bags off in the kitchen before walking back into the ballroom, her boots kicking up puffs of dust in the smoky yellowish light and echoing in the cavernous space.

"How was your walk-about?"

"Uneventful," Brohn says.

"A little scary," Amani pipes in from over at the table where he's abandoned his comfy armchair and is now kneeling across the chessboard from Rain. "Lots of people. Lots of guns."

"It can get rough out there," Mayla warns. "But mutually-assured destruction seems to be the rule of the day."

"Mutually-assured...?" Amani asks, looking up from the game.

"Destruction," I explain. "It's what happens when everyone has the same ability to threaten everyone else, so no one makes the first move."

"In the movies," Mayla adds, "it used to be called a 'Mexican standoff.' Everyone has guns pointed at everyone else, and no one can break the tension without the risk of getting killed, themselves."

"It's called 'zugzwang' in chess," Rain calls out as she moves one of her pieces. "That's when a player is better off not moving but has to because it's her turn. Just the act of moving puts her in a weaker position."

"Well," Brohn sighs, "we came across a few new people today who weren't exactly afraid to make the first move."

"There've got to be better ways to keep the peace," I sigh, turning to Mayla. "We've heard stories about how things used to be. Do you think it'll ever be like it was?"

"I hope not. How it was is what got us to where we are. No. Now that you're here, I'm hoping we can move forward. Do better this time. Be better. I'd like this world to one day be like it *can* be instead of how it's been."

"I like it here," Amani says, pointing to the floor. "In here, I mean. Not out there."

"We like having you here."

Mayla looks Amani up and down before grinning and shifting her gaze to where Sheridyn is sitting glumly in the deep cushions of the armchair where, as far as I can tell, she's been all day. Mayla beckons her over.

"How about if we do something with that hair?"

Frowning, Sheridyn runs her thin fingers weakly through her tangle of frizzy red curls.

"My hair?"

"Would you like me to braid it for you?"

"Braid it?"

"Sure. Haven't you ever had anyone braid your hair?"

Sheridyn's silence is Mayla's answer.

"Come on. I won't hurt you."

Groaning herself up and looking a little green, Sheridyn pads over and sloughs down in front of Mayla, who begins working on her hair. Brohn and I excuse ourselves and slip away to another loveseat in a dark corner on the opposite side of the large room. Perched on the fireplace, Render welcomes us with one of his signature *kraas*!

It's a quiet moment, one I wish we could freeze-frame and live in, at least for a while.

Rain and Amani are bonding over their chess game.

Sheridyn appears half-hypnotized by the rough but nimble hands working their magic on her impossible mane of hair.

Cardyn and Manthy are squirreled away on the other side of the room underneath one of the boarded-up windows.

I'm sitting on the floor and up against the wall where I can feel fatigue catching up with me. Brohn is stretched out with his head in my lap.

"I can hear them, you know," I say through a yawn.

"Who?"

I tip my head toward Cardyn and Manthy who must be a hundred feet away.

Brohn cranes his neck to gaze out across the room.

"Really?"

"Like they were sitting right here."

"What are they saying?" Brohn whispers up to me.

"Cardyn just asked Manthy a riddle," I whisper back, leaning down so my mouth is next to Brohn's ear.

"What is it?"

I tilt my head to pick up Cardyn's voice from across the room. "Why was six afraid of seven?"

"That's an old one," Brohn says, recalling the book *Complete Collection of Pranks, Puns, and Put-ons* we used to read from growing up together in the Valta. "It's because seven ate nine."

Across the room, Manthy bursts into a shoulder-quivering fit of giggles.

I shake my head at Brohn. "According to Cardyn, the answer is 'because seven killed six's family.'"

Brohn frowns. "That's not how the joke goes."

I shrug, and Brohn closes his eyes and grins. Then his grin turns into a chuckle and then a full-on laugh.

"Okay," he says, wiping tears from the corners of his eyes. "Cardyn's version is funnier."

On their side of the room, Cardyn asks Manthy if she knows why the little boy fell off his bike. When she shakes her head,

"No," Cardyn tells her it was because someone threw a washing machine at him.

"What has eleven legs, five feet, and is orange?" he asks her next.

"What?"

"Nothing."

Manthy giggles, and Cardyn launches into another one.

"Scientific fact: If you laid all the veins and arteries from your body end-to-end…"

"Yeah?"

"You'd die."

Now, Brohn and I are both crying with laughter.

Clearly suspicious that we've been eavesdropping, Cardyn calls out to ask us what's so funny.

I lie and tell him, "Nothing. We were just reminiscing."

He seems dubious but goes back to joking around with Manthy.

Meanwhile, Brohn and I enjoy gazing around at the pockets of gentle activity and quiet camaraderie going on throughout the spacious room. He points out how nice the remaining glass prisms from the overhead chandeliers look in this filtered midday light. He runs a finger along the polished wooden floor and wonders aloud if there were ever big dances here.

"You know," he says, "like the ones in the fairy tales with princes and talking animals and motherless women with ill-fitting shoes."

"I sure hope so. Hey. I have an idea."

"Yes?"

"I think we should come back here. When all this is over. I think we should come back here in a year. Or two. Or whenever. And Reno, too. And Salt Lake City and San Francisco. And Odell."

"Especially Odell," Brohn agrees.

"We can have a road trip…see all the old places…see if things are good again."

"It's a date."

"It could take a long time. Years."

"Then it's a *lot* of dates."

I lean down and kiss him to seal the deal.

Brohn reaches up to stroke my hair, and he asks me about my arm.

"It feels surprisingly good," I tell him.

"Someday…," he says.

"Someday what?"

Brohn pulls my face down to his and kisses me. Then he whispers in my ear.

"Someday, 'good' will be *normal* instead of 'surprising.'"

31

WE SPEND the rest of the day and into the night scattered on couches, chairs, and even on the floor throughout the slightly dusty but supremely comfortable ballroom.

In the morning, we awake to the sounds and smells of cooking coming from the kitchen.

Mayla and her crew swarm into the ballroom, plates and trays of food in hand, to feed us once again. They seem to have no shortage of sustenance or hospitality in this otherwise bleak and barren world.

Suffolk and Mayla come over to where Brohn and I are just tying up our boots and ask how my arm's doing, and I tell them the truth: "Better than ever."

"Never seen anything like it," Suffolk says as she inspects the gelatinous cast, now faded to a nearly-invisible blue. "I think this can come off now."

"Really?"

"Well, they usually stay on for a couple of weeks, at least. You can keep yours on longer if you like. But your arm is fine, and this thing'll get itchy as hell before you know it."

That makes me laugh, and I tell Suffolk to please proceed.

Using the sharp tip of one of her long fingernails, she peels back a small panel on the underside of the cast and taps a small input pad.

"Here," she says, holding a thin plastic bag under my arm. "This'll catch the dross."

"Dross?"

"The leftovers from the cast."

As she works the cast off, I flex my fingers and slowly rotate my wrist. I keep expecting there to be some pain or at least some leftover stiffness or discomfort, but the truth is, my arm really does feel totally back to normal.

"Health like yours is rare," Suffolk mutters. "A lot of sick people come through here looking for help. Got medical facilities set up in the basement. We do what we can, but the odds are stacked against all of us. And not by accident, either."

"Around here, health is an old wives' tale," Mayla says, as the pale blue cast disintegrates into dust before our eyes and collapses into Suffolk's bag. "First, they took the fluoride out of the water. Then they lowered all the purification standards. No real doctors left around anymore. Most of us won't live to be fifty."

"It's why we especially appreciate what you've done for us these past couple of days," Brohn says as he joins me in inspecting my arm.

"You seem to have picked up some more of your friend's traits," Mayla says, gesturing to where Render sits perched on the cornice above the door over by the kitchen.

"Ravens have often been associated with magic," I tell them, "including shape-shifting, meaning-making through dreams, rebirth, and healing."

"Kress and Render have been through a lot together," Brohn tells them. "In the Valta, Kress spent more time with him than she did with anyone else."

He leans back and scans me from the bottoms of his eyes.

"I think…yes, they may even be starting to look like each other."

When I scowl at him, he raises his hands in surrender and promises it's a compliment.

"I find you both extraordinarily wise, eminently talented, and devastatingly beautiful," he gushes.

I can't hold my pretend frown anymore and start to laugh.

"I just hope I don't start sprouting feathers," I say, and Mayla and Suffolk laugh along with us as Zidane comes up behind them and wraps his arms around Suffolk's waist.

"Feathers are lucky," he beams, his face burrowed playfully in her neck. "Give you the tickles in all the right places."

Pretending to be annoyed, Suffolk pushes Zidane away, and he skips off to one of the couches where Cardyn and Manthy are helping each other clip on their tactical vests.

"So you're really going?" Mayla asks, suddenly serious.

"We have to," Brohn says, flicking his head toward Amani and Sheridyn. "There are a lot more like them and maybe even the kids from the Unkindness up in that tower, and we know first-hand what's in store for them."

"And it's not good," I add.

Brohn stands up and checks to make sure his guns are secure. "We need to get back to the truck first. We need Olivia to help us with some of the logistics of the place. Can't just go storming in, you know. Between her and Rain, we'll have a plan to get us in and out before the Patriots even know we're in town."

Mayla nods but doesn't look happy.

"What about her?" she asks, tipping her chin toward the couch where Sheridyn is sitting slumped down, eyes closed.

"She's too far gone to help us at this point. Are you okay keeping an eye on her while we check in on Olivia?"

Mayla nods again and says it's too bad I can't share my rapid healing ability. "That little girl could use a good dose of whatever you've got in you."

"Couldn't we all," Suffolk says.

Leaving Render, Mayla and the Unkindness in their Crib, my Conspiracy and I, accompanied by Amani, head out to check on Olivia.

"Do you really think Sheridyn'll be okay?" I ask Brohn as we navigate down the broken front stairs and cross the clearing in front of the house.

"She's in good hands."

"I don't mean right now. I mean long-term. After all this is over."

"I'm sure she'll be fine. She just needs rest and time."

"I was just thinking about what Mayla and Suffolk were saying about my healing."

"What about it?"

"What if someday it *is* possible for me to share it?"

"That would be great," Brohn says.

Walking behind me and draping one hand on my shoulder and clutching at his lower back with the other like a stooped old man, Cardyn groans out that he gets first dibs. "I've got this pain that just won't go away."

"Me, too," Manthy says, gesturing to Cardyn as she walks past us.

"Now that was just uncalled for," Cardyn complains, straightening up.

Making our way back through the tangles of creeping vines and long-dead trees, we muddle along for what feels like an hour before we finally arrive back at the cement tunnel where we left Olivia and the truck.

The six of us climb up into the Pod to find Olivia busily working away, tendrils a multi-colored blur, as she sifts through holo-images and partial schematics of Krug Tower and the surrounding neighborhoods.

"No problems?" I ask her.

"No problems," she confirms.

With all of us gathered around, we fill her in on Mayla and the Unkindness, the Crib, and our brief exploration of the city. We give her the bad news about the impossibility of sending Render out given the danger he'd be in. Olivia then fills us in on the details of Krug Tower, including optimal points of access and possible holes in their security protocols.

"But this is partial intel at best," she warns. "Without Render being able to run his scouting missions for us, the facility is more questions than answers."

"Can we even get into that thing?" Cardyn asks, pointing to the flickering image of the rotating black tower in Olivia's holo-display.

"I was kind of hoping not," Olivia says. She sounds sad, her voice plinking in the stuffy air of the Pod like raindrops on aluminum siding. "I've grown fond of all of you."

"Us, too," I say, leaning over to give her a hug.

"Unfortunately," she says, "there *is* a way in. If you're lucky, you'll just get captured."

"Well," Cardyn says. "That's a relief."

"How is that a relief?" Rain asks.

"I'd rather be captured than killed," Cardyn says.

"How about if we don't do either?" I suggest.

Olivia's monitors hum as she grazes and tickles them with her tendrils. A small receptor implant-pad next to her eye clicks and flickers.

Rain drags a finger along the image and taps a line of identifier code into Olivia's scrolling holo-display. A network of colorful lines appears and snakes in a convoluted maze of veins and arteries throughout the entirety of the tower.

"These are all the building's integrated systems," she explains. "And these are some of the old underground tunnels. Old subway lines. Below-grade avenues. That sort of thing."

"How do you even know how to do this?" I ask.

Rain suppresses a grin but not a blush as she continues to talk us through the logistics of what we're about to do.

Wiggling her fingers around the image, she makes the lines disappear one at a time until only one remains.

"Security. Drone Regulators. Climate Control. Internal Sanitation. Grav-lifts. Emergency Protocols. Electric Grid Plug-ins. Ventilation. Intranet. Communications. Back-up Power Conduits. External Waste Disposal. This last one…External Waste Disposal…this is the one we want. Olivia, can you enhance the terminus of this line?"

Olivia says, "Initiated," and the tower is immediately covered in an array of stats, information tags, and identifier codes.

Manthy points to several of them, Rain nods, and I'm amazed at the ability the two of them have to make sense out of such a jumble of figures, specs, and fast-scrolling lines of blurry green code.

"There's a pedestrian access corridor here at the back with no working retinal or gene-scanners I can see," Rain says at last. "It leads to a Monitoring Station whose only purpose seems to be tracking the fleet of waste-disposal transports."

"There are two security stations, a drone pad, and a comm-relay hub," Manthy adds. "Nothing we can't handle."

"So we can just walk in?" Cardyn asks.

Rain shakes her head. "Hardly. There's a team of Patriot guards on duty at all times. They seem to run inventory and invoicing for all the garbage being shipped out of the tower."

"So, it's kind of the bowels at the end of the tower's digestive system?" I suggest.

Rain points at me. "Exactly."

"Great," Cardyn moans. "We're going to break into Krug Tower through its anal canal?"

"Should be perfect for a sphincter like you," Manthy says.

Cardyn says, "Hey!" and then Manthy, in a very un-Manthy-like move, smiles, blushes, and pushes her shoulder against his.

Cardyn and I exchange a look, him with his eyes wide and the corners of his mouth turned down in a "Hmmm...this relationship just got interesting" expression.

A lot less amused, Rain glares at them over her shoulder as she fidgets with one of the lines of code in the display.

"If you two children are finished..."

"Then it's definitely a weak link," Brohn muses, his hand on his chin.

"Well," Olivia hums. "That's a relative term. There are still more guards, drones, and identity-recognition protocols than we encountered at the Armory in San Francisco."

"Plus," Rain says, squinting at the series of holo-displays, "the building is well over a hundred stories high with the Processor at the top."

"We *suspect*," Olivia clarifies. "Although, based on the power-output readings I've been able to glean and the allocation of military and scientific equipment, that does seem to be the case."

Rain leans forward again and scans Olivia's array of holo-displays. She squints, and I imagine her brain as a collection of digital pathways with every possibility and scenario being considered at the speed of light.

"It won't be easy. But there *is* a window of time. There are regular energy outputs from a bunch of surveillance drone pads, and no one seems to alter or monitor the guards' shift-rotations. Not at this location, anyway."

Rain points to a series of highlighted spots on the display and mumbles to herself.

"If we can get to here. Then here. We should be okay. The problem is going to be the very first step: Bypassing this checkpoint and getting inside the secondary guard post."

A voice squeaks out from behind my shoulder.

"I can get us in."

It's Amani.

We all turn to where he's standing, his head lowered, his hand raised like he's pointing at the ceiling. He looks more like fish-out-of-water kid than like a soldier ready to leap head-first into our Emergent army.

"I can get us in," he says again, with a bit more confidence this time.

Before our eyes, his face goes blurry before returning to focus, only now he looks exactly like the Patriot guard we tossed into the basement the other day. Even his body looks bigger, more robust.

Out of instinct, Brohn whips out his nine-millimeter, but Cardyns shouts, "Wait!" and Brohn realizes what's happening and stands down.

"You have to admit, it's a little disconcerting," he says with a deep, slightly sheepish exhalation.

"A little disconcerting," I agree, as I scan Amani up and down, but I see no trace of the boy we've been getting to know these past few days. "And possibly a *lot* helpful."

Although he's better off than when we first found him, he's not exactly combat-ready. Tagging along with me and Brohn through the dense and polluted streets of Chicago is one thing. Joining a bunch of well-trained but still young soldiers like us on a next-to-impossible infiltration is another thing, entirely. Especially with him leading the way.

The rest of us huddle to the side to confer, and Rain steps up to deliver the news to Amani:

"Okay. You can come with us."

With the new intel and an ace up our sleeve in the form of our shape-shifting friend, we start to say our goodbyes to Olivia in the truck and prepare to head back to the Crib.

"I wish you could come with us back to Mayla's house," I say to Olivia, and everyone else agrees. But Olivia, rotating slowly in front of us, tells us not to worry.

"I can be more help to you from here, anyway. Being a Modified liberates me from a lot of the confines of your physical bodies. That's the gift and the curse of who and what I've become."

When we return to the Crib, Mayla and several of the Unkindness are waiting for us in the ballroom.

As best we can, we fill them in on what we know and on what we plan to do.

"Whether you get in or not," Mayla says, "whether you succeed or fail, you've already succeeded. You've inspired a lot of people these past few days."

No one says it out loud, but Mayla's vote of confidence is like an adrenalin shot to the heart, and we all stand up a little straighter and hold our heads a little higher.

The feeling is short-lived as we say our thanks and goodbyes to Mayla and the Unkindness and, finally, to Render, who slips his consciousness into mine.

I need to come with you.
—It's too dangerous.
There is danger here, too.
—You'll be safe.
No one will be safe.
—Wait...What do you mean?

Render ruffles the dark fluff of feathers protruding in a black mane from under his golden armor, and our connection is broken.

"What is it?" Brohn asks, as we head out the ballroom and through the checkered foyer leading to the front door.

"I'm not sure."

"Render?"

"He's not sure, either. That's what worries me."

Brohn says, "It'll be okay."

In my head, I'm thinking, *I don't see how*. But I decide not to say it out loud.

32

Krug Tower is farther away on foot than it looked, and it takes us the better part of an hour to get there.

Of course, we're slowed down by the need to proceed cautiously.

Chicago is a city—an entire territory, actually—languishing in poverty and always on the verge of violence, all literally in the shadow of the towers where the Wealthies are living it up without a care in the world.

Dad used to tell me stories about neighborhoods back in Boston where I was born where it wasn't safe to go out at night.

"It's easier to commit crimes when everyone is tired, asleep, or too afraid of the dark to think straight," he said.

Here, according to Mayla anyway, things are changing. Crime is getting to be at its worst in the daytime.

"Anyone crazy enough to go out in the height of the radiation cycle," she told us, "is crazy enough to kill you over a portable generator, and handful of nine-mills, or a bag of water."

On top of that, we learned from Olivia about how the major temperature shifts across the country are in the process of turning the major cities nocturnal. On the highway on the way to

Chicago, she showed us shifting thermals and the congregation of people in the few population-dense New Towns around the country.

"There are desert bands where the climate used to be temperate, and there appears to be a wave of frigid air collecting along the north and south tropics," she explained. "Don't be surprised in fifty years to find that the temperate regions are gone, and there's nothing left but desert with patches of unmelted arctic hanging around. The world is turning upside down. Upside down and inside out. And a lot of people are getting lost in the folds."

I didn't know what she meant at the time, but now I think I do.

A few days ago, Brohn said that what the Wealthies, the Patriots, and Krug really steal from us is time. Olivia's observation brings that reality home. The way the people here need to live their lives…it's all based on a distorted and unnatural understanding of time. Days and nights get flipped. It snows in the summer, and there are sand squalls in the winter. The Wealthies don't care anymore about day, night, hot, cold, rain, or snow. They threw all those elements of the natural world into chaos and then built their own skyscraping cities where they could be in total control of their environment. Seasons happen for them when they want them to happen. Daylight and night are controlled from somewhere in the Regulator Centers of those giant towers and arcologies.

It's a sad but true reality: the ones who control time rule the world.

It's daytime now, which means intense heat, but it also means relatively few people around.

"It's strange, isn't it?" I say out loud.

"What's that?" Brohn asks.

"In San Francisco, we operated at night. There was hardly

anyone around when we took down the Armory. Here, it's broad daylight, and no one's around."

"Can you blame 'em?" Cardyn asks, holding up his arm, which is already getting red and blistered. "I'm turning into a human strip of bacon."

"I hate to say it," Rain adds. "But Card's right. We need to get out of this heat."

"Look!" Amani calls out, pointing to an opening in the ground up ahead. "I think it's the tunnel you were talking about in the Pod. Mayla mentioned an old underground transportation system. Is that the one that can get us to the tower?"

Rain pauses for a second, her eyes following two small men who skitter past us and walk down a set of concrete steps into the very opening we're considering trying ourselves.

"Yes," she says. "I think you're right. This is our entryway."

Our descent into the crumbling and unstable remnants of an old subway system is about as close to a descent into Hell as I'd like to take.

The concrete stairs, chipped and decayed, are populated by an assortment of ragged people and scurrying, hairless rats with overgrown teeth and stumpy pink tails.

The rats pay us more attention than the people as we pass.

In a moment of pure cynicism I can't really blame her for, Rain points out that this underground sub-city is a perfect dark and dank space for what Friedrich Nietzsche called "the bungled and the botched."

"But as you may remember," I reminder her, doing my best not to sound too pedantic, "Nietzsche was a big believer in the *übermensch*. The Superman. He talks all about it in *Thus Spoke Zarathustra*. He'd love knowing there were Emergents like us around to dominate the inferior masses."

"You know," Rain says, her voice laced with snark, "sometimes your memory can be a real jerk."

"That's why we need to make better memories for as many

people as we can," Brohn says, leaping heroically to my defense. "Maybe someday, if we manage to pull this off, someone will be out there quoting *us*."

While the tunnel does provide us a direct line to Krug Tower, it doesn't offer much else. The heat and the smell are both worse down here than they are up above.

After a quick jog and what feels like an eternity of breathing through my mouth to spare my nose the torture of the tunnel's stench, Rain holds up a hand to indicate we've arrived at the place where we'll need to exit the tunnel.

"Not there," she says as Amani starts to head toward the stairs. Rain points to a large metal grate riveted to the side of the wall. "There."

"An air access grate?" I ask.

"Exactly."

"It showed up in the specs Olivia laid out for us back in the Pod," Manthy explains. "Those stairs lead right up to one of the Patriot security hand-over kiosks. Not the best place for us to make an appearance."

"Well, here goes nothing," Brohn says as he digs his fingers under the edge of the grate.

With a single quick move, he manages to rip the metal grille from the wall. It clangs when he tosses it onto the wet cement floor, and I worry it's going to attract unnecessary attention. The dozen or so cloaked and huddled people in the shadows don't seem to notice or care one way or the other. Not one of them even looks up.

This time, I lead the way, pulling myself up into the ventilation duct and bracing myself with my hands and knees against the dirty steel panels as I work my way up toward a checkerboard pattern of light.

At the top, I lean against the grate, expecting it to be locked tight like the one below, but I'm pleasantly surprised to have it swing open with just a moderate push.

I clamber out into a concrete stairwell with the rest of my Conspiracy hopping down one at a time right behind me.

Looming above us and blocking out the daylight is Krug Tower. It's clear from here that it's well-protected, but the security isn't perfect. Patriot soldiers patrol various checkpoints, but Brohn, peeking over the top edge of the stairwell, tells us not to panic.

"They've got two things working against them: their complacency and their reliance on drones."

From our hiding spot in the recessed stairwell not more than a hundred yards from the tower, we're able to look out across the narrow mag-way where automated delivery carts, piled high with garbage, shuttle out of a dark tunnel at the base of the enormous structure.

Skimming around above the carts is a small fleet of drones, each with a single surveillance light flickering through a spectrum of pinks and reds.

"Okay," Rain says. "Let's take stock. Everyone armed? Weapons loaded?"

We all pat our belts, pockets, and vests.

War and his men wiped out our arsenal, and the Unkindness, for all the authority and respect they seem to have around here, aren't well-armed. So, we need to make do with the leftovers we scrounged from the Pod.

Sig P226s. A couple of Desert Eagles. A Magpul submachine gun. And, of course, Manthy's silent but deadly Tomahawk axes.

After we've taken full stock, Rain taps one of the feeder-panels Olivia helped install in her vest. A holo-schematic of Krug Tower appears in weak, neon-green. With a quick flick of her fingers, the image is replaced by a zoomed-in view of the Patriot Guard Station, complete with real-time heat-signatures of the guards. We're obscured by the Concealers, and we all breathe a unified sigh of relief to know that the tech is working and that it's actually doing its job and concealing us from the drones.

"I don't suppose you can do your tech thing from here?" Brohn asks Manthy.

She shakes her head. "It's too far."

"All we really need to do is distract this guard here," Rain says, pointing to a red spot on the green thermal image.

"Or I can just walk in," Amani says.

Before our eyes, he shifts again into the Patriot patroller we dispatched just a few days ago.

"I'm not going to get used to that," Cardyn says, and I think the rest of us risk having our heads fall off from nodding so hard in agreement.

Before we have time to process his uncanny feat of disguise, Amani is up the stairs and out in the open, striding forward like he really is a Patriot soldier without a care in the world.

From where we are, it looks like he is on a suicide mission, marching right up to the other droopy-eyed guard, who is sitting drowsily in his glass-walled control station.

But the drone that drops down in front of Amani must see something else, because its facial and biometric recognition scanners bathe him in a halo of red before toggling to green as the drone, apparently satisfied, flies off to resume its patrol along the line of waste-disposal carts.

I nod my head, impressed.

"I don't think our Concealers could have pulled that off."

"One of us should really be with him," Cardyn whispers. He nibbles at the skin on the edge of his thumbnail. "We still don't know how much combat training he got in the Processor."

As we peer out from our hiding place, Amani strides purposefully right up to the guard station like he's been doing it every day of his life.

The guard sits up as Amani approaches and shields his eyes with his hand like he's looking into the sun. He steps out of his guard booth and raises a hand in greeting to the figure he sees as his fellow Patriot guard.

Without breaking stride, Amani flicks the blade of his hand hard against the man's neck. Stunned, the guard doubles over only to be greeted by Amani's knee to the bridge of his nose.

Bleeding and glassy-eyed, the guard stumbles back, flailing at the edges of the doorway as he falls into the glass kiosk, with Amani charging at him and throwing punch after punch until the guard is hammered insensible before he even hits the floor.

Amani lifts the man partway up by his shoulders and drags him behind the administration desk inside the booth as we look on, open-mouthed.

"I'd say he's had a bit of training," Rain says, clearly impressed.

We start to head over, but Amani—still looking eerily like the Patriot soldier—stops us with a raised hand and a flick of his head toward the drones still patrolling overhead.

Slipping behind the guard's desk, he glides his fingers over the holo-panel.

A few seconds later, half the drones glide over to a parking station as Amani steps out of the guard booth. From the far side of the tracks, he beckons us over.

Ducking down, we weave through the small fleet of surveillance drones hovering in pre-docking mode on their way to the grav-pads.

Three more drones buzz overhead, but they continue on their programmed patrol route, ignoring us as if we didn't exist.

"More than a *bit* of training," Brohn says. "Kid looks like he could pull this off all by himself."

"I say we let him try," Cardyn jokes, pretending like he's going to dash off the way we came before Brohn grabs him by the scruff of his vest.

"Get back here."

Cardyn says, "Just joking," and Manthy frowns at him and tells him she liked his *anti-*jokes better.

Together, we approach Krug Tower, and I breathe a strange sigh of relief. Sure, this is the most vulnerable we've been in a long time. But it's also further than I ever thought we'd get. Who knows? If we can make it this far, maybe we can go all the way. Rescue the Emergents. Get safely back to the Crib. Regroup. Head to D.C. Take down Krug. Kick out the corrupt politicians. Reclaim our nation. It's not *that* far-fetched, right?

Inside the guard-house, Brohn asks Manthy again if she can access the building's comm-tech systems.

Manthy surveys the long input panel in front of us before placing her hands on it. She says, "I think so," and leans down with her cheek hovering just above its surface. From here, it looks like she's giving it a big hug, but the agonizing grimace creasing her face and forehead reminds us all of just how painful this ability of hers can be.

It's only been a few seconds, but Cardyn, in his typical paranoid way, is getting antsy and keeps looking around.

Finally, Brohn tells him to relax.

"You're making everyone nervous," he says.

"I can't help it. I get nervous when I'm about to die."

"You're not about to die," I assure him.

"He is if he doesn't settle down," Brohn growls.

Still leaning above the panel, Manthy starts to quiver, and Rain rushes over to throw an arm around her shoulders.

With Rain's help, Manthy stands up, her eyelids fluttering and her hair damp with sweat.

"Okay," she says, her words barely audible as she struggles for breath. "I did the best I could."

"Half your best is better than anyone else's perfect," Brohn says.

Manthy drops her head, but she can't hide the pleased smile of satisfaction playing at the corners of her mouth.

Without the drones to worry about and with only one deeply unconscious guard between us and the next entry portal, the six of us slip easily down a poorly-lit hallway lined with blinking communication charging stations and a bank of orange storage lockers.

"This is already further than I thought we'd get," Rain confesses.

"I was thinking the same thing," I tell her, and she gives me a thumb's up in solidarity.

At the end of the hallway, we're met with another treat: an unlocked door.

"Whew," Cardyn exclaims, dragging his hand across his forehead like he's wiping away nervous sweat. "Looks like this is going to be our easiest infiltration ever."

"Great," Manthy says to me. "He just jinxed it."

"Don't worry," I assure her. "Fate has better things to do than listen to Cardyn."

Stepping forward, I take the lead and peer through the doorway into another long, almost-empty hallway. I flex my hand and rotate my forearm to make sure it really is healed, and I'm happy when the surge of pain I expect to feel doesn't happen.

Down about fifty feet or so, two Patriot guards are deeply immersed in conversation.

I listen for a minute before ducking back into the corridor to report my findings to the others.

"They're arguing about a shift-change."

"You mean they can actually change shape?" Cardyn asks.

Manthy gives him a disgusted, corner-of-the-eye look. "You're joking, right?"

"They're talking about their duty rotation," Brohn says as Cardyn shrugs.

I lean in closer, careful not to let myself be seen. "The taller one wants to go with some commander named Jensen, who apparently lets them get away with shooting loiterers, trespassers, and vandals for fun. The shorter guard doesn't think that's right."

"About time we ran into a Patriot soldier with a conscience," Cardyn says.

I hold up my hand. "Not so fast. He thinks it's not fair that they could have their pay docked for it."

"Great," Rain says with an exaggerated eye-roll. "The one time we think one of these guys might actually have a heart, and he turns out to be the worst of the bunch."

"Not sure what you expected," Brohn says. "You're either a fracker when you join an organization like the Patriots, or else you turn into one along the way."

"So cynical—" Rain starts to say, but I have to cut her off with a raised hand.

"They're heading this way."

"Well, let's give them a proper Conspiracy greeting," Brohn smiles.

We duck back deeper into the corridor except for Brohn who stands with his back to the wall just behind the door.

When it swings open, the two guards walk through and straight into Brohn's lethal forearm swing that smashes both men in the face at once. Before they have a chance to fall backward into the larger hallway, Cardyn and I grab them by the fronts of their security vests and haul them into the narrow access corridor with us. When one of the guards starts to squirm, Rain slides over and punches him twice—once in each eye—until the man sags like a sack of animal pelts to the cold floor.

"That was amazing," Amani gushes.

"They do that all the time," Manthy says. "You'll get used to it."

"You didn't do so bad yourself back there with the guard," Brohn says, giving Amani a brotherly chuck to the shoulder.

Amani can barely get his "Thanks" out through his ear-to-ear smile.

Inside, we have a look around at the interior of the imposing Monitoring Station. It's a secondary station, really. Just a back-up to the big surveillance rooms they probably have in other parts of the facility. This room is mostly for monitoring the tower's own security personnel and coordinating things like garbage runs and such. It's not designed for external surveillance.

Still, it's intimidating just being inside the huge tower.

"I feel like the dog that caught the car," I say. I start to laugh but stop when I'm greeted by five empty stares.

"What's that supposed to mean?" Cardyn asks.

"I don't know," I shrug. "It's just something Dad used to say."

Manthy cringes a little as Rain puts a hand on her shoulder.

"Manthy. We're counting on you to tap into the building's security system."

"Oh, goody," Manthy says in her soporific monotone. "There's nothing I'd rather be doing right now."

"Come on," Cardyn whines. "We still need you."

"And I need to not feel like my brain's been put in a food processor set to 'pulverize.'"

With no way out and knowing we're relying on her, Manthy taps her comm-link and hooks up with Olivia back in the truck.

Together, they perform some miracle of code-interception I can't even begin to understand. My dad may have been a tech genius, but I could never pick it up as easily as people like Rain and Manthy, who seem to speak digi-tech like a second language. Or, in Manthy's case, like a very fluent first language.

"We have control over three hundred and twelve of the fourteen-hundred cameras in the facility."

"That's twenty-two percent," Rain says after a disturbingly quick mental calculation. "Not great, but it skews the odds a bit more in our favor. And the alti-tubes?"

"There are twenty double-decker people-movers. I can't access any of them, but I *can* access four of the hundred and ten alti-tubes and two of the special alti-tube maintenance lifts."

"We'll want the maintenance lifts," Rain says with certainty.

Sliding single-file past a room labeled "Security Station Sigma," we wind our way down a series of black-walled corridors with minimal light, a circumvented security system, and, thankfully, no Patriot guards.

"I just got that," Cardyn whispers.

"Got what?"

"'The dog that caught the car.' I just got that. We got what we wanted, but the thing we wanted is likely to lead to our deaths."

"Welcome to us," Brohn murmurs as he pushes forward toward one of the building's large maintenance lifts down at the end of the dimly-lit corridor.

33

NONE of us has ever been in an alti-tube before. There was an old-style elevator in the office building where my dad worked back in Boston, but I was only five years old at the time, and I don't remember anything about the experience other than that it made me feel sick to my stomach.

Now, my stomach is a tighter and much worse kind of queasy. The sickness I feel is one of absolute terror.

"Talk about being in the lion's den," I say out loud.

"Yeah," Cardyn agrees as we continue to whoosh up to our destination on the 108th floor. "Only more like a den filled with lions, box jellyfish, black mambas, and a couple of great white sharks."

"Don't forget the most dangerous animal of all," I say.

"What's that?"

Behind him, Manthy says, "Humans."

The lift-capsule comes to a gliding stop, the silver door opens, and we're standing face to face with to a Patriot soldier.

Beefy and lantern-jawed, his mouth hangs open at the sight of us, but it doesn't stay open for long.

I strike him under the chin with a sharp uppercut.

The Patriot's gun clatters down the hallway, and his head snaps back as I step to the side. Rain bursts forward and, in one blur of a motion, slides to the floor and thrusts a devastating boot stomp upward into the man's groin. He doubles over and spews a brownish-white mist of vomit onto the floor.

"Ugh," Cardyn and Brohn say at the same time through a sympathetic wince.

A shiver runs through Cardyn's body.

"Right in the flesh-orbs."

I'm just thinking how I can't believe we've made it this far when a piercing wail, accompanied by a pulsing red light on the black glass wall panel, screeches through the corridor.

Cardyn shrieks. "We triggered an alarm."

Manthy leaps to the wall, slaps her palm onto an input panel next to the alti-tube lift, and the alarm goes quiet.

"Oh," Cardyn says into the deathly silence that follows. "That's better."

We brace ourselves for the onslaught of guards, but Manthy must've gotten the system to register this as a false alarm. So it doesn't look like any reinforcements are going to be sent.

That's the good news. The bad news is that our comm-links are off-line.

"Maybe we're up too high," I suggest.

"Damn," Brohn snarls. "They probably have all kinds of channel-blockers in place. I should have anticipated that."

Without any way to contact Olivia to help us navigate, we make our way down the black corridors. It's like the Halo in some ways. Lots of tech. Some signage written in a strange, alien alphabet none of us has seen before.

Amani is having trouble keeping up. "I'm okay," he assures us through a breathy stammer that tells us he's actually far from okay.

"Shouldn't have let him come along," Cardyn mutters.

"We wouldn't have even gotten into the building otherwise," I remind him.

"True."

As we continue on, everyone is following me, which means collisions and a lot of grunts when I come to a sudden stop right in the middle of the hallway.

Render is in my head. I don't know where he is out there in the world, but his consciousness is right here mixing itself in with mine.

Suddenly, I can hear things I shouldn't be able to. Only it's not exactly hearing because it's not vibrations riding on waves into my ears. It's more like the sounds around us have turned into ribbons of color, which I can see and feel and select as I see fit.

I put my hand onto the black wall.

"Behind here," I say. "There are others. Others like us."

"Your eyes..." Brohn says. "Are you connected to Render?"

I tell him I am and that we need to get inside this room.

"Any suggestions how?" Brohn asks.

"Maybe Manthy can tap into the locks?" I suggest. "Or you can see about prying the door open?"

"Or maybe we can just open it," Manthy says, stepping forward and showing us the inch of space between the door and the frame in the wall it slides into.

She slips her hand into the gap and pulls. The door slides open as easily as if it's been greased.

"That's odd," I say, and Cardyn sarcastically praises my gift for understatement.

Glancing back down the corridor to make sure there are no Patriots lurking around waiting to ambush us, the six of us slip into the large, dimly-lit lab.

Inside, there are twelve of those glass prison-orbs lined up along the far wall underneath a bank of mechanical arms. Four have a person inside. The other cells are empty.

"They're alive," I say, but then I wish I hadn't. After all, it was less than a week ago that we encountered a similar scenario in the original Processor where we found Amani and Sheridyn along with six of their friends who wound up victims of Krug's sadistic experiments.

Together, Rain and Manthy dash over to an input panel on the wall. Manthy unlocks the system, and a holo-display of green code springs to life.

"No need for brute force this time," Rain announces as she and Manthy, standing side by side, whisk their fingers through the code, making quick adjustments to the input protocols before Manthy announces that it's done.

On cue, all twelve containment spheres split open like perfectly cracked eggs, and we rush over to collect the four teens who come stumbling out of the last four of the open orbs.

Brohn says we need to hurry and get out, but he extends a hand first.

"Brohn. This is Kress. Rain. Cardyn. Manthy. And Amani."

The sole boy of the three teens steps forward, his tall, lanky, and slightly crooked frame in stark contrast to Brohn's symmetrical package of well-proportioned and battle-hardened muscle.

"I'm Jevaun. This is Nika. And my cousins, T'shelle and Ajana."

"From the Unkindness, right?" Brohn asks.

"The four teens burst into glowing smiles.

"You know about us?" T'Shelle asks.

"Your people have been taking care of us the past couple of days."

I tip my chin toward the empty cells.

"What happened to the rest of you?"

Nika hangs her head. She's shorter than the others, with caramel skin, close-cropped hair, and stunning green eyes. "Not sure. They were taken away and…"

"It's okay. We'll get you out of here."

Ajana and her twin sister say, "Great" at the same time, and, without another second's hesitation, we're sprinting toward the door.

Once outside the lab, we race down a zig-zag of black-walled hallways. The glass panels lining the entire length of each corridor glisten our reflections back at us as we run.

Rain and Manthy lead the way to one of the alti-tubes, which we take down about fifty floors, which they tell us is as far as this one is designed to go.

"I couldn't get access to the express lifts," Manthy apologizes, but Brohn waves her off.

"You're doing great. You and Rain just keep going, and we'll just keep following!"

After a heart-pounding, twenty-floor race down a narrow set of concrete stairs tucked away behind one of the alti-tube shafts, we wind up in a network of maintenance corridors deep inside Krug Tower. Using a combination of the corridors and a series of ladders descending down into deep freight shafts, we're finally able to slip into an abandoned room where we pause to catch our breath and get our bearings.

"Where are we, exactly?" Cardyn huffs.

Rain, admirably not even out of breath, tells us not to worry.

"I know exactly where we are and exactly how to get out. But we have to wait."

"Wait?" I ask. "For what?"

Rain taps her temple. "Thanks to Olivia's intel, I've got the Patriots' patrol schedule up here. They're a dangerous bunch but predictable. A simple analysis of heat signatures is really all Olivia needed to lock down their duty rotation. There's an alti-tube down the hall. It's guarded but not all the time."

Rain checks the chronometer built into the inner wrist of her jacket sleeve.

"We'll stay here for four minutes."

"And then?"

"Then we run like hell."

"What do they want with us, anyway?" Jevaun asks.

I lean up against a slanted, glass-covered monitoring station protruding from the wall of the small office.

"They suspected you of being Emergents."

"Emergents?"

"People like us. People with abilities."

"We don't have any...abilities," Nika says.

"What about the others? There were empty cells in that lab."

"Eight of them," Brohn points out.

"There were three others," T'shelle says, tying her dreadlocked hair back into a thick ponytail. "They got taken away a couple of weeks ago."

"We don't know why," her sister adds.

I look from Brohn to Rain. "I'm pretty sure we do."

"Were they...?"

"Emergents? That'd be my guess."

"They didn't seem...different. Do you think they had abilities?"

"Most likely. Any abilities they have would have been enhanced by how close they get to each other. It could be why they were separated out and taken away."

"What about us?"

"My guess is you were going to be killed. Maybe even today."

"If they don't get what they want," Rain explains, "they either kill you or divert you into the Modified program. Either way, your lives as you know them were about to be over."

A deep crease forms between Nika's eyes. "Any idea where the others could be?"

"We didn't know them very well," Jevaun says.

"Not that that matters," T'shelle insists. "We still care about what happened to them."

"They weren't with you? They weren't part of the Unkindness?"

"No. It was just the four of us. They came later. They got taken away a lot."

"We still have to find them," I say with more urgency than I was planning on letting on. I can't bear the thought of leaving anyone behind, especially knowing what we know about what's likely to become of them. If Hiller had had her way with us back in our Processor…well, chances are we'd be dead or enslaved.

"They could be anywhere in this building," Brohn says.

He's right, but I don't want to admit it.

"What if I try to tap into Render again?" I ask. "Maybe he could lead us to them?"

Brohn hesitates but says it's worth a shot.

"How much time left?" he asks Rain.

"Two minutes."

I concentrate and try to initiate the connection, but nothing happens. So I swipe my forearm implants, but still…nothing.

"Any luck?" Brohn asks, and I can tell he's trying to keep the anxiety out of his voice. He may have tough skin, but even he doesn't want to risk squaring off against however many battalions of Patriot soldiers they have in this enormous building.

"It's almost like a feedback," I tell the others. "Only not quite. Not like static. Not painful. More like the connection's being blocked."

"I didn't think that was possible," Cardyn says.

"Me, neither."

"Either way," Rain advises, unable to hide the urgency in her voice, "we need to be gone. Like, right now."

Brohn leads the way, sliding the door open a crack and peering down the hallway toward the alti-tubes at the end.

"Which one?" he asks Rain.

"The one on the left."

"And we'll be able to access it?"

Manthy says, "Trust me."

And we do.

All of us, eleven in all now, bolt down the hallway as fast and as quietly as we can. Sliding to a stop at the alti-tube, Manthy nudges forward and scans a code into the holo-display of green text and figures projected out from the input panel on the wall between the second and third doors.

At first, nothing happens, and I ask Rain if she's sure about this. Rain doesn't answer, but, next to me, Manthy's eyes slip back and forth between their normal brown and the dull gray indicating her cyberpathy at work, and she promises everything will be okay.

"I can get us out," she says with a huff of confidence.

"Stop bragging," Cardyn pants through a tight smile. "And make it happen!"

The alti-tube door whooshes open, and we clamber inside. The lift is flat on the bottom, but it has slightly curved walls and a cylindrical top, which makes me feel like we're plummeting down in the world's largest lozenge.

"We're at ground level," Rain says when the capsule eases to a stop, its door slipping soundlessly open. "It's a maintenance corridor running parallel to the one where we came in."

We follow Rain out into the corridor where I hear the sound of a stomping boots. I put my hand to the wall.

"They're behind here. Patriots. They must know we're inside."

"Which way are they headed?" Brohn asks.

I flick my thumb back to the left.

"Perfect," Brohn says, breaking into a jog down the hallway to our right. "Let's move!"

With what seems to be an entire legion of Patriot guards thundering into the tower through an access tunnel not more than a hundred feet from where we are, we slip easily out of the building. Crouching low, we skitter under a mag-rail where delivery carts are busy ferrying garbage down a long line, curving out of view around the corner. We slip past the open area with the drone charging pads, hop down into the stairwell, and clamber, one by one, into the air vent. Sliding to the bottom, we bolt all the way back down the underground tunnel, this time moving far too fast to absorb its horror of sights and smells.

Legs and lungs burning, we bolt up the stairs and out into the oven-hot air.

Slowing down at last, the ten of us hack our way through the jungle of brambles, past the clearing outside of Mayla's Crib, and right into the welcoming arms of the Unkindness.

34

As big as it is and as empty as it's been since we were first welcomed in, the ballroom is packed now.

There must be hundreds of the Unkindness. Men, women, and children. Almost all of them have thick dark hair in various stages of dreadlocked length. Their multi-colored shirts, blue and yellow hair-clips, wooden bead necklaces, and robes of reds, greens, blacks, and gold fill the room and light it up like an indoor rainbow.

Then there's my growing Conspiracy. What started out as eight of so long ago it seems, was whittled down to five. Now, with the four new kids we rescued plus Amani and Sheridyn from our original Processor in the Emiquon National Wildlife Refuge, we're starting to feel like the beginnings of an army. The beginning of hope.

Mayla escorts all of us through the tight, happy crowd and over to one of the clusters of couches, loveseats, and settees.

We're just getting settled in when, to our surprise, three teens we've never seen before are shuffled up to us by one of the women of the Unkindness.

"Dova!" Nika exclaims, leaping right into the arms of the three strangers. "Virasha! Evans!"

She hugs each of them in turn before turning to catch our very puzzled looks.

"They're the ones who were in the Processor with us!" Nika exclaims.

Brohn steps forward with the rest of us close behind.

"How'd you get out?" he asks.

The girl named Dova clasps her hands and grins.

"We were in a different room just down the hall. When you overrode whatever security protocols there were, the doors opened, and we were able to hop a maintenance alti-tube all the way down to the Communications Compound. From there, it was easy enough to slip out through the Waste Disposal Terminus. Nice work on the guards, by the way."

"That's when we saw you," Virasha adds.

The boy named Evans, slim and short but very toned and muscular, tells us that's when they followed us.

"It wasn't easy," he says. "You all were moving pretty fast. But we kept up, and here we are!"

Brohn is just telling them that he doesn't care how it happened as long as everyone's out and safe when I notice Cardyn giving the three escaped teens a long stare.

I'm about to ask him what's wrong when the women sitting down leap to their feet and insist we take their seats.

At first, we try to refuse, but we're told, "You must! You must!" and we're all gently but firmly pressed into the couches.

All around us, the Unkindness shout out cheers and lob their "thanks!" They sing out about us being heroes and saviors. The ones nearest to us clamp congratulatory hands on our shoulders and reach over each other to touch us and to try to shake our hands. Little kids, not more than four or five years old, weave their way between the grown-ups' legs and make their way to us, only to stand there staring up, speechless in some kind of reverential awe.

A little girl latches onto Brohn's leg, and he looks down at her, half annoyed, half amused.

"Jevaun's little sister," Mayla explains. "And T'shelle, and Ajana's cousin. All very close. The three older ones getting separated like that...well, it's a nice wound to have healed. Thanks to you."

More people crowd around us, and I can barely hear Mayla over the din.

When Dura folds her tongue back with her finger and thumb and gives a high-pitched whistle, everyone settles down.

Mayla sits in front of us. Some people in the crowd lean in to listen. Others chat with each other in soft whispers around and all throughout the great room. A couple of stragglers lean over the back of the couch to thank us before moving on.

Brohn, Cardyn, Rain, Manthy, and I are squeezed shoulder-to-shoulder on the pink and yellow striped couch with our new friends squished into the matching couches and love seats next to us, and with Amani kneeling in between.

Dova, Virasha, and Evans—the three teens who made it out without our help—stand together in a clutch next to Mayla's cushioned, broad-backed armchair.

Sheridyn has edged her way through the crowd to join us. She stands behind Mayla, her back pressed to the wall like she and the wall are holding each other up. Although her skin is still blotchy, and her arms and legs are wobbly, she looks wide-eyed and oddly alert.

"Mission accomplished," Mayla says.

Brohn shakes one more hand before turning back to her. "Well, one mission. This is just one play in a much larger game."

Mayla swings her head to take in all of us. "Well, there is more talent in this room than any of us has ever seen. You can't blame everyone for being starstruck. It's not every day you get to shake hands with the saviors you've been dreaming about!"

"Saviors," Rain scoffs. "We're still just kids. People need to stop looking for a savior and start taking action against all the brainwashing that's made them think this is the way life has to be lived."

Standing next to Mayla, Suffolk says she disagrees. "You may not think of yourselves as saviors, but you have to admit, you saved a lot of people today."

"You have gifts, and you're using them in the right way," Dura adds.

"Everyone's good at something," Cardyn shrugs. "We just happen to have heightened abilities in certain areas."

"Heightened beyond what's humanly possible, you mean," Mayla says.

"So what's next for the great Conspiracy?" Suffolk asks with a laugh, although I can barely hear her above the hum and buzz of the crowd filling the room behind us.

Brohn rubs a hand along the stubble coming in on his cheek and jaw. "We have to get to Washington, D.C. It's where Krug and the Deenays have their headquarters set up. It's the hub of Krug's entire operation and our only chance to stop him."

"If our new friends here are willing," I say, giving a broad smile to the seven newly-liberated kids, "and with their parents' permission, of course. Emergents or not, together, we have a good chance of fixing a lot of what's been broken about our country for a long time now."

"Consider the Unkindness at your service," Mayla says with a grand flourish.

"I've got to ask," I say. "You're the nicest people we've ever met. You help so many, including us. Why did you decide to call yourselves the 'Unkindness'?"

Mayla looks up at Suffolk and Dura who put their hands out, palms up.

"Honestly, I don't know. We're not the founders. We kind of inherited the organization."

"Can I tell you something surprising about yourselves?" I ask coyly.

"Sure."

"We call ourselves the Conspiracy. It's a term for a group of ravens. And Render, as you know, is kind of our patron saint."

"What's the surprising part?"

"'Conspiracy' isn't the only name for a group of ravens. There's another one."

"And that is?"

"An Unkindness."

Mayla, Suffolk, Dura, and several of the other members of the Unkindness who are in earshot burst into a pealing, windchime chorus of laughter.

"You don't say," Mayla pants, wiping joyful tears from the corners of her eyes.

"I do say. And I also say it's not a coincidence that our paths have crossed."

Mayla holds up her hands. "I don't doubt you. I don't think anyone in this room will ever doubt anything the lot of you say from this point on!"

"That's great," Brohn says, leaning forward now, all business. "Because what we're going to do next in D.C. is going to take a lot of will and a lot of sacrifice, but it's going to take trust more than anything else. And I don't mean trust in us. I'm glad you don't doubt us. But if we're going to pull this off, we have to have faith that there's a truth in the world beyond what we've all been brainwashed to believe."

Pushing herself away from the wall, Sheridyn's eyes go big like she's just witnessed a nuclear explosion. "How are we supposed to take over an entire government?"

"We take our truck east," I tell her. "We gather up as many supporters as we can."

"Emergents, you mean."

"If we can find them," Brohn says. "There may not even be any left for all we know. But there *are* a lot of good people left out there. People who've been programmed to accept the lies in front of their faces. People who've been beaten down. People who are ready to face the truth about the Eastern Order, about Krug, and about what this country has turned into right under our noses. We'll gather as many as we can. The same ones who have nothing to lose. That'll be our answer to Krug. That'll be our army."

"And you *are* accepting applications, right?" Mayla asks. She tilts her chin toward the bursting-at-the-seams room around us. "A lot of people here are tired of being stepped on."

"Or tricked into stepping on each other," Suffolk says from next to her.

Mayla nods her agreement, and Brohn looks around at our growing Conspiracy.

"It's a long way to D.C.," he says at last.

"And, from what we understand from Olivia," Rain adds, leaning forward so we can all hear her, "it's at least a three-day drive through some pretty rough parts of what's left of the country."

"You've been through Chicago," Mayla says. "You've seen how we live, what we're capable of becoming. I think we can handle it."

"What about vehicles?" Cardyn asks. "We have our truck. But it won't fit the entire Unkindness."

He looks over his shoulder at the jubilant crowd. A man has brought out a fat, dented guitar, and he and a woman start singing a peppy song over on the far side of the room by the kitchen as the voices of dozens of others join in until they've got a rollicking chorus filling the huge room with a melodious refrain.

"We can arrange for other transportation," Mayla assures us with a laugh. "We know people in some pretty low places."

Inside, I'm excited, but I try not to show it. Our plan is working. Our army is growing. My mind is filled with images of all the oppressed people of the country joining us in an impossible mission. We'll gather up the Unkindness. The Unkindness will bring others into the fold. We have the five original members of my Conspiracy, Amani and Sheridyn, and the seven new Emergents we rescued from Krug Tower. Plus, Olivia and Render. Okay, so it's not Genghis Khan and his 13th century million-man army, but it's one heckuva start.

With the revelry kicking into high gear, Jevaun's father comes over and throws his arms around his son and his twin nieces, all of whom hold on tight like they'll never let this hug end.

As the singing sweeps through the ballroom and as trays of food and water are brought out, the rest of us stand up and confer with Mayla.

"I say we don't waste any time," she says with a girlish squeal. "Let's celebrate tonight! Tomorrow, we'll start arranging for supplies, weapons, transportation, the works."

"It won't be easy," Brohn says. "Or fun."

"I don't expect it to be any of that. But I do expect it to be a… liberating experience. For all of us."

"So that's it?" Cardyn says, raising his voice to be heard above the singing, cheering, and the now dancing throng. "We're really going to do this?"

"It's been the plan all along," Brohn says, giving Cardyn a playful shove to the shoulder.

"That's unfortunate," Dova says as she stands up from the couch where she's been sitting, arms folded.

"Unfortunate?" I ask, wondering if I heard her right. "What do you mean?"

"Unfortunate that you all feel ridiculously empowered enough to think any of that can work."

"Or even that's it your right to try to make it work," Virasha adds, also standing up.

With the sound of the guitar still lofting around behind us, the area we're sitting in is suffused in a split-second of stunned silence.

"What's happening here?" Cardyn asks, looking around. "Wait. I know you three," he says before turning to face me. "They're the ones from that underground bunker War had me in."

"And now we're putting a stop to this," Evans says. "We're putting a stop to all of you."

On the big wall behind Mayla, the boarded-up windows disappear. Behind us, we hear confused shouting and turn to see that the four doors on the long interior wall and the swinging kitchen door are all gone.

Suddenly, we're inside a huge steel box, crammed in by the hundreds with no way out.

Sheridyn steps forward, her skin glowing a luminous neon-blue.

Then, it's like all the oxygen in the air around us has been instantly sucked away. We all thrust our hands to our throats, straining to breathe.

The air inside the big ballroom goes wavy, swept through by a rolling heat distortion. The walls burn red before glowing a shimmering greenish-blue. The music and singing stop and give way at first to confused murmuring and then to a crescendo of panicked realization as half the people in the room clutch their throats and drop to the floor.

Before our eyes, Dova, Virasha, Evans, and Sheridyn fade away into a wispy fog of nothingness. And just like that, they're gone, and we're trapped.

After all the risk and heroics, after all the training, planning, and combat…we're caught off guard, and we're standing here, open mouthed, more helpless than we've ever been.

Our immobilized confusion doesn't last long.

Brohn shouts out, "Run!"

But there's nowhere to run to. No exit. No escape.

Brohn and Rain solve the problem for us.

"It's an illusion!" Rain shouts.

She vaults over the couch and shoves her way through the crowd with Brohn right behind her.

Shouldering their way through the rest of crowd, Brohn reaches where a door should be. Rain screams at him to open it.

"There's nothing to open!" he cries back.

"Trust me!"

Brohn lowers his shoulder and charges against what looks to be an impenetrable steel wall.

The wall shudders and shimmers in strained waves of distorted color. With people shouting and screaming behind us, Brohn hits the wall again, and sure enough, a door appears. Brohn gives it one more run, and the door goes smashing off its hinges and slams down onto the hallway floor.

With the heat rising from unbearable to deadly, Brohn and Rain shout for everyone to get out.

Urging the Unkindness out first, we burst from the ballroom, scrambling with dozens of others down the hall toward the front door.

Manthy and I each pick up two of the little girls who have been knocked down in the rush to escape.

Bursting out onto the front porch, we stumble down the broken stairs and wind up face to face with Dova, Virasha, Evans, and Sheridyn, all flanked by a line of Patriot soldiers, guns at the ready.

With the Unkindness swarming out around us, Brohn, with one child under each arm, leaps down the steps and lands on the open patch of land in front of the house. He shouts at the children to run before turning to help others out of the house, down the steps, and toward the woods.

Still standing on the front porch, bathed in the intensity of the blue heat, I try to do the same, but Evans leaps onto the porch, grabs me by my vest, and slings me down the stairs. I hit the ground hard, my face and arms scraping against the rough terrain as I slide to a stop.

Evans leaps down after me as I scramble to my feet.

He tries to punch me, but I easily redirect his strike away from me with a hand to his forearm. I take a shot at him, but I hit nothing but air. I try again, but he's too fast. His reactional reflexes are off the charts.

Fortunately, he doesn't have eyes in the back of his head. If he did, he'd see Rain storming up with a wrinkle of fury burrowed between her eyes.

She unleashes a stone-hard side kick to the area just behind his knee, and I hear tendons snapping as he shrieks and rolls to the ground, clutching his wounded leg to his chest.

Like Evans, Dova is impossible to hit. Cardyn and Manthy team up to try to stop her, but every punch, kick, elbow-strike… they all hit nothing but air.

"She's precognitive!" Rain calls out from next to me where she's just knocked a gun out of one of the Patriots' hands. He bends down to pick up the weapon, but his head snaps violently back as Rain connects with a swift knee to the bridge of his nose.

"She knows how you're going to attack!"

In the chaos, it's fallen to me to take on Virasha, but, like the other members of my Conspiracy, I'm frustrated by my inability to take her down. She's not very tall or powerful-looking, but the girl I try to punch is vapor, so I try again. But I wind up swinging wildly into the air, and I stagger off balance in the process.

Every time I'm sure I've got her pinned down, the ghost of what she was fizzles away, and she's suddenly behind me.

Then, a blurry wave of flame engulfs the house and all the rest of the men, women, and children of the Unkindness along with it.

The screams from those still inside fade into nothing, disappearing into the menacing silence of death.

35

Outside of Mayla's Crib, we're herded by Dova, Virasha, and a platoon of Patriot soldiers onto a bare patch of rough, rocky ground and are forced to our knees, our hands over our heads. One of the soldiers tends to Evans, who is still writhing on the ground in pain, while six of the other Patriots stomp up behind us to latch zip-cuffs onto our wrists.

I want to resist, to struggle, to fight to the death, but my mind is a haze of static. My muscles are limp and lead-heavy.

I want to keep my head up, but I also want to keep my eyes down at the same time to avoid seeing the carnage around us. I can't bear to face the sight of what's happened or the thought of what's yet to come.

Brohn is kneeling to my right, his back hunched over in defeat, with Rain on the other side of him. Her normally perfect olive skin is now a patchwork of black ash and crimson blisters running along her cheek and neck. On my left, Cardyn is bleeding from a long gash stretching from his forehead down to his jawline. On his other side, Manthy is staring off into nothing, shocked it seems, her face frozen in a wide-eyed state of crippling terror.

From the far side of the clearing, a fleet of Patriot mag-jeeps comes gliding up through a wall of vines and brambles. The vehicles haven't even come to a complete stop before the Patriot platoons inside come piling out, weapons drawn. They charge after the Unkindness who are trying to escape down the path leading away from the house or who go diving blindly into the surrounding jungle.

In full hunter-mode, the Patriots pursue them at top speed, catching the ones they can and shooting dead the ones they can't.

A Patriot soldier, thick-necked and heavily armored, walks back out of the brambles. He has Jevaun draped over his shoulder. He's dragging Nika along the ground behind him. Another soldier has each of the twins, T'shelle and Ajana, by an ankle. Like his partner, he drags the girls' lifeless bodies along behind him.

Screams and cries mix with the stomp of boots, the shouted orders, and the smoky, thundering discharge of fired weapons.

Coughing and bleary-eyed from the toxic cloud still consuming the house, I can barely register the specifics of the commotion. It just feels like all hell has broken loose, and my friends and I were unlucky enough to be standing in the doorway when the demons burst forth.

I reach down to summon more strength, but my reserves are depleted, my energy is gone, and I'm too disoriented to do anything other than surrender at last.

The unfairness of it all, the cruelty, ties a tight knot in the pit of my stomach. My eyes are burning like they've been doused in acid.

Only a hundred feet away, the Crib remains bathed in a shimmering, flameless wave of heat and radioactivity. The aurora of every blue, green, and silver on the color spectrum would be beautiful if it weren't so deadly, if it weren't suffocating everyone still inside.

The pulses of radiant energy from the burning house are

intense, and I can feel the rolling emissions blistering the skin on my neck and arms. A toxic coppery stench fills my nose and mouth and sears the back of my throat. The implanted micro-tech ports in my forearms sizzle scarlet and scorch every pain receptor in my body with fiery lighting strikes that burrow their piercing way into my spine.

Apparently immune to the radiation and heat finally dissipating into the air, Sheridyn stands in front of us, hands on her hips like she's the triumphant hero of the day instead of the despicable traitor who just betrayed the very people who saved her life.

"You're scared," she says flatly. "You're wondering how this happened."

"You're like us!" I shout. "We had a chance to work together, to put things right."

"Put things right? Do I look *wrong* to you?" she asks.

"You look like…someone…who betrayed the future…of humanity," I stammer.

"Now why would I do that?" Sheridyn asks, smiling sweetly. "We *are* the future of humanity. You. Us. You just got too caught up in your righteous, save-the-world heroics to realize it."

Next to me, Brohn blinks hard and tries to stand up, but the guard behind him grips him by both shoulders and orders him to stay down.

Brohn, however, is in no mood to follow orders.

Lunging to his feet, he drives his shoulder hard into the soldier, who flies back like he's been shot from a canon.

With a surge of strength I've never seen from him before, Brohn sends a flood of raw power flexing through his shoulders and arms, and he rips through his zip-cuffs like they were made of lightly-braided straw.

The Patriot soldiers spring into action, charging at Brohn with stun-sticks.

Brohn shrugs them off, and I get ready to leap up and join

him when a flash of flickering light blasts through the clearing and envelops him in its shimmering sea-green aura.

His hands to his throat, Brohn collapses back to the ground between me and Rain.

Sheridyn walks a few steps closer to us, shaking her head.

"You still don't get it, do you? After all you've been through. After all you've learned and after everyone you've outlasted…."

She stares with admiration at her own glowing hands for a full five seconds like she's seeing them for the first time.

"Our abilities aren't super powers. They're not parlor tricks. Heck, they're not even extensions of natural abilities like you might think. Do you want to know what they are? I'll tell you."

Sheridyn leans down to face Brohn, who doesn't seem to register her presence.

"They're a key," she says with an ironic laugh. "A key to why we dream. A key to a door that keeps getting slammed shut. A key to survival. And this time, people like us can finally be on the right side of that door."

Moving away from Brohn, Sheridyn sits down cross-legged in front of me and takes another second to survey the death and destruction around us. Behind her, Patriot soldiers drag the captured Unkindness—some of them still struggling, some lifeless—through the clearing and over to a line of mag-transporter trucks where they're tossed in like sacks of garbage.

Some of the Unkindness have guns and try to fight back. They fire out of blind desperation, but they're weak and disoriented. Without mercy, the Patriots unleash a furious salvo at them from three jeep-mounted M61S Vulcan six-barreled rotary canons.

The screams of hundreds of people mix in with the screams of twenty-millimeter rounds fired at six-thousand rounds per minute to create a horrific cacophony of death and destruction all around us until it looks like the ground itself is bleeding.

A harsh buzzing fills my ears, and I'm having trouble focusing my eyes. Even though she's sitting less than three feet away from me, Sheridyn's features are blurry. Her voice is an overlapping series of echoes.

"You're Emergents. You and your friends here. Amani, too. But Us? We come from another place," she says, tilting her head toward her fellow betrayers, her voice practically a shout over the clamor of gunfire. "We come from dreams," she says, as if from the end of a long, empty tunnel. "We're Hypnagogics."

"Hypna…," I manage. "Kella said something about…hypnagogia…"

"Kella? Oh, right. The other Emergent. Don't worry about her. We have plans for her. Wisp, too. And Granden."

"Granden…"

"Yes," Sheridyn says, reaching out and putting a hand on my leg like she's comforting a small child who's lost her favorite pet. "We know about Brohn's sister, and we know about Krug's traitorous son. We have something special in mind for the others, but Krug wants to see to Granden, personally."

"What…what *are* you?" Cardyn stammers through a curled-lip snarl.

"Me? I'm an alpha emitter," she says matter-of-factly, giving Cardyn a glib grin.

"Basically, she attracts and can redirect radioactive isotopes out of the atmosphere," Dova explains as she absently inspects a patch of burned fabric on the sleeve of her jacket.

Virasha, her head held nobly high, walks up to join them. "She's the one who just stopped you from stopping us."

A wave of adrenalin surges through me, but it fades just as fast, and I can barely get the words out. "How can you do this? After all they've put us through."

"What Krug did, he did *for* us, not *to* us. What the Patriots put us through—the isolation, the elimination of the adults, the Processor—"

"'Elimination'?" Rain shouts from where she's kneeling on the other side of Brohn, a Patriot guard behind her with his hand firmly on her shoulder. "It was murder. Mass murder. They killed our parents. Aunts, uncles, teachers…everyone!"

"Don't be so dramatic," Sheridyn says, standing up and brushing dirt from her palms. "This is the Garden of Eden, and gardens get weeded. It was all a test. You failed. We passed."

Now I'm not even trying to stop myself from crying. "You passed by siding with the enemy."

"If there's one thing all of us should have learned by now," Sheridyn says, looking like she's suppressing a giggle, "it's that the enemy is whoever you need it to be."

"Don't let yourselves be used like this," Cardyn mutters and then repeats, louder the second time. From his knees, his hands bound behind him, he swings his head back around to make eye contact with the guards lined up behind us. "You're the only ones who—"

Sheridyn shuffles backwards, her hands clamped over her ears.

"Stop him!" she shouts to the Patriot guard looming behind Cardyn. "He's a Persuader!"

Following Sheridyn's command and without a second's hesitation, the guard flips his rifle around in his hand and swings it, barrel-first like a baseball bat, into the side of Cardyn's head.

The sound of the crack of steel on bone is horrifying, and I scream at the top of my lungs, certain Cardyn is dead until I see his shoulder dig into the ground as he tries to sit back up.

The soldier stops him with a boot stomp to the back, and Cardyn collapses down into the dirt, unmoving, but at least still breathing, his face twisted in pain.

"Don't worry," Dova says. "You'll still contribute to the cause. But not as saviors or soldiers."

"No," Virasha laughs. "You're going to be guinea pigs."

"Subjects," Dova says.

Sheridyn steps forward again and leans down, cupping my chin in her hand. "And we don't mean the subjects of a king."

"Although you'll be that, too," Dova adds.

"That's right," Sheridyn says, pushing my face away hard. "You'll be subjects in the labs here in Chicago."

Sheridyn points up to where Krug Tower looms over the city like an obsidian tombstone.

"See, they're going to use you to figure out what makes us who we are. I'm sorry you had to waste so much time and effort breaking into Krug Tower. It was such a short visit. I'm pretty sure this time, you'll be staying for longer. A lot longer."

Sheridyn nods to the Patriots behind us. I feel a sharp sting in my neck, and I fall into a hellish nightmare where I can't catch my breath as I slip down and drown in a sea of my best friends' blood.

EPILOGUE

When I open my eyes, I'm suspended in one of the clear prison orbs inside a vast, high-ceilinged room that looks like a transport hangar. The walls are crisply white. On the far side, a dozen drone charging stations hum softly blue. A narrow black glass input panel runs the entire length of one of the walls.

There are no signs of life.

I don't know what's happened to Brohn, Cardyn, Rain, and Manthy.

I don't know if Olivia is safe in the Pod.

I don't know if Amani is dead or alive, a victim or a traitor, a friend or a foe.

Render is gone.

And not just physically. I concentrate and try to connect with him.

Nothing.

I swipe a contact pattern into one of my arm implants, but there's still no connection.

I thrash against the magnetic forces holding me in place, but it's useless. I can move my arms and legs, but even that's pointless since there's nothing for me to do with them. I've been in this situation before. I know I can't do anything from inside. I need help from outside.

As if in answer to my prayers, a rectangle of silver light materializes on the white wall near the charging stations, and a door appears.

A person walks over and stands in front of me, the figure's features distorted momentarily by the glass orb and by the fog swirling around in my head.

I blink the person into focus, and the smiling face of Sheridyn appears.

Not an answer to any prayer I've ever made.

She looks young again, her hair unbraided now and pulled back into a fiery orange ponytail. Her skin is freckled and pale. There's a lightness to the sparkle in her watery green eyes like she's got a secret and not a care in the world.

I can't believe this is the same girl-turned-monster who killed so many so fast right before our eyes. All like it was nothing. Like she was shooing away a swarm of gnats.

"We found your truck."

She raises a finger to her lips before I have a chance to say anything.

"And your poor Modified friend."

Sheridyn holds up a dangling mass of graying tendrils that sag from her clenched fist like wilted angel-hair pasta.

"Olivia!"

"Was that her name? I guess we didn't have time to do proper introductions."

"What did you do to her?"

"Don't worry, Kress. You fret too much. Olivia is in one of the labs. Well, *parts* of her are in one of the labs. One of the Neuro-tech Inquest labs, to be precise. Parts of her are in the Disassemble and Salvage Terminal. The rest is in the Incinerator."

My eyelids flutter, and I clench my teeth, struggling to hang onto consciousness, to fight against the wave of horror at what's happened. How did everything so right go so wrong and so fast?

I want to scream at Sheridyn through the glass. No. I want to lunge through the glass and kill her with my bare hands. I want to ram my boot through that smug smile of hers, make her pay for what she's done. Make her sorry she ever met us.

That's the worst part of these prison orbs. I'm suspended in the air, isolated and alone. Friendless. Weightless. Helpless. At least with chains, you have something to struggle against. Prisons have bars. Pits have walls. Here, I have nothing holding me back except the invisible, irresistible force of a mag-grav system, so I feel light, like I'm flying. Like I'm Render hovering in a gentle thermal. Yet, I couldn't be less free at the moment.

On the far side of the room, a large portal slides open to reveal wispy clouds drifting through the pink-hued sky. In the distance, the horizon curves away, and I'm shocked to realize we must be a mile up in the air.

A heli-barge hums up on grav boosters and eases into the hangar, settling with a whisper onto a landing array of shimmering silver circles. The heli-barge's doors slide open, and a man, lanky but pot-bellied, steps down the ramp and into the light.

It's President Krug, himself, in all his sweaty, greasy glory.

His crisply ironed blue suit and spotless yellow tie stand in disconcerting contrast to his scraggly goatee and that oily black hair. The long red and white striped scarf around his neck whips and thrashes in the high-altitude wind until the big bay doors behind him hum shut, and the ends of the silky scarf droop down on either side of him. His black dress shoes, as reflective as the black glass panels on the walls, are polished to a high shine.

Six beefy Patriot soldiers march down from the heli-barge's ramp to form a semi-circle behind him like a heavily-armed consort of scowling backup singers.

Waving his entourage still, Krug walks across the hangar

toward me, the hard heels of his dress shoes clicking like horse hooves on the sterile white floor.

"That was quite a stunt you pulled back in San Francisco," he says as he approaches my prison of curved glass.

His voice is rough. Aggressive. A handful of rusty nails wrapped in a strip of sandpaper.

"Honestly, we never saw it coming. Nice job of staying underground. But you poked your head out. Now, there's no going back."

Krug fiddles with one of his cufflinks and sighs like this is all a burden to him, like he regrets having to chastise a disobedient child.

I stare at him through the glass, hoping my hatred will somehow turn into a dagger I can thrust into his evil heart.

"What do you want with us?"

"Honestly," Krug says, tapping his finger to his temple, "I want what's in here. Even after all the analysis by the En-Gene-eers, we still don't really know what makes you tick. Sure, we know a bit more about your genetic deviations. We've mapped out your genetic code, identified your molecular markers, and even accomplished some positional cloning. But why do only some of you develop these abilities? And why only when you're in isolation and when you hit a certain age? Why can't I do what you do? You know, the whole 'telempathy' thing you do with that bird. That's what you call it, right? 'Telempathy'? Or Brohn's impenetrable skin. Rain's perfect mind of advanced analytical expertise. Cardyn's persuasion. And Manthy. Dear, sweet Manthy. With her on my side, I can go global. Tap the network. Bypass any nation's firewall. Decode any country's military encryption system."

Krug pauses to drag the back of his hand across his mouth and fiddle with his marble-sized golden cufflinks.

"They say in the land of the blind, the one-eyed man is king. Well, I plan on being a fully-sighted king in the land of the blind, deaf, and mute."

SURVIVAL

He takes a deep breath and puffs out his chest like he's reeling himself in.

"But right now," he says after another deep breath and as he runs his hands up and down the sleeves of his tailored jacket, "I can't do any of those things. I'm just a flesh-and-blood human. But you. You get to be an Emergent. You get to have special abilities. Doesn't seem fair, does it?"

With my body immobilized, I point at the sphere I'm trapped in and around at the enormous transport hangar.

I refuse to cry when I say, "None of this is fair. We're just kids. You killed thousands. You lied. You invented a war—"

Krug puts up his hand and cuts me off.

"Millions. I've killed millions. Well, technically they've been killing each other."

Krug gives a hissy laugh, runs his finger and thumb along his dyed jet-black goatee, and gives me a nasty stare. He must be reading the brew of fear, anger, and confusion I've got swirling around behind my eyes because he asks me if I'm wondering what happens next.

When I don't answer, he says, "Okay. I'll end the suspense. You're about to be tested. Studied. Examined under conditions I would *definitely* wish on my worst enemy. All those doubts and limits you have in your head…we're going to smash them until you're sure you can't take another ounce of pain, and then, just when you think it's all over, we're going to get mean."

I'm crying quietly now, but every tear just seems to egg Krug on.

"We're going to break you, Kress. Take you apart and lay all the little pieces of you out on a table. We figure it'll take a few months. Maybe up to a year. It all depends on how much you decide to cooperate. Call it a prison sentence if you like. Or the beginnings of the greatest experiment in human history. Frankly, you should be honored. When it's over, though, when we've gotten to the bottom of this Emergents mystery you've become, when we've solved you and when you're mine in every sense of the word…that's when the next step in human evolution will begin, and I'll be on the top rung of the new genetic ladder."

"We'll die before we help you," I hiss.

"Ha. Right plan. Wrong order. First, you'll help. *Then*, you'll die."

Krug straightens his tie and does up the buttons on his double-breasted blue sports coat.

"Anyway, I heard you were coming for me. I figured the least I could do was be ready for you when you arrived." He gestures to where Dova, Virasha, and Evans, a mound of heavy bandages on his injured knee, have walked into the hangar to stand behind Sheridyn, who is now standing just behind Krug's shoulder, practically rubbing her hands together with glee.

"As you can see," Krug says, "I'm *very* ready."

And then he smirks at me. "Are you?"

Sheridyn's skin and eyes glow radioactive green as she steps up next to Krug. He gives her a nod, and she walks a few steps forward, her small hand splayed out like a starfish on the curved glass of my spherical cell.

The glass shimmers a luminous cobalt blue, and the air in my lungs burns blistering hot. The anti-grav shuts off, and I collapse down into the curved bottom of the orb.

I look through the glass at Krug and Sheridyn and at their entourage of evil standing behind them, watching my suffering, planning my fate, waiting for my death.

I think about Cardyn, Rain, Manthy, and Render. And I think about Brohn. Indestructible Brohn. I'm not ready for us to end. Did we come this far for nothing? Did we survive so much just to be betrayed and fail?

All the wisdom, clichés, and platitudes I've ever read and always believed go racing through my mind:

The human capacity for survival and renewal is awesome.

Cheaters never prosper.

The meek shall inherit the earth.
And the bad guy never, ever wins.
Did the bad guy just win?

In the end, there's a voice in my head. But I don't know if it's mine, Brohn's, Render's, or any of the millions of writers whose works I've read that now live in my memory.

You must be ready at any moment to sacrifice what you are for what you can become.

It's the last thought I have before the shadowy blackness of unconsciousness overtakes me, and I close my eyes and drop my head, my face pressed to the cold glass as I lie curled up. Alone. Disconnected. Defeated.

The last thing I see and hear through the glass is Krug standing over me, laughing.

—*End of Book 1 of the Emergents Trilogy*—

ALSO BY K. A. RILEY

Resistance Trilogy

Recruitment

Render

Rebellion

Emergents Trilogy

Survival

Sacrifice (Coming in November 2019)

Synthesis (Coming in 2020)

Seeker's World Series

Seeker's World

Seeker's Quest

Seeker's Fate

Athena's Law Series

Book One: *Rise of the Inciters*

Book Two: *Into an Unholy Land*

Book Three: *No Man's Land*

For updates on upcoming release dates, Blog entries, and exclusive excerpts from upcoming books and more:

https://karileywrites.org

Printed in Great Britain
by Amazon